IN THE

Camera crews were busy setting up what looked like an important shot. Light technicians worked to cast just the right amount of light while sound technicians checked microphone placement.

And me, Mr. Starstruck, stood there sucking it all in.

Which is when I suddenly felt my body take over and jerk me out of the doorway a scant second before a bullet splintered into the wall right where my heart had been a blink earlier. Bits of masonry dust flew out at sharp angles. No report shattered the air, however.

Whoever'd shot at me was using a sound suppressor.

I jerked sideways just as the next round whizzed past me and into an unsuspecting cop. His chest exploded and his eyes went white almost immediately. Another heart shot. The shooter wasn't taking any chances.

Another burst of brick exploded next to my ear, showering my cheek with concrete, drawing blood.

The shooter was getting closer . . .

**Books by Jon F. Merz in
the Lawson Vampire series**

THE FIXER

THE INVOKER

THE DESTRUCTOR

THE SYNDICATE

Published by Pinnacle Books

(Please visit
http://www.zrem.com
for more information.)

THE SYNDICATE

Jon F. Merz

PINNACLE BOOKS
Kensington Publishing Corp.
http://www.kensingtonbooks.com

First Pinnacle Books Printing: October 2003

10 9 8 7 6 5 4 3 2 1

Printed in the United States of America

ACKNOWLEDGMENTS

I owe an enormous thanks to Donna Mangubat—a brilliant dancer and extraordinary woman—for her help and advice regarding all aspects of dance. Much of this story would not have been possible without her.

One

Darkness enveloped everything.

I couldn't see a damned thing.

Even with my incredible vision, a cloud of darkness hid everything from me. I felt vulnerable. I could be attacked from any angle and never see it coming.

"Lawson."

The voice was a sick, harsh whisper coated with the promise of extreme violence. I wheeled around, searching for the source. None revealed itself.

Again the voice spoke. "Do you remember me?"

Something about it seemed familiar. Something about it tickled the back of my mind. I could feel the adrenaline coursing through my veins. I could hear my heartbeat drumming against my bones.

And I knew.

Cosgrove.

He laughed then and it seemed to echo off unseen walls all around me. I pivoted, jumped, and threw myself from position to position hoping to stay one step ahead of him.

"You remember. Don't you?"

My throat felt tight. Suffocating. Squeezed between the forefinger of fear and the thumb of hesitation. "I killed you."

An unseen punch crashed into my jaw and snapped

my head back. I felt my teeth grind together. I tasted blood. It was a helluva shot.

I brought my hands up to ward off the secondary blow, but none followed the initial strike.

"You didn't kill me, remember? I warned you about that. You chose not to listen. I told you I'd be back. I swore my vengeance."

I shook my head. It wasn't possible. I'd staked and decapitated him. There was no possible way he could ever come back. Not after what he did. Not after what I did in return.

A kick to the groin doubled me over. I felt my bowels drop toward my feet but I sucked them back in, steeling myself and hoping he hadn't just crushed my testicles.

"Do you believe me now?"

"NO!"

The shout that erupted from me did a lot to restore my confidence. If I could only see through the darkness. If only I could see him.

But the darkness didn't clear. Instead, it suddenly became unbearably hot. I felt a rush of energy go by my right side. I jumped. Another energy burst zipped past my left side.

"Lawson."

The voice had changed. Cosgrove had vanished seemingly. He'd been replaced by something softer. But I knew the softness was only a disguise to mask the pure evil residing behind it.

Something slammed into my chest. I flew back and hit the ground somewhere beneath me. Wind jumped out of my chest. I heaved and struggled to get to my feet. Colors swirled around my eyes.

"What about me? Do you remember me, Fixer?"

I tried to stand. Another bolt of energy slammed into my chest. I flew back again and felt my shoulder crack when it hit the ground.

What the hell was going on?

"Say my name, Fixer. Say it!"

I'd seen her killed, too. It couldn't be.

"Arvella?"

Her laughter oozed through the air like an evil mist. "Very good. I'm so glad you remember me."

"You're dead. I saw you die."

"Maybe you didn't. Maybe I fooled you. Maybe now I've come back for my vengeance."

Impossible.

Another voice joined Arvella's. "I'll bet he doesn't remember me."

Another man. The vague hint of an accent told me who it was immediately.

"Petrov."

A shot rang out. I felt a hot burning sensation sear my right bicep. I grunted and spun, fishing behind my right hip for my own gun, trying to ignore the pain.

But my gun wasn't there.

I was unarmed.

"I could toy with you," said Petrov. "I could kill you as easily as I draw a breath. Look at you. Already wounded and we haven't even begun yet."

We?

A whisper tickled the back of my neck. "You were such a good fuck."

I whirled.

Shiva.

A low growl suddenly sounded in front of me and I felt a claw slash across my chest. Sharp nails cut open my flesh. Blood poured out of my body. I could feel the sting of sudden pain. I could smell the rush of fresh coppery blood.

My head hurt. My arm was hurt bad. I could tell the wooden fragments had nailed an artery. A few minutes longer and I wouldn't be much of a problem to anyone.

"You're dying, Lawson. You're almost dead now. We told you we'd be back. We told you that you'd never be rid of us. This is your day of reckoning. Welcome to hell."

Cosgrove's laughter erupted once again. I always did hate hearing that sick bastard's laugh. Arvella's spirit-invoking chants emanated from somewhere off to my right. I could hear Petrov chuckling as he ratcheted the slide on his gun, chambering another round to finish me off. And Shiva's growling came from both behind and all around me.

More voices joined them. More evil vampires I'd long since executed for crimes against our society.

All of them had come back.

All of them had returned for their revenge.

My past had finally caught up with me.

"This can't be. This can't be possible. I saw you all die. I killed you. You're all dead!"

They spoke with one voice. "You can't kill us, Lawson. You can never be free of us. You can never be free of what we have all become to you."

The pain in my body increased. My head felt light. Their voices echoed inside my skull.

My stomach rumbled.

Woozy.

I sank to the ground.

Retching.

Heaving.

Bleeding.

Was I dying?

Was it all true?

Had they all come back from the dead? Had they all come back to take me off to hell?

The darkness abruptly began to clear. Slowly it became a lighter shade of gray. The voices receded in volume. The pain in my head lessened, but only slightly. I could sense something happening on the fringe of my consciousness.

A figure stood in the gray mist—smaller than a full-sized man.

The mist cleared some more and I could make out a few details. I could see his face.

I winced.

He was horribly disfigured.

He smiled at me, his teeth coated with fresh blood.

He mouthed something that I couldn't make out.

What was he trying to tell me? What was his message?

My head exploded in pain again. I cried out and felt myself sinking toward the black fuzziness.

I passed out.

For a while, I had no thoughts. No sensations. I floated in limbo—exhausted, bloody.

And almost dead.

I woke to the sound of incessant ringing.

The phone.

My head throbbed like I'd just gotten back from a ten-day pub crawl with my good buddies Jim Bean, Johnny Walker, and Captain Morgan. My stomach heaved like a blue whale was about to be born through my mouth.

I sat up quickly and instantly regretted it. I looked

down, convinced that there'd be claw marks across my chest.

Nothing.

I looked at my arm. No gunshot wound.

I breathed deep.

Another dream. A bad one at that.

The last time I had bad dreams, I later figured out they'd been some type of warning. Was that happening again now? And if so, what were the dreams warning me about this time?

And what the hell was making that damned noise?

I slid my legs over the edge of the bed and felt my bare feet touch the cold wood floor. I needed to start wearing socks to bed.

I got up, stifled the urge to puke my guts out, and padded out of my bedroom.

I used to have a telephone in my bedroom but I'd ditched it a few months back. There are times when I like to sleep unaffected by pain-in-the-ass telemarketers.

Now I was actually glad the stupid thing had woken me up. I wouldn't have wanted to go on with that dream for much longer.

I padded down the hallway and took the stairs to the second floor to my office. My leather swivel chair accepted my body with a small squeak of protest. The red light on my desk phone blinked like an epileptic flasher.

I needed to get a phone with a better ring. This one sounded like an old nuke war alarm.

I picked the receiver up.

"Yeah?"

"Lawson?"

"Yeah."

"It's Uncle Phil."

My eyes opened a bit wider. I don't have much in the way of family. Uncle Phil is one of the few relatives I have left. His call caught me off guard. A total surprise. I almost forgot about my intense headache and vomit-ready gut ache.

I checked the clock. *Six in the morning?*

"A little early isn't it?"

"I need your help."

"What's up?"

He paused. His next words faltered and stuttered out of his mouth in a broken staccato sentence. "Are you . . . still, you know, a . . . Fixer?"

"It's okay to say the word, Phil."

"Well, are you?"

"They haven't canned me yet." Not for lack of trying, though.

His voice emanated relief. "Good."

"Is something wrong?"

"I think so. Yes."

I felt like a dentist trying to pry out a particularly stubborn wisdom tooth. "Anytime you want to tell me what it is, Uncle Phil."

"It's Marilyn."

My cousin. Phil's daughter. Last I knew, she lived in New York City. "What about her?"

"She's missing, Lawson."

"How missing? Like she hasn't called you in a week or two or something?"

"She hasn't been *seen* in over a week. Her roommate doesn't know where she is. She hasn't called. I'm worried to death about her."

"Maybe she's gone somewhere."

He wasn't listening. "She could be dead. Kidnapped. I don't know."

"Calm down. It's probably not something so bad as that."

"I'm beyond remaining calm, Lawson. I don't know who else to turn to." He paused again. "I've only got one question to ask you: can you help me?"

Family, even the little I had left, was important to me. As such, I only had one possible answer.

"Yes."

Two

My personal family history isn't something I normally discuss in great detail. It's a bit messed up. That, in and of itself, is a rarity in the vampire world. Most vampire families have blood lines running back hundreds of years. Family trees in my society look more like capillary networks than an actual tree.

My dad died young. I miss him every day. Life has a way of snatching the most precious things from us and leaving behind the shit we'd all rather see gone. God, whatever God you happen to pray to, must have a sick sense of humor. When my time came, I was going to have a serious sit-down with the big guy upstairs and see just what the damned score was.

My mother died a few years after my father—killed in what got officially ruled as a car crash. I was away at the time, on a field-training exercise as part of my Fixer work. It wasn't the type of thing I could just get up and walk away from.

I missed the funeral.

Uncle Phil had made no bones about the fact he thought that was completely inexcusable on my part. It was also probably the only reason I'd clued him into the fact that I was a Fixer at all—to get the guy off my back.

He might have accepted the excuse grudgingly,

but a big part of me suspected he still harbored some resentment.

Especially since Phil remained convinced to this day that my mother was actually assassinated. I looked into the matter but found nothing to substantiate it. And every time I tried to get it out of Phil as to why he thought she'd been killed or what he thought she'd been involved in, he just clammed up.

I left it alone.

The funny thing about having your parents dead and gone is the sense of isolation you feel. Think about how many years of your life you spend under the watchful eyes of the people who brought you into this world. Then, one day, they simply aren't there anymore.

Have I mentioned what a champ I am at depressing the crap out of myself?

I could hear Uncle Phil pacing on the other end of the phone line, all the way down in New Jersey. He lived in a big house on a new development parcel that hadn't spent much money on trees. The area Uncle Phil lived in looked as flat and boring as an anorexic runway model.

"I don't know what to do, Lawson."

"When'd you hear from her last?"

"Two weeks ago. Her mother's worried sick."

Knowing Phil's wife, that wasn't much of a stretch. "She still living in New York?"

"Yeah, trying to be some superstar dancer. Parading up and down Broadway, trying out for cruise ships, music videos, all that crap."

"She must love all the support she gets from her family about her career choice."

"You know how much she set me back putting her through NYU?"

"You gonna tell me anyway?"

"$32k a year."

I whistled. "Impressive."

"Impressive? Hell. Now she's got some pad on the Upper East Side. She's charging everything on my credit cards to the tune of three grand a month."

"You try weaning her off the plastic?"

"Ah, shit." He sighed again. "You know she's my little princess."

"Yeah. I know it. Makes it a real bitch when she's got to grow up, though."

"Might not be relevant now, anyway."

"What kind of talk is that?"

"Well, shit, she vanished a week ago. I'm trying to be realistic. She might be dead."

"She might not be."

"I'm not a dreamer. And I'm not some innocent fool. I know what goes on up there in the city."

"Stop shocking me, Phil." My cat Mimi came by looking for some attention. I scratched her behind her left ear and she rolled her head into my hand. "You want me to find her?"

"Please."

"What if she doesn't want to be found?"

"What the hell is that supposed to mean?"

Phoebe came by and I patted her some, too. "Means she might have disappeared for a reason. Maybe she's tired of living on daddy's dime and wants to make her own path. It happens you know."

"Not with Marilyn it doesn't. Last time I mentioned her getting a job, she freaked out and wouldn't talk to me for a month."

"When was that?"

"Year ago. Just before graduation."

"She see the Council?"

"Yeah. They said she should be in entertainment."

"They set her up down in NYC?"

"Hell, no. They told her she should explore New York. *I'm* the fool who set her up. Damned Council."

"But they were going to put her in touch with the right people."

"Supposedly."

"You don't sound too convinced that they did."

"Fuck, Lawson. If they set her up right, would I still be getting credit card bills that look like the GNP for Abu Dabi?"

"Guess not." I drank some more orange juice. "So, what do you think they did?"

"You want to know what I think? I think they sent her to see some of those bastards that run the Syndicate."

I sighed heavily into the phone. I glanced at the clock. *Shit.* Quarter to seven and already my day was in the crapper.

Phil said, "You there?"

"Yeah. Remind me next time not to give you my phone number."

"Why's that?"

"Because fucking with the Syndicate isn't really the best way to prolong your life."

"Shit, Lawson, you're a Fixer. What do you have to worry about? I thought you were the guys who go everywhere and do everything with complete authority."

"For the most part, that's true." I took a breath. "Problem is, the Syndicate doesn't exactly like Fixers much."

"They still answer to the Council, don't they?"

"Supposedly. Officially, yeah. The real truth is the Council leaves them alone for the most part. Unless something really bad goes down, we're not supposed to dick around with them, either."

"Cushy friendship. I knew all those decrepit fools were on the take."

"It doesn't necessarily mean they're on the take."

"Doesn't mean they aren't, either."

He had a point. "Well, what if Marilyn did see some guys in the Syndicate? That wouldn't necessarily explain her disappearance. I can't recall the Syndicate thinking it wise to kidnap every vampire that comes to see them at the Council's behest."

"Yeah," said Phil. "I know. That's why I was wondering if you could poke around and see what might have happened."

"You want me to poke around in Syndicate business?" That was like taking a toothpick and needling a hornet's nest.

"Would you?"

Outside, the sun seemed to be shining brighter than a few minutes ago. Getting involved in Syndicate business would be bad for my health. Guaranteed. But Marilyn and Uncle Phil were family. Hell, they were pretty much the only family I had.

"I'll check it out."

"You'll have go to New York."

"Seems to be the logical step."

"I know how much you dislike that town."

"It's not that I hate New York. I just prefer Boston. Remember, I grew up here. I'm biased."

"Yeah," said Phil. "You call me if you come up with anything?"

"Yeah." I hung up and stared at the phone.

The Syndicate. I sighed. Think of a vampire Mafia and you got the Syndicate. They controlled the fringe elements of vampire society. While they didn't do anything outwardly illegal per se, they danced on the edge enough to cross over every now and again. They controlled a lot of strip clubs, brothels, and bars in most of the cities in the world. They had a lot of crossover with show business types, too. A lot of Syndicate interests took root on Broadway and in Hollywood. They delved into the fashion worlds of Milan, Paris, Tokyo, and New York.

Drugs were forbidden, even for them. While they might not have respected the Council to the degree most of the rest of our society did, they also knew not to fuck up their good position. If they dealt drugs, they'd all die. The Council would mobilize a Fixer strike team and we'd go in and kill them all. Every last one of them.

It had happened once before.

And I didn't think the Syndicate would want it to happen again.

It also didn't help that I was known to the Syndicate.

The last time I'd shown my mug around their part of town, I'd caused several of their number to depart for the afterlife. I still had bad memories of having to back my way out of the building they used as their headquarters.

I don't much like backing out of things.

And if looks could have killed me, I would have bought the farm ten times that night and died a few more times just for good measure.

They didn't like me very much.

And here I was getting ready to go messing about with them all over again.

A breakfast of arsenic and cyanide never looked so appetizing.

Three

I called Niles next.

He answered on the second ring. "Good morning, Lawson."

"Got the Caller ID installed, I see."

"I took me awhile to figure it out. But yes. I did."

"Nifty. I'll come straight to the point: I need some time off."

"Uh . . . that might be a problem."

"It's not really all that negotiable, Niles."

He paused. "Can I ask why?"

"Family matter."

Another pause. "Lawson, you don't have much in the way of a family."

"Thanks for reminding me."

"Sorry, it's just that—"

"Let's just say that the little family I do have needs my help right now. Is that fair enough?"

"You're being serious."

"You bet."

He paused a third time. Niles was my Control. Usually, that meant he gave me my assignments and basically directed me. He wasn't my boss as much as my contact with the Council. Niles and I were still working out the peculiar dynamics of our relationship. In recent months, I'd grown to respect the guy. A little.

For me, that was impressive.

"It's just that right now Boston's in such a state of flux. What with the head of the Council dead and all."

"Belarus got what he deserved. You know it as well as I do."

"I know that, Lawson. It's just that he had a lot of friends. Powerful friends, you know what I'm saying?"

"There won't be any trouble. They know they'd get terminated if any of them started kicking up dirt and dust. Now is not the time for them to get delusions of grandeur."

"I hope they all feel that way, too. But I'm not overly optimistic about it."

"Jeez, Niles, you're becoming as much of a cynic as I am."

He laughed into the phone. "You're starting to rub off on me."

"That might be bad."

"Or it might be good."

"Fair one."

"This family thing you're going off to handle—is there anything I can do to help?"

"Wish there was. I'm not sure how thrilled the Syndicate will be if two of us hit town."

"You're not serious."

"What?"

"The Syndicate?"

"I didn't go looking for this, Niles. It just showed up on my doorstep this morning like the bastard case it is."

"Christ."

"I could use him, sure. If you talk to him, put in a good word for me, okay?"

He paused. "Can I ask for a check-in every two days until you get back?"

"You can ask."

"I'm asking."

"I'm answering. Every forty-eight hours. No problem."

"Thank you."

"You can run interference while I'm gone?"

"Oh sure, no problem."

"Can I ask one more favor?"

"You will anyway."

"You are starting to know me."

"What's the favor?"

I hesitated. Hell, I wasn't even sure why I was about to ask it. Then again, it never hurts to be prepared. "If I miss a check-in, will you send the cavalry?"

"We don't have much cavalry to send, Lawson. You have anyone in mind?"

"Send Wirek if you can. And Arthur. They'll be more than enough."

"Anyone else?"

"Well, you can come if you have to."

He laughed again, but it was an uneasy laugh this time. "Sure, wouldn't miss messing with the Syndicate for the world. I'm sure if I live through it, the memories will be lots of fun."

"Fun?"

"That was sarcasm."

"Got it."

"Those guys won't give a rat's ass that you're a Fixer. Watch your back, Lawson."

I hung up thinking about how bad my life gets every time someone says that to me.

I drove to New York.

A few months back that would have meant a road

trip in my wonderful black Ford Explorer. But some asshole had demolished it with a shaped charge left under my seat. The explosive was meant for me. They only got the truck because they used cheap Soviet surplus that smelled like marzipan. I happened to sniff the crap seconds before my asshole met my skull on the way to a moon-shot death.

Now I drove a Mercedes.

I think I explained before that vampires don't usually want for much. Most of us have enough money to live quite nicely on. So the Mercedes wasn't really all that much of a budget pinch. Plus, the damned thing drove like a dream, cornered tight, and would undoubtedly help me blend into the world of the Syndicate, which I was going to inevitably run into.

Lucky me.

The Massachusetts Turnpike shot me west. Around Sturbridge I turned off and onto 84 south into Connecticut—land of the bad drivers. In between grinding my teeth and watching for Connecticut State cops who have been known to use Yugos as unmarked patrol cars, I drove into Hartford and then slid onto 91 South.

91 dropped me onto 95 South like a bad hangover. 95 has never been one of my favorite roads to drive on. Potholes, maniacal trucks, and a lack of anything decent to eat dog you every inch of the way to New York. Fortunately, the route I took meant that I was on 95 for about an hour or less depending on traffic.

According to Uncle Phil, Marilyn had a pad on the Upper East Side. I caught FDR Drive and got off just below the United Nations—because I like that exit—and started checking to make sure I hadn't been followed. It was a slim chance, but I follow the rules whenever I can.

I crossed over onto Third Avenue and headed north toward the East 50s. As I cruised through the slim side streets looking for parking. I caught sight of a camera crew and wondered which show they were shooting. After all, this was New York. Next to Los Angeles, I figured there was more square footage of camera crews and actors than anywhere else in the world.

I found a space only five blocks from Marilyn's apartment and muttered a whole bunch of thank yous to a few gods. Parking this close to my target was a real miracle down in the Big Apple.

Rain began splattering my leather jacket as I walked back toward the apartment building. I don't know what I hoped to find there, but I've read enough detective novels to know you always start with the place the victim was last seen.

Who knew? Sometimes folks have a habit of turning up where you least expect them.

I rang the buzzer.

The doorman inside looked up from his paper and waved me in.

I smiled and entered the building. "Thanks."

"Rain'd soak you through in another five minutes."

"Didn't hear a thing about storms on the forecast."

"Never do. Weathermen are worse than psychic hotlines." He eyed me. "You don't live here."

"No. I'm looking for someone who does, though. Marilyn Hansen."

He smiled. "Sure, I know Marilyn. Ain't been around in a dog's day, though."

"How long is that?"

"Few weeks. You the boyfriend?"

"Cousin. In town and hoping to see her. I don't have much family." Might as well tell the world.

"Shame. But she ain't here."

"She move out?"

"Nah, still keeping the place. Just that she's not around."

"You got mail for her?"

"In her box."

"The box holds two weeks' worth?"

He shrugged. "Never got all that much to begin with."

"You have a key?"

"'Course not."

"You wouldn't let me see it anyway, would you?"

"How'd that look? If word got out I let some stranger see a tenant's mail, I'd be humping sidewalk in a heartbeat."

"Not a fun way to hump."

"Better if there's a nice warm woman underneath."

"Amen to that."

He glanced back at his paper. "You so interested, why don't you ask her roommate some about her?"

"She had a roommate?"

"Has. Had. Another gal. Name of Teresa."

"How come Teresa doesn't have Marilyn's mail?"

"Marilyn had a separate mailbox."

"Teresa home now?"

He had already picked up the phone. I listened as he spoke a few words and then replaced the receiver. He nodded. "Says to go on up. Number 216."

"Guess I'm not a stranger any more, huh?"

He just grinned. "We'll see."

Phil hadn't held back on making sure his little princess got the kind of pad she thought she deserved.

I wasn't familiar with rents in the Big Apple, but I'd say my cousin's zest for a nice apartment was probably setting Phil back somewhere on the order of $20,000 a year.

I know a helluva lotta folks who work their asses off just to make that each year.

The elevator doors slid back with a vague hiss. Thick red carpet covered the hallway, the sort of rug that footsteps make no noise on.

As I banked a right off the elevator, I heard a door open ten feet down the hall. I imagined Marilyn probably lived with an unattractive roommate. Marilyn had always had something of an inferiority complex when it came to other women.

I was wrong.

"Lawson?"

I hate it when my mouth and tongue stop functioning, but it did take me just over three seconds to regain my composure. I did a passable imitation of a nod and she stood back, letting me into the apartment.

Teresa was slim but not in the disgusting rail-thin way too many women are nowadays. There was a lithe quality to her. Sinuous. Sleek. Like a jungle cat stretched out on some savanna, basking in the warm glow of an afternoon sun and contemplating killing something to eat. She had black hair that fell to about her shoulders and warm eyes shaped like plump almonds.

Judging from the way she moved, I guessed she was a dancer.

She sat on the leather couch and studied me. "Marilyn never mentioned a cousin."

"I'm the black sheep of the family."

"Oh, really?"

"No, but the truth is a lot more boring."

"I haven't seen her in about two weeks, if that's what you're here for."

"It is."

"I can't help you."

I looked around and then back at her. "You're a dancer."

"What makes you say that?"

"Way you move."

Her eyebrows wiggled a little. "You saw me walk from the door of the apartment to the couch."

"That's right."

"Very confident in your assumptions."

"I've seen dancers before."

"What—dated them?"

"No. I've seen them." I glanced around again. The furniture looked as expensive as the view. "Am I right?"

"You're right."

"Marilyn danced."

"Yes."

"That means you might have danced together, right?"

"Is that some vague lesbian innuendo?"

"No. It's a perfectly legitimate question."

She grinned. "I don't get many of those."

"I'll bet."

"That was innuendo."

"Maybe."

She grinned again. "Yes. Marilyn and I danced together every once in a while. We were both hoping to land some dream gig. We went to auditions, had meetings with our agent, and we hoped against hope to find a blockbuster stint that would catapult our careers into stardom."

"A lot of past tense in what you just said."

"Well. Marilyn is gone. And me? I've got to some-how pay the rent on this apartment. Dancing isn't exactly the easiest lifestyle to maintain. It doesn't lend itself to the hours of a nine-to-five job."

I could have shed some light on exactly how difficult the life of a Fixer is, but I chose not to. Teresa didn't look like she'd be all that interested in vampires anyway. "What's the rent on this place?"

"Why?"

I sighed. "Call me curious, okay?"

"$3500 a month."

"Is that all?" I grinned to show it was a joke. She bit, but only just.

"It's more than I can make, I'll tell you that."

I took out my wallet and removed one of the folded up blank checks I keep in there. For some reason, I've never liked carrying checkbooks. I wrote out a check and handed it to her. "Put that in the bank. That should take the heat off you for a while."

Her eyes widened when she saw the amount I'd written down. "Why are you giving me a check for twenty thousand dollars?"

"Because I need your help finding my cousin. And I can't get your help if you're too busy looking for work to pay the bills on this place."

"You want my help?"

"Yes."

"For twenty grand?"

"Consider it a fair trade."

"I'd say you overpaid."

"I'm an optimist. I like to think I'll get my money's worth."

She leaned forward. "You're serious."

"I am very serious about finding my cousin. I'm also

serious about needing your help. Now if you'd rather not help me find Marilyn, that's your prerogative. I'll just take the check and go."

She looked at me and a bright warm smile spread across her face. It was the kind of smile I'd enjoy seeing more of. "I'd love to help. I really would."

At last, my day was getting better.

Four

Teresa was the kind of girl everyone on the street checks out. As we walked toward my car, I counted a dozen people who took more than a passing interest in her. And in me. People always look to see what kind of man is with a beautiful woman—if only to confirm or refute whatever judgment system they have in place.

But for a guy like me, who usually flies under radar as much as possible, that kind of attention wasn't something I particularly enjoyed. Even if I *did* enjoy having Teresa walk beside me.

"You drive a Merc?"

I shrugged. "I stole it from a rest stop in Connecticut. Hop in."

She stopped.

I paused. "Well, it's not like the old guy who'd been driving it was even giving her a decent workout. At least I drive over the speed limit."

She stood there with a very firm look etched across her face. I don't usual put people into such moral quandaries so soon after meeting them. I grinned. "It was a joke."

She hesitated another minute, nodded, and got into the car. "Where are we going?"

I turned to her. "Well, I was hoping you'd be able to

suggest an avenue we could explore. Tell me about your lives, what you did, where you went, that sort of thing."

"Are you a private eye?"

"I play one on TV."

She smirked. "Do you always tell this many jokes?"

"Only when I'm around beautiful women. Otherwise, it just comes out as sarcasm."

"So, I should consider myself . . . lucky?"

"I was thinking that was me, actually. Let's get back to Marilyn."

"You sound like a private eye."

"You know that from talking to them?"

"No. From watching them on TV."

"Surest way to become a pseudo-expert."

"You're dipping into the sarcasm now."

"I'm just asking questions."

"It's not the questions you ask." She looked out of the window. "It's how you ask them. Like you've done this kind of thing before."

"I'm addicted to *Magnum, P.I.* episodes in syndication. Does that explain it?"

"Not even remotely."

"Best answer you'll get."

She sighed. "Start at the studio."

"What's that?"

"The studio. Where we danced. We got some assignments from the program director on occasion."

"Whereabouts?"

"Broadway. Down by Little Italy. You know how to get there?"

"I think so."

"Hit Broadway and I'll direct you from there."

I nodded and slid the car out onto the street. "While

I drive, why don't you tell me about the last time you saw Marilyn?"

"Two weeks ago. I thought you knew that."

"I'd like you to elaborate somewhat on it. Was this the first time she vanished? Did she disappear like this before?"

"A few times she'd be out all night. We used to go clubbing a lot. Maybe we'd meet some guys, that sort of thing. We didn't keep super-close tabs on each other. We knew enough about each other, but you have to remember—we're both dancers. Sometimes we'd go for the same jobs. You get what I mean?"

"A little rivalry never hurts things."

"Well, just so you don't go thinking we were sisters or something like that."

There was no way Marilyn would have ever let herself get too close to Teresa. Being that she was a vampire and all. "So, she never came home that night?"

"No."

"When she left, the last time you saw her—tell me about it."

"She was dressed well. Like she was going to dinner or something. Marilyn always did have better luck landing the rich older guys."

"You think she met a rich older guy?"

"She was wearing a small black dress. Spaghetti strap number. Deep plunging neckline. Definitely a step above our usual club garb. She mentioned dinner."

"She get picked up by anyone?"

Teresa shook her head. "A cab took her to wherever she was going."

"And that was it?"

"Yeah."

"But we're going to the studio."

"You asked for my help. This might help."

"She ever go to the studio dressed like you just described?"

"Of course not."

"So what—you think the dinner might have been connected to a job?"

"You never know." Teresa pointed. "Pull up there and park."

"There's no meter."

She just looked at me. "So?"

I find it tough to argue with that kind of logic so I slid the Mercedes into the space and we got out. Teresa reached the door first and swung it open. A small brass sign read Broadway Center for Dance and we walked up a flight of linoleum steps caked with dust and small bits of paper.

"Cozy."

Teresa didn't notice. I watched her backside swing as she moved up the steps. For a moment, I forgot about everything else. But just for a moment.

The scent of sweat tinged the air the way it always does at gyms and like places. I'd had that smell ingrained in me for years. It was always present at the martial arts school I worked out at in Boston.

I heard music as we crested the steps. Someone was playing Tchaikovsky. I usually prefer Vivaldi, but then again, I don't dance.

"Classical ballet?"

Teresa nodded. "There's jazz, tap, modern, hip hop, pretty much everything. Do you dance?"

"About as often as I get root canals."

"What's the matter—got no rhythm?"

"I've got rhythm. It's just that it usually abandons me on the dance floor."

Teresa smiled. "You know what they say—guys who can't dance can't perform well in the sack, either."

"Who says that?"

"People. Girls. It's a well-documented fact."

"Well, whoever did that research must have missed interviewing me. I've never had any complaints."

Her smiled deepened. "Maybe they faked it."

I shook my head. "I won't even dignify that with a response. Where's the program director?"

"That's him over there. His name's Raoul. He's a bit of an ass."

And he looked it; although far be it for me to judge a book by its cover. Raoul stood about an inch taller than I did. Thinly corded muscles wrapped themselves around his body like anorexic pythons. I had a tough time deciding whether the pencil-thin moustache he wore made the black spandex unitard any easier to take. I gave up trying when he walked over.

"Teresa. Sweetheart." He kissed her on the cheek and I thought I saw a glancing brush of his tongue on her skin. Teresa jumped slightly but kept her revulsion in check. I admired her resolve. If Raoul did that to me, I'd cut him a new airhole.

He took his time being lecherous with Teresa but finally cast a glance my way. He looked over the black leather jacket, jeans, and turtleneck I wore with obvious disdain. Apparently I wasn't dressed properly.

"Who is this?"

"His name is Lawson. He's Marilyn's cousin."

"Really."

I smiled my best friendly smile. "Sure am."

"You're wanting dance lessons?"

"Oh no. I leave the dancing to the professionals.

I'm more of a cut-to-the-quick kind of guy. I don't have much time to dance around things."

"Really."

"Yeah. I'm looking for information on where Marilyn is. Teresa here thought maybe you'd have some ideas."

"Did she?" He laughed, but there was no mirth in it. "Silly girl, Teresa is. Obviously, I have no idea where Marilyn is. I mean, I run this studio. I don't truly have the sort of time to nose about in the lives of my dancers."

"You ever give her any jobs?"

"On occasion. A dancewear catalog assignment down in Memphis. A commercial. A video now and again. Nothing too high profile."

"What about other stuff?"

"What other stuff?"

"You ever rent the girls out?"

Teresa's eyes exploded white. Raoul kept his composure in check. "You aren't serious."

"Seems like a legitimate question. I've known less likely fronts for prostitution before."

"That does not surprise me one bit," said Raoul.

"The question still needs an answer."

"This is ridiculous." Raoul crossed his arms and did his best to look intimidating. "I won't stand for such an accusation."

"Wasn't really an accusation. If it had been, I would have said something like, 'you're pimping your best looking dancers and there's a chance my cousin got mixed up in it and might be dead now.'" I smiled. "See? I didn't say it like that."

"However you want to describe what you just did, I

won't have it. I think you should leave now before it gets unfriendly around here."

"Unfriendly?"

He moved closer and tried to peer into my eyes with what I guessed was his killer look. "You are beginning to get on my nerves, Mr. Lawson."

"It's just Lawson. No need for the mister stuff."

He leaned closer. I smelled garlic and onions. His breath stank. "Leave now, Lawson. While you are still able to do so on your own two legs."

"And if I don't? Are you going to remove one of my legs?

"If I have to. I can also get the police down here and have them charge you with trespassing."

"Standing here asking questions is trespassing? Wow, New York gets tougher laws every time I come down here."

Raoul put a hand on my arm. "Time to go."

It was a bad move. I looped my arm over his and cranked it up, affecting a tight armlock. Raoul's whole body seized up. Too bad, that made the lock work even better. He tried to squirm out of the armhold but I moved my knee in behind his and leaned some weight in, making it tough for him to move around.

I leaned in close. "Now that we're nice and friendly-like, let me tell you something, Rollo."

He gasped. "Raoul."

"I don't give a damn what your stupid name is. But I'll tell you what: I don't like what I've seen in the last five minutes. I don't know what you're up to, but judging from what I feel, you're a sleazeball. I don't know how, I don't know what you're into. Yet. But I'll find out. And if I find out you've got something to do with my cousin's disappearance, I'll be back for you. And you will not like what happens then."

I cranked the armlock tight, grinding the bones together for effect. "You got all that?"

He nodded weakly. "Good." Teresa looked like she was going to pass out. I nodded to the door. "You ready?"

She gave me a meek nod and I let Raoul go. He stood there massaging his shoulder. I thought he was going to cry.

Teresa followed me downstairs. At the bottom, I glanced back up and saw Raoul standing there attempting to bore a hole in me with his eyes. I let my own eyes go stone dead and looked right through him. He got the message and disappeared back into the studio.

I sighed. Something definitely did not feel right about that guy. And it wasn't just the black unitard and pencil-thin moustache.

Something told me I'd be seeing the slime bucket again real soon.

Five

"You look shocked."

"I'm mortified!"

I thought that was a bit extreme but didn't say anything. Truth was, Teresa'd probably never seen Raoul manhandled that way before and it must have jarred her some. But guys like Raoul get their kicks from oozing slime all over women who need their help in one capacity or another. I don't much like that type of behavior. And every once in a while, I actually get the chance to do something about it.

Teresa stalked back to the Mercedes. "You know, this may not matter much to you, but I've got to train there. I've got to go back and see that . . . man. You almost breaking his arm like that isn't exactly going to be healthy for my career."

She leaned against the car. I couldn't help myself. I smiled.

"What the hell are you grinning at?"

I shrugged. "Well, it's just usually when women get pissed off like that, they storm away from me and never look back."

"That must happen a lot."

"Actually, it doesn't. But I figured I'd just bluff my way through it. Obviously you aren't mad enough at me to stalk away."

"And ride the subway back to my apartment? Don't be ridiculous."

I slid into the car. "And here I thought it was because you're concerned about Marilyn and want to help me."

She got in. "I am concerned about Marilyn."

"Have you gone to the cops?"

"Her father didn't want me to." She glanced away almost as if she expected me to ream her out for not doing so. But I knew Phil wouldn't have wanted the human authorities involved in vampire business. That's why yours truly was down there.

I leaned back against the seat. "So, did I hit a nerve with Raoul there or what?"

"You almost broke his arm."

"That's not what I meant."

"I know."

She stayed quiet for a minute and then sighed. "I've heard he does it."

"No firsthand experience?"

She looked at me. "Jesus. You ever hear of tact?"

"My tact tends to go out the window when I'm trying to save somebody's life. Check me out any other time and you'll find me as etiquette-bound and circumspect as the next guy."

"That's not saying much."

"Touché."

"You really think Marilyn's life might be in danger?"

"It's a possibility. Why don't you tell me a little bit more about what you've heard about unitard-boy upstairs?"

"Marilyn mentioned he'd approached her a few

times about being an arm trophy for some rich old guys who wanted a nice night on the town."

"He ever come right out and suggest she sleep with any of them?"

"She never said. I think it was pretty well implied, though."

"Having just met the slimeball, I'd tend to agree."

"I'd heard other rumors from some of the other girls who dance there as well."

"What kind of rumors?"

"Just the same things. Raoul made it sound like some sort of legitimate escort service—go out with these geezers, have a few drinks, look good, and make some decent money."

"You know any escort services that are legit?"

"On the surface, aren't they all?"

"I've never called any. I wouldn't know."

"You think Raoul got to Marilyn?"

"Maybe. You said she was off to dinner, dressed up and looking sharp."

"That could have been for anyone, though."

"And you also said the way she was dressed was a cut above what you all usually wore to the clubs."

"Yes."

"And while you didn't, as you said—keep super-close tabs on one another—you would have at least known if she had a boyfriend or lover she was serious about."

"Sure."

"Serious enough to go out wearing a little black dress."

"Yeah."

"The Raoul theory is looking better all the time, don't you think?"

"Unfortunately."

I glanced at my dashboard clock. Wristwatches and I have never gotten along. The stupid things jump off my wrist first chance they get. "You hungry?"

"Are you proposing a date?"

"I was thinking dinner first. Marriage usually comes later."

She smiled. I smiled. She smiled some more. "Aren't we supposed to be looking for Marilyn?"

"We are. We've been conducting some very thorough research. And now we need sustenance. You can't find a missing person without some food."

"I thought you'd be pissed off."

"About what?"

"My reaction to what you did back there."

I put my seat belt on. "You know, Teresa, I do a lot of things I'm not always sure are the smartest choices at the time. Sometimes, some of those things come back and bite me on the ass in a real bad way. I don't claim to be perfect. Never have. But I do things the best way I know how and hope they work out in the end. I don't expect anyone but me to understand how I work. And I don't expect to win anyone's approval for what I do, either."

She kept watching me. Her eyes were fairly intense. "You're an honest man, I'll say that for you."

"Man" didn't exactly cover it. But she nailed the honest part and that was fine with me. "How about that dinner?"

"You know a place?"

I nodded. "I've been to town a few times before. I know a few spots."

She smiled. "All right then."

* * *

"I've been dancing since I was twelve."

We'd found a pub we both thought looked good on West 56th Street, a few blocks away from Carnegie Hall, almost on the border of the Upper West Side. The dark brown wood panels and high-backed booths afforded us a lot of privacy. I didn't think we were that much in need of privacy yet, but I kept my hopes up. A single bulb overhead cast some light across our plates of food. "What got you started?"

Teresa smiled. "Parents. It's always the parents, isn't it?"

"Sometimes. Sometimes the kid actually wants to do it."

"My mother wanted to be a dancer. She wound up married in suburban New Jersey instead, with four children."

"Thus endeth the dream."

"Temporarily."

"Oh?"

"She lived vicariously through my accomplishments."

"The American way. Live your dreams by imposing them on your kids."

"You're a bit of a cynic, aren't you?"

"Some people would call it realistic."

"Some people would call a cow a horse and bet money on it to finish first in the Kentucky Derby."

"Okay." I bit into my cheeseburger. Teresa picked at her tuna salad.

"Once I started dancing, though, it was like something clicked with me. You know that feeling?"

I shrugged. Agreeing that I'd felt the same thing the first time I killed a rogue vampire in the name of protecting the Balance didn't really seem to be the best way to keep the momentum building.

"Well," she continued, "it clicked for me. I studied every dance style I could. Ballet—both Russian and American—Tap, Latin, Swing, Ballroom. I loved them all."

"Got a favorite?"

"Jazz. I like the improvisational attitude it has."

"You ever dance to Dexter Gordon?"

"I don't think so. He a jazz musician?"

"Something like that, yeah."

She kept going. "I came to New York to study dance in college."

"Where?"

"NYU. I had a great time. Even had a little cat I'd smuggled into the dormitory."

"You like cats?"

"They're easier to hide in a dorm than dogs."

"Wow, your love of them blows me away."

"I like dogs just as well. I had fun with the cat." She shrugged. "It wasn't a life changing event."

"You had many of those?"

"No."

"How old are you?"

"Twenty-four."

That made me a hundred and thirteen years her senior. Us dirty old men were always hawking the young girls. "Give it time. I'm sure you'll have your share."

"You say that like you know firsthand."

"Yeah."

"But you don't look all that old."

"And how old is that?"

"Midthirties. Maybe."

"Appearances can be deceiving. I'm actually over a hundred years old."

She grinned and plopped a piece of tuna into her mouth. "Yeah. Sure."

So much for the truth. "What happened after NYU?"

"The cruel reality of the big city—the big wide world waiting for a sucker thinking they can actually live their dreams."

"That was woefully poetic."

"Woefully?"

"It was on my 'word-a-day' vocabulary-builder calendar."

"It's the truth, though. People in this town trying to forge their own path are a dime-a-dozen. How many of the folks I pass each day are like me, trying to keep their heads above water and find the courage to not give in to the pressures of getting a nine-to-five job?"

"Probably lots."

"No 'probably' about it. I've seen too many of them. What makes me different from any of them? What makes my chances of success any better than theirs?"

"I don't know. Determination? Perseverance? Luck?"

"Luck more than any of the others you mentioned."

"Maybe."

"Definitely. This is a hard town to thrive in if you buck the system."

"Life's not supposed to be easy."

"Sure it's not. But it's not supposed to be a royal pain in the ass all the time, either. Is it?"

"Depends on your life." I happened to think mine qualified as the pain-in-the-ass lifestyle grand champion of all time. But then again, I'm biased.

"You aren't much for explaining the mysteries of the universe, are you?"

"I'm just enjoying my cheeseburger."

"That's it?"

I smiled. "View's pretty good."

"Pretty good?"

"Well, I don't want you thinking I'm going to fall all over you and gush like some sixteen-year-old."

"You don't seem like the gushing type."

"Probably not."

She leaned across the table. "So, what do you do?"

"I solve problems."

"For a living?"

"If you can call it that, yeah."

"And you're solving this problem?"

"The Marilyn problem? Yep. Trying to."

"You get paid for doing this?"

"No. This is family."

"But other times."

"Other times, I do this professionally. And I get paid for it."

"Was this your dream?"

"Doing this?" I almost choked stifling the laugh. The sheer lunacy of the idea cracked me up. Imagine having my destiny decided for me by the Council and thinking it was my dream to live a lonely life devoted to killing those vampires that would threaten the Balance. *Comical.*

"You okay?"

I nodded and took a sip of the Sam Adams in front of me. It was just the Boston lager. I was waiting for the Winter brew, which was a damned fine beer in my book.

"I'm not so sure I ever thought of my job as a dream."

"So it never was?"

"Sometimes it seems like things just happen. Call it karma, destiny, kismet, fate, what have you. I don't think I could ever say my career was a dream."

"That's sad."

"It's my life."

Teresa patted my hand. Her skin felt smooth and cool. "You're an interesting man, Lawson."

"A lot of people think I'm an asshole."

"I don't think you're an asshole."

I looked up and smiled. "Raoul thinks I'm an asshole."

"*Raoul* is an asshole."

"Fair enough."

"So, what happens next?"

"We finish our meal. I take you home. I go and find a hotel to crash in."

"You haven't taken care of that yet?"

"Didn't seem to be a rush earlier. I wanted to talk to you, maybe get started. Sleep's overrated anyway. I knew a guy once who told me I could sleep when I was dead. Guess that stayed with me."

"The long sleep."

"The longest."

"You have a hotel in mind?"

"Not yet."

"I could suggest a few places."

"Okay." I nodded. "What are you doing tomorrow?"

"Audition. First thing."

"What's the job?"

"Music video."

"Raoul set that up for you?"

"No. My agent."

"Did Marilyn have an agent, too?"

"Sure."

"Should we talk to him?"

"Her, actually. And I wouldn't bother. Marilyn's agent is also my agent. And I'm still here."

"So, you aren't worried."

"Should I be?"

I wanted to say no. But part of me felt that we'd both be saying yes sooner rather than later. The realization didn't make my cheeseburger taste any better.

Six

I dropped Teresa off at her apartment and headed toward midtown east. Before I could check into a hotel and grab some much-needed sleep, I had a few formalities to address.

Not that I particularly enjoyed doing so.

I slid into a recently vacated parking space and headed toward the red brick building on Third Avenue. A set of stone steps lead up to the entranceway and I paused before cresting them.

I leaned on the buzzer and waited.

The door opened ten minutes later. I'd apparently woken him up. Judging by the way he answered the door, keeping his left hand out of sight, I knew he was hiding his piece in it.

"Yeah?"

"*Fyar Chuldoc Erim.*" It was the pledge of the Fixers everywhere, in our ancient language, Taluk. It meant Duty, Loyalty, Honor.

His eyes popped open. "*Malang dol hachvem.*"

The reply to my phrase meant "Before all, the Balance" and was the required response. He looked me over and then offered his right hand.

"I'm Kohl."

I shook his hand. "Lawson."

His eyes widened a little. "You're some ways from Boston. What brings you here?"

"You know my name."

He shrugged. "Just from the stories."

"Would it help if I said they weren't true?"

"Nope."

Fixers are required to check in with the resident Fixer of another city whenever they're on their turf. I didn't like the idea of alerting too many people to my presence, but I try to obey the rules when I can.

"I'm here on family business."

He grinned. "Our whole career is a family business. Give me a little more, would you?"

"My cousin's missing. She lived down here."

"Someone could have requested a formal investigation. I could have saved you some time—a road trip even."

"My uncle isn't the type of guy to go and request an investigation from the Council. He freaked out enough when he found out I was a Fixer."

"So he called in a marker, did he?"

"That's about it. Yeah."

"You want to come in? It's better than standing out here on the stoop."

I figured by the time I got around to booking a hotel, I'd have about as much luck finding a room as finding Tia Carrere waiting for me when I arrived. It wasn't going to happen. At least not tonight.

I followed him inside.

It was a fairly nice office setup. Fixer stations outside of Boston are generally low-key facilities that house the Fixer and sometimes his Control. Or they have the option of getting regular houses or apartments. Kohl must have noticed my curiosity because he cleared his throat.

"I just got transferred over from Madrid a few weeks back. I haven't had a chance to scout out some real digs yet. I'm bunking here for a while."

"And your Control?"

"Vacation in Cancun."

"Cancun? That place is overrun with drunken students year-round."

"That's what I said. He said it was a great place to hunt. A guy's got his preferences I guess."

"I guess." I sat down on a couch opposite a television set in the reception room and waited for him to drop into an armchair opposite me. "Kohl sounds German."

"It is German."

"If you just got transferred over from Madrid, who'd you replace?"

"D'Angelo. He put in for a switch to Honolulu and it finally came through. Lucky bastard."

"How long'd he have New York for?"

"Five years near as I can figure."

"You up to speed yet on the city?"

"You mean have I had a chance to get acquainted with all the scumbags running around this place?"

"That's one way to put it, I guess."

He smiled and laid his pistol on the side table. "Answer's no. I've got a stack of case files on my desk that need closure. I haven't had a chance to do any covert community policing as such."

"Guess it's a good thing I came on down then, eh?"

"How do you figure?"

"You wouldn't have had time to look into a missing person case."

"Oh, I don't know. If I knew it was a favor for you, I might have found the necessary time."

"Yeah? How'd I rate that kind of preferential treatment?"

"You're a famous guy, Lawson. Fixers everywhere know all about you. You're the one."

"The one what?"

"The one who killed his own Control and lived to tell the tale."

"I never said a word."

Kohl smiled. "You know Controls gossip like old ladies. Word spread pretty fast. Besides, even if it hadn't, a call for a replacement Control for Boston is a pretty unusual thing to come down the pipeline."

"I guess." I made a mental note about poor operational security. "So, what can you tell me about the city that you've found out so far?"

"What do you want to know?"

"I know the Syndicate's down here. What's the deal on them?"

"You planning on messing around with them?"

"Hopefully not."

Kohl nodded. "They run some fringe enterprises. Nothing too overtly illegal. They stay in line most of the time. They seem to respect the Council's right to administer harsh justice if they step out of line."

"Really?" The stories I'd heard about the Syndicate didn't seem to jibe with Kohl's assessment.

"D'Angelo apparently had a pretty decent relationship with them. He kept them in check but gave them the necessary room to operate. Maybe even some respect."

"I don't even know why they're tolerated. What they do, it could expose us all. And the cleanup would be horrendous."

"The way D'Angelo explained things to me, the

Syndicate provides some sort of vital inroad to certain aspects of society we need assets in."

"That a fancy way of saying they give us sleazeball informants and information in exchange for turning a blind eye to what they do?"

Kohl shrugged. "Don't know. I haven't even met them yet."

"Who runs the show?"

"D'Angelo never knew. He said they worked through cutouts. He met middle managers—that's it."

"Nice they respected him enough to show him the way to the top."

"Yeah, well, I'm trying hard to keep the good vibes going. I don't need the Syndicate stirring up a kettle of shit and pouring me a cupful."

"I'll keep that in mind."

"Please do. Your reputation precedes you, Lawson."

"Meaning what?"

"Meaning I know you have a penchant for administering your own brand of justice. The Council tolerates it because you get results. But along the way you stir up a lot of trouble. Trouble like the Syndicate, I don't need. Not right now. Not ever. We clear?"

"Sure. I'll do my best to make sure you don't get any shit."

Kohl grinned. "Thanks. Now what was your cousin's name?"

"Marilyn Ferro."

"You want, I can ask around. Shake the trees a little bit and see what falls out."

I didn't mention Raoul and the fact that I'd rattled his tree pretty hard already. "Yeah, that'd be good."

"Where are you staying?"

I glanced at the clock over the mantle and frowned. Already heading on midnight. "Nowhere yet."

"You don't have a hotel?"

"Didn't have time. I drove down this morning and spent the day interviewing the roommate. Then I came here."

Kohl frowned. "You should have come here first."

"Yeah. Probably."

"No probably. You know the protocol."

"Oh, for Christ's sake, Kohl, I'm here now."

"What if you'd gotten in the shit earlier today? I wouldn't have had any idea what was going on. Things could have gotten out of hand and I'd be left holding a rotten bag of—"

"—shit, yeah I know. Okay. Consider me reproached, okay?" I stood. "It's late and I've got to find a place to crash or the homeless are going to have make room for one more down in Washington Square."

"No more homeless down there. Giuliani cleaned 'em up and moved 'em off years ago."

"Great. Thanks for the tip." I walked to the door.

Kohl followed. "You all set with a gun and ammunition?"

"I brought some."

"You have the number here?"

"Yeah."

"You get into trouble, you give me a call, all right? None of this handling stuff by yourself shit."

"As if."

He eyed me. "Like I said, Lawson, your rep precedes you. And yes, you most certainly would."

I stuck out my hand and he shook it. "I'll call you if I need you. My word on it."

Kohl nodded and disappeared back inside. I walked down the steps and back into the Manhattan night.

Then me and my reputation crawled back into the Mercedes and went looking for a hotel with vacancies.

Seven

Lady Luck dealt me a hotel outside of Times Square. The last time I was down in the city, Times Square still catered to the freaks, perverts, and bums. Now it looked like a neon Mecca of upscale shops and eateries. At least the change meant the hotel was a few steps above the flop-pads that used to be there.

I crawled into bed and scored maybe five hours of solid sleep. I prefer a lot more than five on most nights. But I don't always have the luxury of sleeping late. I take what I can get and roll as best as I know how.

Considering I hate sleeping in hotels, I was almost surprised I slept as long as I did. Something about not having the comforts of my own bed really makes it tough for me to fall asleep. Plus, hotel-room doors are never quite secure enough to make me feel at ease.

Next morning, I picked Teresa up at her place around eight o'clock. We grabbed a quick breakfast at the diner around the corner from her pad. Well, it must have once been a diner. Now, it had been converted into an overpriced upscale kitsch pseudo-diner that served roasted red potato home fries instead of the old brown and pockmarked Idaho spuds I prefer. And the price for a cup of orange juice was outrageous. But since it was orange juice, I paid anyway. Got to have my OJ.

Teresa wore a bulky sweatshirt that made her upper torso look too amorphous for my taste. But the Spandex pants she wore showed off her incredible lower body. And when she slid into the booth, her hips blossomed beautifully. I'm a sucker for a good set of hips.

"So, where's the audition today? Is it at some big Broadway theater?"

She grinned around the rim of her coffee cup. "Most auditions are held in scummy old buildings where the producers can rent the space out for cheap. Broadway theaters cost a lot unless they're staging the show there."

Images of *A Chorus Line* went flying through my head. So much for my preconceptions about the dance industry. "You said it was a music video last night."

"It is. Ever heard of Blake 7?"

"Wasn't that an old sci-fi show in the UK a few years back?" I used to dine on a steady diet of *Doctor Who* and other Brit SF whenever I had the chance. But I hadn't seen any of the new stuff.

"I don't know about that. But they're the hottest boy band to come out of London in the past three years."

"Wow." I took a sip of juice. "Three years, huh? That's gotta be some sort of longevity record."

"You're being sarcastic again."

"Me?" I switched on my Brit accent. "Perish the thought, luv."

She ignored my accent. "Anyway, there should be about three hundred dancers there trying out for the video today."

"And how many spots are they looking to fill?"

"Three."

"Three? As in 'comes after two'?"

"Uh huh."

"Great odds."

"I told you the dance business was tough."

"You work against those kind of odds often?"

"Not often. All the time."

Three hundred to three were the kind of bad odds I normally deal with as a Fixer. I thought about offering Teresa a new job. "So, where is this place then?"

"Old warehouse down by Wall Street."

"There are warehouses near Wall Street?"

"Down by the fish market, sure."

I could smell the fish guts already. "All the glitz, huh?"

"The glitz comes later. Right now, it's just sweaty, smelly hard work."

Breakfast didn't last as long as I wanted it to. Especially since Teresa didn't have much to eat, just a protein energy shake. I paid the bill and we headed out.

We found our way down Broadway to John Street and banked a left there. Teresa directed me toward the South Street Seaport, which looked similar to Boston's Fanueil Hall. I remembered then that the same architectural firm had supposedly designed them both.

"You can park anywhere around here."

I glanced out of the window. "Uh, where exactly? There are no spaces."

"Over there."

"That's a loading dock."

"So?"

"You want me to park my new Mercedes where it can be towed? Do you have any idea how attached I've become to this car?"

She frowned. "You're not one of those weird guys who names his car, are you?"

"I haven't had this baby long enough to think up a name yet."

"What happened to the car you had before this?"

"It was blown up."

She looked at me and I smiled. Her mouth started to move, but then she simply closed it and looked straight ahead out the windshield. "You can park over there."

A truck had pulled out of a space and I slid in thanking the gods for good timing. I got out and slid a lot of change into the meter. "I'll have to come back and put more change in this thing every hour?"

"We'll be a while," said Teresa.

I followed her along the underside of FDR Drive. Ahead of us, the streets were slick with the hosed-down guts and oil of the million fish that had passed through these rickety storefronts only hours previously.

"New York's fish market is one of the biggest in the world."

"You should see Tokyo's," I said. "It's huge."

"You've been?"

"Been and smelled, yeah."

"That's the building up ahead."

A gray-white old cement building that looked like it might have once been a textile plant poked out among the brick and corrugated steel shutters that ruled this section of town. As we drew near, I could already see a number of dancers heading inside.

"Is this going to be okay—me being with you?"

"Sure, tell 'em you're a reporter or something."

"You mean . . . lie?"

She glanced at me and I broke into a grin. She smiled. "More sarcasm?"

"Call it playful facetiousness. I'm not always sarcastic."

"Right."

Steps led us inside the building where a huge throng of women waited. Most were clad in leotards and leg warmers with dance shoes already on. Teresa looked suddenly overdressed until I saw her peeling off the sweatshirt. She wore a sports bra underneath that did little to conceal the fact that the interior of the building was a bit chilly.

I cleared my throat. "Where should I wait?"

"I have to check in," said Teresa. "Come along and tell them what you're doing. They'll probably give you a great seat."

Someone who looked like he might have played Raoul's understudy—just a helluva lot more effeminate—manned the check-in table. He looked up at me and his eyes narrowed as he broke into a thin smile.

"Can I help you?"

"Yeah, hi, I'm Joe Lansing. I work for the *Albuquerque Free Press.* I'm doing a story on dancers and I've been assigned to follow this woman," I pointed at Teresa, "around town for a few days while she goes on auditions and stuff."

"The *Albuquerque Free Press?*" He said the name like it was coated with dog shit.

"That's right."

"That's in New Mexico?"

"I hope so."

"Never heard of it."

"Well, we're not one of the majors, but we're getting there. You should have seen our subscriptions jump after last year's 'Soda Cans for Suburbia' drive."

He cocked an eyebrow, which I'm sure he felt looked really imposing. I thought it made him look like a Caucasian Charlie Chan. I didn't offer him that opinion, however.

"All right. You can sit in the back and be quiet. And I mean make no noise whatsoever."

"What if I have to breathe?"

"Do it quietly."

"Okay. Thanks."

"That won't be too much of a struggle for you, will it?"

"Not until my asthma kicks in."

"You have asthma?"

"No. But I've been seriously considering acquiring it."

"You aren't funny."

"Well, I'm not a comedian."

I felt Teresa's eyes boring into me. I smiled. "Thanks for your help."

"Oh, it's my pleasure."

Teresa and I moved off. She nudged me. "'Soda Cans for Suburbia'?"

"I thought it was catchy." I winked at her. "Good luck."

I wandered over to the main audition room and found plastic molded chairs at the back of the room in varying pastel shades. Teresa had mentioned this would be a long audition. Three hundred dancers would take a while to get through, unless they all sucked.

I doubted that would be the case.

Twenty minutes after we got there, the auditions began. Ahead of me, three men and two women sat at a table and ticked off items on a checklist while the same monotonously mechanized boy band song played endlessly through a pair of speakers in the room. Waves of dancers worked through a series of steps led by a choreographer who called the moves in time to the music.

Some of the dancers were excellent. They seemed in sync with their bodies and knew how to let the music flow through them. Others looked about as uncomfortable as I would have looked decked out in spandex and leotards trying to dance my way through the Macarena.

The numbers dwindled quickly at first. Waves of hopefuls fell to callous disdain. Their destinies in this case decided by the simple call of the numbers taped to their chests and backs. I saw the tears welling at the corners of painted eyes; I saw the pouty lips pursed together trying in vain to quell the disappointment.

And I saw the professionals who were used to the disappointment of failure, but persevered. These would be the ones who would eventually find some measure of success.

Finally, after an hour of nameless faces coming and going, I saw Teresa's group come into the room. I settled back, concentrating on how well she danced.

And she did. She seemed to know the song already, so that helped. And she followed the choreographer's lead with practiced precision. Her hips swayed, bounced, bumped, and grinded just the way his did. They seemed to be in perfect unison.

I lost track of the other dancers in her group. I was more interested in watching Teresa anyway.

Her group moved off. Numbers were called. I held my breath.

They called Teresa.

I saw her smile and give me the thumbs-up. I nodded and felt happy for her.

Smaller waves of dancers filed in now. There seemed a marked improvement in their precision having run through the steps once before. It amazed me that they were able to dance the set after only having done it once before. Not only was incredible style a necessity, but a photographic memory seemed essential as well.

Teresa came back in and made another round of cuts.

The groups got smaller. I glanced at the clock on the wall overhead and saw that three hours had passed. If I hadn't been looking at Teresa so much throughout it all, I might have realized my ass had fallen asleep hours ago.

Walking was going to be quite a challenge when this was all over.

The music stopped abruptly. One of the men stood up and called a break for lunch. I stayed seated, willing bloodflow back into my hindquarters.

Teresa came over, a sheen of sweat glistening across the top of her breasts. I briefly considered offering to lick it off. Her sports bra was splotchy in places with perspiration. She breathed easily, though, and I knew she was in remarkable shape.

"How are you doing?"

I shrugged. "Me? Oh, I'm fine? Why do you ask?"

She smiled. "Those chairs aren't all that comfortable, are they?"

"You could say that."

"Is your bum asleep?"

"What makes you say that?"

"You haven't moved yet."

I nodded. "I think it's well on its way to gangrene."

She smiled. "I need some lunch. Want to come along?"

"I've got no place else to be."

We walked back out into the cool autumn morning. Around the building, scores of business types walked with briefcases in hand and cell phones glued to their ears.

"Odd sight seeing dancers and the corporate world combining out here, huh?"

I nodded. "Sure seems so."

"What did you think of the morning so far?"

"Grueling. I had no idea it was this tough."

"This isn't the worst it can be. I've been to some even tougher. Broadway shows are really devastating. I usually need a day to recover after them."

"Have you ever done one?"

She shrugged. "Not yet. But that's the dream."

"Well, you looked good to me. I'd say you're a shoe-in. But then again, I'm uneducated in the ways of the dancing world. Plus, I'm extraordinarily biased."

"Extraordinarily?"

"Oh, yes."

"I appreciate the confidence. And your bias. We'll see how things go after lunch, though."

"Will your agent be here then?"

"She might come down, yeah. She handles a lot of the girls here today."

"I'd like to ask her some questions."

"Well, sure." Teresa looked at me. "I mean, that's why you're here with me today, right? To see Marilyn's agent. Otherwise, what would the point be of being here?"

"To lend you moral support."

"You think my morals need support?"

I raised my eyebrows. She just laughed and kept talking. "You could be out looking into other possibilities for clues."

"Clues?"

She grinned. "I'm new to the whole private eye world."

"I never said I was a private eye."

"You never said you weren't, either."

"I love talking with you. I feel like I'm waltzing conversationally with a primed grenade."

"Be careful where you put the pin."

"I wouldn't expect a dancer to know about that."

"One of my brothers was a Marine. He was killed in Panama."

"Sorry."

"Forget it." She kept walking.

I caught up. "What's for lunch?"

Teresa pointed. "Carbohydrates and lots of water. You like Italian?"

I started to nod, but I stopped.

Ahead of us, I saw something I didn't like.

Raoul.

"What the hell is he doing here?"

"I don't know." Teresa frowned. "But he's with my agent."

Eight

From Teresa's reaction, I knew something was up. "What's so weird about that?"

She frowned. "They've never met near as I can tell."

That sure as hell didn't seem to be the case. "The way they're chumming around, I'd say they're a little bit more than passing acquaintances."

"Yeah." Teresa kept walking toward them. I wasn't so sure a follow-up run-in with Raoul was a good thing, but I didn't have much choice. I followed Teresa over.

Raoul saw us first and his eyes squinted accordingly. His moustache looked as ridiculous today as it had yesterday. I smiled at him and he blanched. Always nice to know I have that effect on people. He tried to fake a smile at Teresa.

"How are you doing?"

Teresa shrugged. "Fine. I'm back in after lunch." She turned her attention to the woman. "Rebecca?"

Rebecca stood about four feet eleven inches tall and very close to the same in width. The dark red lipstick splashed across her face added something of a clownlike appearance to her visage. I wanted to ask where her bright red nose was.

She spoke with a thick Brooklyn accent. "Teresa, darling. How are you?"

"I didn't know you knew Raoul."

"Oh, certainly. We go way back."

"Do you?"

"Oh, sure. He sends me talent every now and again that he feels might just have what it takes to make it to the big time."

I grinned. "What a guy."

Rebecca turned to me. "And who, pray tell, is this lovely specimen of a man, anyway?" She glanced at Teresa. "You didn't tell me you had a boyfriend."

"He's not my boyfriend."

Rebecca's eyes lit up like burning magnesium. She must have been about forty-five although the crow's feet scratched on her face looked like they had been there for ages. "Really."

I smiled my best smile. "My name's Lawson."

She took my hand in one of those crappy half-palm handshakes that feel like you're fondling a bowl of cold, wet spaghetti. "Charmed. Please call me Rebecca."

I smiled some more. "You know, Rebecca, I've never met a woman outside of England who used 'pray tell' and 'charmed' before."

"Well, the Brits don't have a monopoly on grace, you know."

Maybe not, but Rebecca certainly wasn't positioning herself to acquire any. "You're Teresa's agent."

"Indeed I am."

"And you were Marilyn's agent as well."

Rebecca clapped a hand over her heart. "Have I been fired? As far as I know, Marilyn is just off on a little vacation or something like that." She put a stubby hand on my arm. "You know how young girls are."

"Not really, but I'm a quick study."

"Oh, they're always off on little sexual rendezvous

of one sort or another. She probably met someone and they skedaddled for a bit of time is all."

I didn't say anything so she continued. "I'm sure she'll turn up again. And when she does, I'll still be her agent. I've found her some very nice jobs, I have."

"Did Ragu here recommend Marilyn to your agency?"

Raoul's eyes blazed. "My name . . . is *Raoul.*"

I just shook my head. "Grinding your teeth isn't good for your gums." I looked at Rebecca. "So?"

"I rely on Raoul to scout dance talent for me. In this case, he recommended Marilyn. A little later on, Marilyn brought Teresa in to see me. It's all worked out quite well so far."

"Except for one thing: Marilyn's missing."

Rebecca nodded. "Yes. There is that."

"As far as I'm concerned," I said, "that's all there is to 'that'."

Rebecca's friendly demeanor slipped just a speck. "Raoul was telling me as much."

"How utterly swell of him to do so." I smiled at Raoul. "How's the arm?"

He looked away. Teresa cleared her throat. I took that as my cue to back off some. Ever the attentive monkey, I did just that and let Teresa speak.

"Rebecca, do you have any information about the jobs Marilyn went on that might help us track her down?"

"What's this 'us' stuff, darling? The way I understand it, Mr. Lawson here—"

"It's just Lawson."

She looked at me. "What?"

"There's no mister. It's just Lawson."

She looked at me like she was trying to figure out

why I'd interrupted her monologue with such a seemingly trivial piece of information. After five seconds of silence that I supposed was her way of chastising me, she continued.

"The way I understand it, Lawson here"—she glanced at me and I smiled—"is the professional looking into the disappearance. Not you. You, sweetie, have a dance job to win for the Blake 7 music video. I'd suggest you keep your mind focused on that and let the rest of us worry about Marilyn's whereabouts."

I grinned. "The rest of us?" Since when had this become a team effort?

Rebecca smiled at me. "Naturally, I'm as interested as you are in finding dear Marilyn."

"What happened to your sexual rendezvous theory?"

"Oh that's just one possibility."

"Really."

"There could be more."

"I'm listening."

She smiled. "It's probably better if we talk some other time. But I want you to know that I am definitely interested in finding her."

"If only for the financial rewards?"

"I beg your pardon. I am not as callous as that. I have a personal interest in seeing Marilyn safely returned."

"And what interest is that?"

Rebecca smiled. "Well, how good would it look if one of my clients turned up missing and failed to return?"

"Pretty bad. But it ties back in with the financial."

"I liked her as well."

"Ah, nice. Now it's personal."

Raoul frowned. "I told you this was a waste of time."

I ignored him for the moment and zeroed in on Rebecca. "What did you mean just now when you said you wanted to see her 'safely returned'?"

"Exactly what that means."

"And where would she be safely returned from?"

"Her . . . vacation."

I wasn't sure that's what she meant at all. I glanced at Teresa who had a frown on her face directed at the two of them. "Are you sure there's not something else happening here that you might want to disclose now rather than later?"

"There's nothing to talk about."

"Because, you know, if it turns out that I find there was some information withheld, that's liable to make me a pretty cranky dude."

"Why are we wasting time on this man?" Raoul piped up again.

I eyed him. "You're starting to annoy me. I suggest you shut up and not speak for the remainder of our little chat here."

He clammed up and scowled instead. I smiled at Rebecca. "I'd like to see your files."

"What files?"

"The files on where you send your clients. The jobs, the pay rates, the whole damned ball of wax."

"What good will that do?"

"It might give me some interesting leads to go on."

"Leads?"

"Yeah. Clues."

She nodded. "Oh, yes. And what would you do with those leads if you came across something of interest?"

"Obviously I'd run it down and see where it took me."

"Showing you my files wouldn't be the most prudent thing for me to do. As a businesswoman, I need to make sure clients and contacts understand the confidentiality of my work."

"Not showing me your files could prove just as disastrous a business decision."

"Is that a threat?"

"Does it really need to be?"

She eyed me for another minute and then looked at Teresa again. "Not your boyfriend?"

"Nope."

"Well, maybe he should be. I like his pushy style. He's got the attitude you need to make it in this business."

I almost choked. "Thanks."

She squeezed my biceps and smiled. "Strong, too. Come by my office today at three o'clock. Teresa will tell you how to get there. I despise giving directions and I'm awful at it anyway."

"If I come by will you show me the files?"

"Of course."

"Fine. It's a date then."

Her eyes lit up like she hadn't heard that word in twenty years. The way she looked, she might well not have.

She flashed me one last smile, looked at Teresa, and grinned. "Don't forget to go in there and knock 'em dead. Get that job. Believe, believe, believe."

Teresa nodded. "Got it."

"She's doing great," I said.

Raoul sniffed like he'd inhaled a line of bad cocaine. Rebecca smiled patiently. "You have a trained eye, I assume?"

"Me? Nah. But I know a good dancer when I see one. Teresa's amazing. I think she's got a good shot at landing a spot."

"Well, we'll see if your psychic powers are as impressive as your good looks, Lawson. See you at three."

She turned and waddled away with Raoul shooting me one last death glance before turning around. I watched them go and then glanced at Teresa. "Those two seem a lot more pal-around than they ought to be."

"What are you thinking?"

I shrugged. "Nothing concrete yet. It wouldn't be wise to take too big a jump just now. I want a look at her files, though. I want to see where she's sent Marilyn."

"It's going on twelve now. That's three hours for her to get back to the office and purge anything she doesn't want you to see."

"True."

"You don't care."

"I care. I'm not expecting to see much in the files, though. Maybe a name if I'm very lucky."

"So why go?"

"So I can lean on little Miss Rebecca there a bit more without Raoul hanging around. Divide and conquer."

"You think she knows?"

"She knows something."

"And Raoul?"

"I don't know. Maybe he's a hitter."

"What's that?"

"Business term for someone with muscle. An intimidator, sometimes a killer. The way he hung on Rebecca there, he looked like a bodyguard."

"A bodyguard that doubles as a dance instructor? Lawson, do you think you might be reaching here?"

"Undoubtedly. But I've also seen some very weird pairings of occupations before, so Raoul's doesn't seem all that alien to me."

"That makes one of us."

"We'll see how much of a believer you are when this is all over."

"You think this is going to turn out bad?"

"I've never known Marilyn to just take off and not leave any sort of contact information for her family."

"So the answer's yes."

"The answer could well be yes. Yes."

"I'm still hungry."

"You can eat even though you've got to go back in there and dance for God knows how much longer?"

"I'm not really thinking of it in terms of eating, per se. Right now, it's just fuel. I need to gas up for the next round of workouts."

"You mentioned Italian. You still interested in that?"

"Absolutely."

"Lead on."

She pulled on my arm and then stopped. I raised an eyebrow. "Yes?"

"She was right."

"Who was?"

"Rebecca."

"About what?"

"You do have an impressive physique."

I grinned. "Teresa, are you flirting with me?"

"Low blood sugar can make me do strange things."

I smiled. I'd have to remember that.

Nine

Rebecca looked different in the ambient light of her crowded, paper-heavy office. For one thing, her body seemed to ooze over the sides of her chair. I wondered how she could be comfortable. But the biggest difference was her hair. The fluorescent bulbs made it look about five different shades of bright orange. She caught me staring at it and smiled.

"You know, I have to look in my underpants to remember what my real hair color is."

I almost choked. The visual alone should have killed me.

"You must be a real kick at the hairdresser's." I glanced out the window. Rebecca kept the blinds pretty low even though the afternoon hadn't peaked yet. Long shadows drew themselves out across the office. It felt pretty gloomy.

"You didn't really come here to look at my files, Lawson. Did you?"

I turned around to face her. "You've had upwards of three hours to get rid of anything that you might not want me to see."

"I've never purged anything in my life."

I almost smiled. That fact seemed fairly obvious given her girth.

"I've got nothing to hide, Lawson."

"So you wouldn't mind if I checked your drawers?"

Her eyes lit up again the way they had back down by the South Street Seaport. "You name the time and the place, baby. You can check out my drawers any time you want."

I smiled. I'd lobbed that one out there and of course, she'd hit it back. Good. Maybe I could play that angle up. Hopefully I wouldn't have to play it up too far or for too long.

"You and Raoul seem friendly enough."

"Are you jealous?"

"I saw him in a unitard. He didn't give me or anyone else a reason to be envious."

She smirked. "Close relationships are essential in this business. Hell, in any entertainment field they're important. You can't just have an on-again-off-again with these people. On one end, I need to know who is looking for what kind of talent. On the other, I have to know the people who get to see that raw talent first. Can you imagine if I tried to run around scouting good dancers? I'd go crazy."

And probably lose about a hundred pounds, which wouldn't have been a bad move. "You use Raoul to do the scouting for you?"

"He does some, sure. But he's only one dance instructor. There are hundreds of studios and schools in Manhattan. More in the boroughs. I need to know a couple of the key movers and shakers out there. These guys have the reps, so the talent comes to them. I go to the instructors, listen to the recommendations, and see for myself what they've got that I can work with."

"And what does Raoul get out of your relationship?"

"Prestige. He can use the fact that he's supplied me

with talent to recruit more students. And that helps line his pockets with more cash."

"What about a percentage of what you make off the talent he sends you?"

"Depends on the situation. In rare circumstances he might. Say a commercial spot that generates a lot of residuals, he'd get some. But run-of-the-mill assignments don't net him anything in terms of cash."

"There seem to be some vagaries built into this business."

"That happens in any business, dear."

"Not all."

"Mmm." She looked at me. "And what business are you in, Lawson? I mean, besides the psychic prediction business."

"I'm just a guy looking for my cousin. That's all."

"And when you find her?"

"'When'? Are you being optimistic now?"

She smiled. "Why, are you being pessimistic?"

"It's my nature."

"You've done missing persons cases before?"

"Not necessarily that. But my outlook tends to be a bit jaded."

"And what jaded you?"

"Life."

She thought about that for a moment. I could see her debating about whether to try to counter it with some pseudo-psycho-babble bullshit, but she decided against it. And that was fine with me.

"You still haven't told me what you do for work," she replied instead.

"Do you have a job for me?"

"No. You look too much like you go around killing people."

"Just the bad ones."

She held my gaze but only for a second. Not many people can hold my gaze without flinching. I smiled to soften the atmosphere, but only just a little.

Rebecca shuffled some papers on her desk. Finally, she lit a cigarette and inhaled deeply. "Are you here to kill me?"

"What makes you think I wasn't joking?"

"The look in your eyes when you said it. They went stone hard. Cold. I've never seen anything like it before. Well, maybe once. But I never had any reason to doubt it. I see even less reason with you."

"I'm here to find Marilyn," I said. If it turned out Rebecca was involved in her disappearance and possible death, then I'd be back to settle the score with her. There didn't seem much point in saying so, however. Especially since it appeared that Rebecca already sensed enough to keep her on edge for a while.

"Tell me more about Raoul."

"What's to know? He's a washed-up former dancer. He had a shot at Broadway but he snorted it up his nose and bled it out of his mouth. He found himself in the gutter for a few years. By the time he finally yanked his guts out of Skid Row, his prime time had passed. He did what so many other aging wanna-bes do—he opened a school and now lives somewhat vicariously through the dreams of his students."

"You must see that an awful lot."

"Naturally."

"How long's prime for a dancer?"

"Depends on the dancer. Depends on the dance style. Sometimes these kids peak at twenty-two. Sometimes they peak at thirty. A few peak much, much older, but they're the ones who hit it big early on and can then cruise somewhat on their laurels later on. They've got the credentials to do so. For the others, well. . . ." She trailed off.

"What?"

"Well, this isn't the sort of business you can just decide to pick up halfway through however many years you've happened to draw for this lifetime. You want to be a dancer, you start early. Ballet lessons. Jazz. Tap. Later on you move into improvisational, interpretive, performance art pieces, or you specialize in something. You try your damnedest to hit it big. You go to grueling auditions that last for hours, and you hope. You pray."

I saw the faraway look in her eyes and knew. "How long did you pray?"

Her eyes softened and I saw some moisture glistening at their corners. "I started dancing at seven. In Queens. By the time I was seventeen, I was here in town, working in clubs, cheap roles in Off-Broadway shows. I kept going on auditions. I only had a little money. But I had faith, you know? I had this glimmer in my heart that told me if I just hung in there long enough, something—anything—would happen. I would have settled for anything."

"What happened?"

She chuckled a little bit. "What happened? Lawson, *time* happened. You just hear any of what I said? This isn't an old gal's game. Can you imagine the endless hours of trying, followed by endless hours of waiting to hear, and the horrendous amount of stress you have to deal with? It burns you out faster than you'd think. It nearly incinerated me."

"But you didn't open a school."

"Oh, no. Not me. You see, while Raoul does indeed

have some credits to his name, I have little more than grainy memories of dancing in clubs that used to populate Times Square. Shitty red neon nights that blazed and then died in the back closet of my mind."

I whistled. "You got a way with words."

"It's not the words, dear. It's the life I lived."

"So no school."

"You know many banks that make a habit of giving out loans to ex-strippers who want to open up a dance school?"

"Not many."

"Try none."

"That was my next guess."

"I started eating too much. I could blame it on a number of things, but the truth was I let my discipline slip. All those years of never missing a workout, never eating the wrong foods, never letting anything distract me from my goal. It all went to shit."

"Discipline's not the sort of thing you can ever take a break from. It doesn't build up like a reservoir you can drink from when the times are tough."

"I know that now." She gestured to the refrigerator in the corner of the office. "A little too late to be sure, but I know it now."

"You get a lot of dancers through here?"

"I get enough to make a pretty decent living."

"And how good of a dancer was Marilyn?"

"Good."

"Not great."

Rebecca frowned. "I don't know how to put it exactly. Like you said, there are a lot of vagaries in the biz. And that's not just talking about the business ones. Sometimes you see a dancer and you know there's something not there all the way. It's tough to describe. Something's not quite right. And that something holds them back from reaching the highest levels of their craft."

"Marilyn lacked that?"

"I saw her one time during an audition. She'd made it through a few of the callbacks. They'd come down to having the girls in costume, just to see how they each looked. I don't know, maybe the producer got his rocks off looking at girls in cabaret outfits."

"Those outfits have fishnet stockings?"

"Sometimes."

I started to say I couldn't blame the producer but kept it in check. "So she was in costume."

"Yeah, and anyway, about a third of the way through the show, part of her costume starts to come off. Not a lot and certainly not something that would have damaged her good reputation."

"What are we talking about here?"

"Certainly not like her crotch was exposed for the world to see. Her bra, though, it became visible."

"Her bra."

"Right. Like I said, not devastating by any means. Happens all the time to costumes. Damned things are shit for the most part. A lot of costumers moonlight and try to break into the fashion world during the day. You can guess where their minds are at."

"But it mattered apparently to Marilyn."

"Mattered quite a lot. She got flustered by it. Kept moving her hand up to try to keep the material of the costume covering herself. All it was was a bit of exposed neckline and bra strap, but she treated it like she'd been caught strumming the cello on the subway."

"Strumming the cello?"

"Yeah. You know . . . masturbating?"

"Wow, is that what women call it?"

"One of the things, sure. Why—what do you guys call it?"

"Never mind." Marilyn hadn't necessarily been squeamish about her bra showing. Or maybe she had been. But even more importantly, if she hadn't covered herself up, her birthmark would have shown—a blotchy patch of skin that marked every member of the vampire race. An oddity like that might have raised a few eyebrows. Of course, given the number of tattoos people have—maybe it wouldn't.

But to Rebecca, Marilyn had simply been overcome by modesty. Well, that was fine. I'd let her continue to think that.

"You're saying that sank her."

"Yeah, her modesty cost her that job."

"Weren't there other jobs?"

"A few. Not many. I think her confidence was waning."

"She hadn't been trying for all that long, though. She only graduated from NYU a few years back."

Rebecca shrugged. "What can I tell you? It's different for everyone. Some of them hang in there for years, deluded by their own confidence. Others burn out really fast. Marilyn might have been one of the fast ones."

"You think she was?"

"I'm just telling you what I saw."

"And that's all you've got?"

"For now. She shows up again, there might be another chapter to write yet."

"Hopefully one with a happy ending."

Rebecca nodded. "Be nice if it was. God knows I could use a little happiness right now."

I started for the door and then stopped. "Tell me something."

"Yes?"

"What about Teresa?"

"What about her?"

"She a better dancer than Marilyn?"

"Maybe not in the technique department. But she's got the attitude it takes to win. And she knows it."

I nodded and let myself out.

I wasn't at all sure if I'd learned anything useful from my talk with Rebecca.

Ten

Outside Rebecca's office on Houston Street, I paused for a moment. It was a little after four o'clock and a throng of corporate types swam down the sidewalk, intent on walking somewhere they undoubtedly thought was important. All around me, the city surged—almost oblivious to my existence.

But something felt wrong.

I'd been in enough hairy situations to recognize hair standing up on my neck or butterflies in my stomach as warning signs. And since I always try to pay attention to my instincts, I listened this time as well.

I stepped off the stoop and melded into the crowd. As I walked with the humans around me, I tried to pinpoint the exact nature of my feeling. Was it immediate danger? Was it more a sense of impending uneasiness associated with Marilyn's disappearance? Was it some lowlife about to conk me over the head and grab my wallet?

I moved past a subway station and then turned left down West Broadway. Thick electrical cords ran all over the sidewalk and street. Heavy trailers sat parked like juggernauts awaiting their activation. And a different throng of people, far unlike their corporate counterparts, scurried to and fro carrying out tasks.

A movie set.

I'd never stepped into one before and I found the whole thing so fascinating that I almost forgot about the gnawing edge of uneasiness tickling my subconscious.

Almost.

What I'd told Rebecca about discipline was the truth: let it ebb for one moment and you'd lose it entirely. Constant guard against becoming lazy or slipshod is the only way to keep what you've worked so hard to attain.

That idea was drilled into my head—all of the recruits' heads—during my time at The Academy, the Fixer training camp in the Northeast Kingdom of Vermont. Over and over again, the drill instructors had harped on staying sharp. No rest for the Fixer, they'd told us. We could rest—we could sleep—when we died.

But the scene fascinated me. I paused and slid into a nearby doorway to assess the situation. Ahead of me I could see several of the folding chairs typically used on movie sets. I couldn't make out who might have been starring in the flick because I was too far away.

Camera crews were busy setting up what looked like an important shot. Light technicians worked to cast just the right amount of light while sound technicians checked microphone placement.

And me, Mr. Starstruck, stood there sucking it all in.

Which is when I suddenly felt my body take over and jerk me out of the doorway a scant second before a bullet splintered into the wall right where my heart had been a blink earlier. Bits of masonry dust flew out at sharp angles. No report shattered the air, however.

Whoever'd shot at me was using a sound suppressor.

My right hand went immediately for my gun, but I stopped.

The movie set crawled with cops.

There was no way I was going to be able to draw and take out the threat without bringing down all sorts of unwanted heat.

I hugged the closest trailer and began walking ahead. The direction of the gunshot told me the shooter had to be across the street. If I could keep the trailer between us, I'd at least have some degree of cover.

I risked a quick duck down and tried to look under the trailer across the street. No luck, the stupid trailers sat virtually flush with the street.

I stood back up and then continued walking.

Right into a cop.

"Hold on a second, pal. This is a closed set—"

I jerked sideways just as the round whizzed past me and into the unsuspecting cop. His chest exploded and his eyes went white almost immediately. Another heart shot. The shooter wasn't taking any chances.

I dove over the barrier and rolled, yanking out my own gun as I did so. Forget worrying about the cops, I had more important things to concentrate on—like living.

I came up in a low crouch and kept moving, trying to find some cover. Another burst of brick exploded next to my ear, showering my cheeks with concrete, drawing blood.

The shooter was close.

Around me, people were starting to notice, which wasn't a good thing. The first thing they saw was the dead cop. The second thing they saw was me ducking and scooting all around trying to keep a low profile. From the way things looked, it appeared that I'd shot the cop. And now I was sneaking around hoping to pop a major celebrity.

Hysterical screaming, the natural human by-product of gunfire or just seeing a gun, erupted from scores of people on the set. This kind of attention I definitely did not need right now.

Or at any other time for that matter.

I had to get off the set.

Ahead of me a small alley led off the street past an antiques stores advertising kitsch from the 1970s. I checked out my reflection running past the store window, which boasted old metal lunchboxes decorated with cartoon scenes.

No bullets came at me.

The air in the alley was cooler. Bricks sprung up on either side of me and a tinge of urine tickled the air and my nose. I wanted to reach the end of the alley before the shooter got behind me. With only six feet of width, there wasn't a lot of room to move.

If the shooter hit the alley, he'd be able to draw a nice bead on me. And that would be the end of ol' Lawson.

But since I still had some things left on my 'to do' list, I increased my speed until I broke out of the other end and turned the corner. I slid my gun back under my coat. Apparently, the wild shouting and screaming over on the movie set hadn't permeated this street. Or maybe you got used to screaming when you lived in a city this big.

People swirled around in dizzying numbers, but no one paid much attention to me.

I could hear sirens already cutting through the city traffic. Celebrities always did rate a lot better care than regular humans. After all, if there weren't celebrities out there making movies that let everyone forget about their humdrum existence, what use would there be to life?

I hated the idea of leaving my Mercedes anywhere near Rebecca's office. It wouldn't take an astute cop to figure out the cause of the ruckus on the movie set could well have originated with the out-of-towner who'd parked his car a few blocks away.

But I also didn't want a shooter with a suppressed pistol following me into the crowd. For one thing, I wouldn't be able to hear the sonovabitch. For another, looking over my shoulder isn't my preferred method of walking.

I stepped off the sidewalk and hailed a cab.

Inside, the driver, who looked like he might be from Bangladesh from the slope of his cheekbones, had an audio language tape of Urdu playing. Over and over again, a high twangy voice kept telling him how to say "tomatoes" in the dialect. If that kept up too long, there was no way I was going to make it back down to the Financial District.

As it was, I lasted barely two blocks before a red light gave me the opportunity to slide a few bills into the front seat, wish the driver well with his Urdu lessons, and step back out into the swirl of human traffic.

I doubled back on my trail and broke protocol.

I headed back toward Rebecca's office. I wanted my car back. Moreover, I was pissed off at having a shooter on my tail already. I'd only been in town for a day and already someone wanted me gone. Usually it takes me at least forty-eight hours to piss off everyone in the surrounding vicinity.

I guess I was improving.

Another cop car sliced through the traffic, its lights flashing but with no siren. I smiled. In Boston, most emergency vehicles need a plow to get the oblivious drivers out of their way. Flashing lights and sirens don't impress Boston drivers one bit. I knew a guy who once remarked how rude it was to have to move over for an ambulance when people needed to get home.

Human compassion blows me away.

I boxed around the movie set, using parallel streets to make my way back toward Houston. Rebecca's office didn't look like much from the inside. It looked like even less from the outside in the coming evening light. But I'd grown up knowing that appearances can be some pretty deceptive shit. And Rebecca apparently made out well enough to afford the high rents of Manhattan.

If Marilyn hadn't been landing jobs because of what Rebecca perceived as a confidence problem, someone else must have been. Any agent, dance, literary, or otherwise, needed to have some clients that could produce. After all, fifteen percent of nothing is nothing.

And Rebecca didn't look like she was making nothing.

What about Teresa?

According to Rebecca, she had the attitude even if she was a little lacking in technique. Well, I'd seen attitude win out a helluva lot more often than technique, so I wasn't sure that a lack of performance couldn't be remedied by spirit.

Then again, Teresa had claimed the poor house when I'd shown up yesterday. So if she wasn't scoring the big jobs either, who the hell was keeping Rebecca afloat in that dingy office of hers?

And more importantly, who put a shooter on me at this early stage of the game. According to my mental calculations, which rank right up there with remedial addition, I'd only talked to a few people: Teresa, Kohl, Raoul, and Rebecca.

Oh, and Teresa's doorman . . . Now there was a guilty party.

I caught myself grinning at my own joke and shut the smile down. New York's got enough weirdoes standing around on the streets without my adding to the mix.

I walked the neighborhood a few more times trying to determine if anyone was staking out my car. I should have gotten Kohl to slip me some New York plates for the Mercedes. Having Massachusetts plates on the car made it stand out like a sore thumb. And the fact that it was an expensive ride made it even more so.

But after thirty minutes of checking, the area seemed clean.

I walked over, crossing the street between cars to make it look like I was just a jaywalking asshole rather than the owner of the car. I slipped my keys into the lock and dropped onto the leather seats, gunned the engine, and then flew out of the space.

I checked my rearview mirror but saw nothing. Whoever'd been shooting bullets at me earlier must have decided it wasn't worth sticking around right now.

And that was fine with me.

I eased the car downtown. Rush hour traffic surged around me. I hoped Teresa wasn't waiting for me to get down there. I hoped her audition was going well and she was still in the midst of proving herself to the casting directors.

I was wrong.

She was standing outside of the building, all bundled up when I got there. I couldn't see any trace of sweat. It must have already dissipated.

She slid into the car. "You're late."

"Yeah. I am."

"What happened?"

"I ran into someone who wanted to cancel my library card."

"What?"

"A shooter. Someone tried to nail me as I was coming out of Rebecca's office. Obviously, they missed."

"Oh my God. You're serious?"

I glanced at her as I caught the on-ramp to FDR Drive. "Of course, I'm serious. Why the hell would I lie?"

"I'm not saying you're lying. It's just that . . ."

"What?"

"Just that you seem so nonchalant about the whole thing. I mean, someone shooting at you—God, I can't even think about what I'd do if that happened to me. I'd freak out."

"Most people do the first time."

"First time?"

I shrugged. "It's happened before."

"And what—you're *used* to it?"

"I wouldn't say I'm used to it, per se. You never get used to it. But it does tend to come with the territory. I acknowledge the possibility that it could happen and try to keep on going with my job."

"That's some outlook on life you got there, Lawson."

"Don't laugh—I'm penning a self-help series. Should sell record numbers, don't you think?"

"I wouldn't give up the day job just yet."

"Well, there's one good thing about them missing me."

"Only one?"

I winked at her. "Maybe more than one."

"And that is. . . ?"

"If they'd gotten me, you'd have no way of getting home. You would have been standing there for hours."

"Don't count on it."

"No?"

She smiled. "I would have given you five more minutes and then I was leaving."

"I got there in the nick of time."

"Lucky me."

Eleven

I needed a change in strategy. Not that I'd really even had one to begin with, aside from tugging on a loose thread and seeing how much came off in my hands. But having a hitter on my tail—someone who knew how to shoot vampires dead—mandated I up the ante some. How, I didn't know for sure.

Sometimes in this business you shoot for anything and hope it comes up aces.

Sometimes you get deuces.

That's the nature of the beast. I've known guys who parade around pretending they've got a clear-cut idea about how to handle everything that drops down in their path. It's bullshit. Even for professionals, the time comes around every so often when you've got a job to do but no idea how best to go about it.

I dropped Teresa off at her apartment and then headed for the Fixer station to speak with Kohl. Fresh off the boat or not, I was hoping he could clue me in on who might have set a shooter on me this early into the game.

The obvious choice—that being Raoul—didn't seem likely. Raoul was a blowhard and he might very well be dirty. But he didn't strike me as having the kind of clout or financial wherewithal to hire a pro hitter. Rebecca fell into the same boat.

Especially since they were both humans.

I was less sure, though, about Kohl.

Truth was, there probably used to be a time when a Fixer could trust a fellow Fixer. Back when your word was as good as spilling blood for each other. Those times are, well—long gone. And from personal experience, I don't trust anyone without investing a lot of time into researching their background.

But Kohl should know a few things—even if he hadn't coughed up much dirt the night before.

And if he was dirty, well I'd be walking into an ambush. But at least then I'd know a few more facts than I knew now.

The word simple doesn't pop up in my life very often. So I wasn't all that surprised to find Kohl out when I reached the building. I parked two blocks up from the office and waited for him.

I spent the better part of forty minutes counting how many women walking by probably didn't have panties on and how many of the men walking by did. I came up about even. But since I had no way of knowing for sure, I gave up and fiddled around with the radio dial.

I'd parked far enough away from his place that I wasn't all that obvious. And a black Mercedes isn't a rarity in Manhattan, so I wasn't especially concerned that Kohl would notice me.

Unless he was looking for me.

Marilyn's disappearance was rapidly taking on the appearance of something else entirely. I'd thought I'd eventually come up with either a body or a live vampire. Missing persons cases usually end in one of those two ways.

What concerned me now was that as a result of some

gentle prodding, I'd triggered a chain reaction. Someone had ordered me clipped. No warnings, no gentle
hints to get the hell out of town. Just a double-tap and
a pat on the back. Someone was going through a lot of
trouble to make sure I didn't find Marilyn—alive or
dead.

But why?

Had Marilyn taken a job that went bad? Had Raoul
pimped her out as some classy call girl and she'd gotten roughed up by a client? Was she in something
deeper altogether that I hadn't even touched on yet?

No answers spilled out of my cranium. I cracked the
window and let in some of the autumn evening. I
found a classic rock station playing Foreigner and slid
the volume up for "Hot Blooded."

Kohl showed up around eight o'clock.

He came striding down the sidewalk with what
looked like a bag of Chinese take-out in one hand. I
could tell by the way his left arm hung that his piece was
under his armpit. He hadn't mastered the abbreviated
walk that helps conceal the fact you're packing a piece.

I would have expected better from a Fixer.

I slid out of the Mercedes and shut the door quietly.
I didn't want Kohl to see me approach. I like keeping surprise on my side whenever possible.

And a good thing I did, too, because as I was
covertly exiting the Merc, Raoul showed up.

I fought the overwhelming urge to duck by the side
of the car. What the hell was unitard-boy doing here?

The alarm on the Mercedes was silent, so I keyed
that and pretended to pay attention to whether it had
triggered or not. Out of the corner of my right eye, I
watched Raoul go up the steps and head inside with
Kohl.

More thread seemed to be unraveling.

The problem was how far would it come off? Were Kohl and Raoul into something? Why would Raoul even be at the office? How did he know Kohl?

I came up the steps slow, in case they were still in the vestibule. I didn't want my appearance to startle either one of them. In fact, I hoped I'd be able to get inside without them knowing it. Maybe I'd catch some valuable intel from their conversation.

Prior to obtaining any spoken nuggets, however, I'd have to get past the alarm system. Fixer stations have pretty decent security systems.

My old friend and mentor Zero would have been able to get through the door in under a minute, no questions asked. He'd spent a lifetime studying alarms, locks, and all the other gizmos that lull otherwise rational people into feeling secure.

I was a door-kicker.

In the past, the only route I knew how to take was through the front door with a gun blazing. Crude, but it usually worked for me. The few times it didn't weren't enough to convince me to reconsider my entry techniques.

Zero's death, however, did.

Since his demise over a year ago, I'd taken up a lot of his habits and hobbies. He'd embraced the old ways and could speak Taluk fluently. He knew a lot about our traditions. Hell, he'd impressed an Elder I knew named Wirek on more than one occasion. And that wasn't the easiest thing to do.

One of his skills I'd embraced was lock picking. I was nowhere near his level of mastery, but I felt pleased with my progress. When I'd had spare time up in Boston, I'd spent a few days with a guy known as Lucky Louie.

They called him Lucky because Louie had managed to cheat and steal his way through most of Las Vegas. And he'd done it without getting iced by the mob bosses who still had hooks in the scene out west.

Among Louie's many skills, aside from his unbelievable approach to counting cards at the Blackjack table, was an almost supernatural ability with electronic alarm systems. Louie didn't need schematics; he had the soft touch that the safecrackers of old were famous for. I'd seen Louie simply look at an alarm pad, rub it gently and stroke the right keys, and the entire system disarmed.

I studied the alarm pad inside the vestibule and prayed some of his good luck had rubbed off on me.

But I had to rely on some modern technology to help me out of this jam.

From my coat pocket, I withdrew a small black box and clamped it over the alarm pad. I flipped a small switch on the side of the box and kept praying. The tiny screen lit up as numerical combinations flew across it.

After thirty seconds, three numbers showed in luminescent green.

I punched them into the keypad and there was a small beep and click as the door unlocked. I slipped inside the cool interior of the building.

Kohl hadn't left any lights on in the vestibule but it didn't matter all that much. Vampires have great night vision. Not as good as the lycanthropes, but we're pretty good anyway.

I headed straight for the doorway to the right, where Kohl and I had had our talk.

I saw nothing but more darkness.

Turning left, ambient light spilled out from behind a door at the end of a long corridor. I hugged the wall, careful not to disturb the paintings that hung along the walls.

I caught snippets of conversation as I drew closer.

I eased my pistol out from behind my right hip and brought it down in a low-ready position. I couldn't see any door hinges on the frame, which meant it opened inward.

A good thing, since in the past I'd had some bad experiences with kicking in doors that opened outward.

The voices grew louder as I got closer.

I couldn't quite make out what they were saying, though.

I leaned against the doorjamb and thought about my next move.

On the one hand, I could kick in the door in my usual Lawson style and just point my gun at Kohl and Raoul until one of them talked. There was no guarantee either of them would, however. And that would leave us in some sort of standoff. I'd either have to kill them both or back out of there and run for my life.

I wasn't crazy about either of those options.

Choice number two involved me listening at the door as long as possible and trying to make something out of the voices beyond the door. Then I'd sneak back out the way I came and try to make some sense out of what was going on around here.

I wasn't thrilled with that choice either.

But I hate standoffs, so I stayed put.

And I didn't hear squat.

After ten long minutes, I sighed and eased off the

doorjamb. Was it enough for me right now to know that there was a connection between Kohl and Raoul? Did I have enough to start shaking a few trees in other areas and see what fell out?

And could I stay alive for another day with a shooter waiting for me?

I thought yes, so I moved back down the corridor. It occurred to me halfway back that if I'd thought this through on the stoop, I could have saved myself a lot of stress and discomfort.

But then again, I now knew what the alarm code was. If things kept heading the way they seemed to be, I'd be needing it again very soon.

Back outside, the cool autumn twilight greeted me by whipping up a cool breeze that dried the line of sweat breaking out across my hairline. I took a deep breath and headed back to my car.

No one took any shots at me as I crossed the street, so I felt especially good about that. Inside the Mercedes, I took my cell phone out of the glove compartment and placed a call to Niles.

He answered on the third ring. "I've been waiting to hear from you. Everything okay?"

"Wicked nifty."

"Sarcasm already? That's so unlike you, Lawson."

"Don't I know it. I need you to run a few things down for me."

"Name 'em."

"Check on a Fixer here in New York named D'Angelo. Apparently he recently got reassigned to Honolulu. I also need some background on a Fixer named Kohl."

"You busy making friends in all the wrong places?"

"You know me."

"I know you. How soon do you need the information?"

"Is five minutes ago too soon?"

"For you? Never. For the computer records division over at the Council, yes. You know those guys keep bankers' hours."

"How long?"

"They open at nine-thirty tomorrow."

Nine-thirty. That was almost twelve hours away. I hated the thought of having to sit and wait all night. I could have called my friend Benny the Phreak and had the information inside of five minutes, but then afterward, I'd have to kill Benny. Benny didn't know I was a vampire and it needed to stay that way.

"Niles, maybe you could call someone and wake them up. I sorta need this information a little sooner than later."

"What do you have that won't wait until morning?"

"I don't know."

"That's a great start."

"I'm pulling on this thread and I want to see where it leads."

"I thought you were tracking down your missing cousin."

"I am."

"But you're asking about Fixers assigned to New York now. What gives?"

"There might be a connection."

"How so?"

"I don't know. In fact, I probably won't know until nine-thirty tomorrow morning."

He sighed. "Wish I could do more."

"Maybe you can ask the Council to get a special

twenty-four-hour records clerk to man the systems in case this happens again."

"Sure, I'll bring that up at the next 'suggest a change' luncheon. Should go over like a breeze."

"Now who's being sarcastic?"

"Not me. I'm just being honest. I'll call you back tomorrow morning when I have something."

"Thanks." I switched the phone off and sat in the darkness watching the brownstone. In truth, as much as had happened today, I didn't feel like I'd made any progress whatsoever.

Have I ever mentioned how frustrating this job is?

Twelve

Niles called me at ten-fifteen the next morning, just as I was finishing a breakfast of fresh-squeezed orange juice and a ham and cheese croissant in my hotel room. I'd had a hit of juice earlier, so I felt pretty good.

That is, until I heard Niles speak.

"You've got problems. Anyone ever tell you that?"

"I think I might have heard that once before."

"In your case, I'd think probably a bit more than that."

"What's your point?"

"Point is—you do have problems. I ran the information down and what the computer spit out does not look good."

"I'm already blissfully excited."

"First off: there was a Fixer named D'Angelo assigned to New York. He was never transferred to Honolulu."

"Uh . . . did anyone tell him that? There's no sign of this guy anywhere down here."

"Yeah, that's another part of the bad news."

"Well, where is he?"

"We have no damned idea. That's just it."

Great. I sighed. "What else?"

"You'll love this: according to the Fixer Academy, there's no record of a graduate by the name of Kohl ever passing through its gates."

"What about a name change?"

"Why would he do that? There's no need to. We don't put you guys undercover all that often. You're the ones we send in to mop up the bad slop. He'd have no reason to change his name. If he told you his name was Kohl, then I'm assuming that's exactly what it is."

"Okay, let me make sure I got all this great news down pat: I show up at the Fixer office here and announce my presence."

"As is standard protocol."

"And the guy I take to be the local Fixer introduces himself as Kohl, claims he only arrived in town recently. And the guy he replaced is sunning himself on the shores of Maui."

"Lots of beaches in Hawaii, Lawson. He could be on Kauai, too."

"Yeah, great. Thanks for pointing that out."

"I'm here to help."

"Now you tell me that there never was a reassignment for D'Angelo. So presumably, D'Angelo ought to still be kicking ass and taking names here in the Big Apple."

"Not getting lei'd in Hawaii. Correct."

"You working on a stand-up routine, Niles?"

"There's an open mike night at the local boys bar. I've been looking for a hobby."

"Swell. Now, the most obvious questions are: where is D'Angelo and who the hell is this guy Kohl?"

"Those are important questions."

"Well, they seem to be."

"You forgot 'where is my cousin?'"

"I didn't forget. I'm simply breaking down the information into family and business related."

"You mentioned they might be connected. Does it seem that way any more now?"

"Unfortunately."

"So, what's your next move?"

"I guess I'll be doing a lot of cat-and-mouse surveillance. I've got to see how far this thing runs."

"I don't need to tell you that D'Angelo going missing is a pretty important task right now."

"And let me guess, it just got heaped onto me?"

"Well, you are the eyes on the ground right now. We don't have anyone else who'd be able to come in there and do as good a job as you will."

"Flattery now. You guys must be desperate."

"Find out where D'Angelo is. Find out who the hell this Kohl character is. Find out what the hell is going on down there. And find your cousin, too."

"All on a day's pay? Piece of cake."

"You see? It's that can-do attitude that makes life worth living. I don't doubt for a second that you'll come out on top of this thing."

"Thanks for the vote of confidence."

"Say it like you mean it. Something else bothering you?"

"Someone's trying to punch my ticket. Tried once yesterday."

"Already? You've only been in New York for two days."

"Three if you count today."

"That's early even by your amazing standards."

"Someone's getting spooked."

"Well, you've got two good suspects in D'Angelo and Kohl."

"D'Angelo's a suspect?"

"He is until he turns up and can explain where the hell he's been hiding for the last few weeks."

"Good point."

"Anything else I can help you with?"

"You've been helping?"

He chuckled. "It's all news, Lawson. Whether you see it as good or bad is up to you."

"Now you're calling me a pessimist."

"I wouldn't dream of it. Have fun chasing down your prey."

He rang off and I finished my orange juice. Thinking about what Niles had told me, it occurred to me that in all my years with the service, I'd never heard of a Fixer going missing. Sure, a few of them dropped out of sight after retirement, but not while they were on active duty. D'Angelo's disappearance was as weird as it comes.

And Kohl's appearance didn't make things any less suspect. Especially the revelation that Kohl might not even be a Fixer at all. He'd known the Taluk greeting code that Fixers use. How had he gotten that information?

I got my car from the garage and headed across town. I wanted to follow Teresa around again, if only to admire the way her hips swung when she walked. But following her around, while it might have been good for my libido, wasn't going to get this case solved.

Fact was, Niles was right. Things seemed even more certain now that Marilyn's vanishing was connected to D'Angelo and Kohl. And let's not forget Raoul. Whatever a dance instructor was doing at the local Fixer station last night was beyond me.

But I had a hunch that if I stuck close to Kohl, I might just figure it out. And hopefully, I'd do it before the shooter could plug me full of unwanted bullet holes.

As I drove, I kept an eye peeled behind me. It was an elementary gesture. No professional would let himself get tagged. And Manhattan is a pretty good place to tail people because the gridlike pattern of streets lets you run parallels pretty easily. A four-car team can box a suspect for days without the mark ever knowing it.

But I kept looking anyway.

I got to Kohl's office by eleven. I chanced a call into the office just to see if he was there. I made sure I disabled the caller ID function on my phone before I called.

Kohl's voice came down the line. "Hello?"

"It's Lawson."

"Hey, amigo, what's up?"

"You going to be around this evening?"

"Sure, where else would I be?"

"It's been quiet?"

"I'm still wading through D'Angelo's backlog. But yeah, it's been quiet."

"It's not going to be for much longer."

"What the hell does that mean?"

"I've been shaking a few trees. You know, just to see what might possibly fall out of them."

"And?"

"Something fell out."

"Something big?"

"Could be."

"And you want my help. Is that it?"

"You probably know the city a lot better than I do. And if there's any involvement with the Syndicate, I'm going to need an intermediary."

"You think it might involve them?"

"It might."

"You don't know for sure?"

"I'll know a lot more by the time I see you tonight."

"Oh?"

"Yeah. I've got a few people to see today. Plus, I've got to shake a shooter who picked up my trail yesterday."

"Someone's gunning for you?"

"He wasted a few good rounds trying to yesterday."

"At least your reputation doesn't lie."

"Damned thing gets me closer to death than I'd like. I'll see you later on tonight."

"Okay, be careful."

I hung up and smiled. Letting Kohl know I knew something might just shake him up a bit. And if he wasn't the top boy on this thing, maybe he'd go running to whomever was. I felt fairly certain Kohl had been brought in to fill D'Angelo's vacant slot.

But for how long?

D'Angelo's vanishing act wouldn't go unnoticed for long. His Control would be back from chasing down fermented college students soon and the gig would be up. That is, if D'Angelo's Control was even still alive.

Truth was, he could already be dead. Along with D'Angelo.

What the hell had I stumbled into?

I didn't have time to theorize. The front door of Kohl's office opened and he came out, locked the door and then hurried down the steps. He climbed into a blue Toyota parked around the corner and slipped out into the traffic.

And when he did, I pulled out as well.

I kept about four cars in between us. Kohl didn't know what I drove, so I felt reasonably comfortable at that distance. And I stayed far enough back so he wouldn't be able to pick up details on my license plates.

Another question popped into my head: how did he know about me? He'd said that my reputation had preceded me. Was it assumed I'd be coming down here to look for Marilyn?

Or was this whole thing just a trap to kill me?

Kohl eased onto Broadway and headed uptown. I didn't recognize the area; but then again, I'm not nearly as comfortable in New York as I am at home. I like the city just fine but I don't know it like the back of my hand.

Although, Kohl certainly seemed to know where he was going.

We cut back down and under FDR Drive, then sprinted clear across town to the West Side. I recognized it as Kohl's own method of making sure he hadn't picked up any tails. That meant things might get interesting.

Another thirty minutes and we'd come back to the east side again, just shy of the Financial District. Kohl's car meandered down around the fish markets.

I cracked the window and nearly gagged—fish oil and slimy guts cooked in the gutters, broiled by the autumn daylight.

At Gold Street, he pulled over and parked in an illegal space. Being a few cars back, I'd been held up at a stoplight. This was problematical. If Kohl continued on foot and I was still at the light, I'd lose him.

As he got out of the car, the light changed and I slid forward. I stayed off of Gold and nudged myself into a space by a pharmacy. I got out just in time to see a meter maid headed my way. Well, let her ticket me. It'd go right to the accounting department back in Boston anyway.

Kohl was already a full block ahead of me by the time

I picked him up again. He seemed to be moving a lot faster than anyone else on the street. That fact alone made it easy to track him. I stayed well back. He kept looking around every thirty steps or so. The last thing I wanted was him turning around and eyeballing me.

We dipped past a sushi joint and he bore right down the sloping streets toward the East River. He passed a shipping museum and then went down a side street.

And instantly everything changed.

The sunlight that had been beaming overhead seemed to disappear altogether. Gray buildings closed in one either side of me as I followed behind him as quietly as I knew how.

Heavy steel shutters caked with residue and oil and grease and a million other sticky things barred entrance to most of the buildings. I could see loading docks that must have bustled at three in the morning, locked up tight for the day.

And still Kohl kept walking.

Where were we going?

At last, he stopped by a small set of steps leading up to a heavy gray door on the second floor of a squat building. He took another look around, but I'd already stepped into a nearby doorway. When I looked again, he'd climbed the steps and stood by the door.

It must have been unlocked because he simply pulled on it and then disappeared inside.

I couldn't see any video surveillance, but that didn't mean it wasn't there.

I sighed, knowing what I had to do and hating it very, very much.

I started up the steps after Kohl.

And a minute later, I was inside the building, too.

Thirteen

Darkness.
Absolute.
Ambient noise.
Funny smell.
Those things ran through my mind immediately upon entering through the door, which turned out to be unlocked anyway.

The darkness hit me first. It didn't seem to be the kind of dark that you could acclimate to within a few minutes. There seemed to be something more . . . dense about this darkness. Almost like a thick cloak had been draped over my eyes. I couldn't see a damned thing. I'd have to grope and fondle my way through it. Hopefully, I wouldn't kill myself in the process.

The ambient noises I heard sounded distant. Like they were farther in the bowels of the building. I could hear water dripping and then hitting the floor with a predictable splat pattern. I heard some pings, some metallic noises. All of them largely unclassifiable.

But I couldn't hear any voices.

I knew Kohl was in here somewhere. But he wasn't making much noise right now. Which meant he might be laying in wait to ambush me.

It wouldn't be the first time I'd walked into an ambush.

And it probably wouldn't be the last. That is, if I happened to survive this caper. Despite all my training, there are plenty of times when I act like an impulsive fool. In the past, that's come close to killing me.

Maybe I've got a death wish.

I sniffed the air again. Short intakes of breath better convey scents across the olfactory senses situated high in the nose. I made out mildew, must, and copper. But there was something else that I couldn't quite place.

I had to move.

I had to get farther into the building.

I wanted to catch up with Kohl.

But I didn't take a step.

Instead, I eased myself down until I was squatting on my haunches. And I waited.

Vampires, as I've said before, have tremendous vision in the darkness. But even my eyes were having serious trouble penetrating the ebon environment. After about twenty minutes of squatting, I was at last able to make out what looked like a railing in front of me. I reached for it and my hands touched cool, wet metal.

I stood and let my hand act as a guide. Ten feet in, the railing sloped downward, suddenly curving abruptly.

A ladder.

If I'd just started walking, I would have taken a header off the ledge and probably broken my neck. A broken neck is a royal pain in the ass to work around.

And if I'd fallen, it would have alerted anyone in the building to my arrival.

I reversed myself and eased a foot over the edge until it touched a rung. I braced my hands on the ladder and started down.

I hit the next level thirty rungs later. The ladder ended.

The darkness dissipated on this level. I looked back up and frowned. It was as if a cloud of black hovered around the ladder.

Weird.

My eyes took over and guided me ahead. On this level, a great many pipes ran overhead and beneath the metal planks underfoot. My rubber soled boots kept my steps pretty quiet though. Plus, the ambient noises seemed louder on this level, at least enough to mask my approach.

I ducked through an entryway and saw steps leading down.

I took them.

At the bottom, I had to again duck through another entryway. I felt like I was on a submarine the way the entryways were designed. But I wasn't. I was in a building that simply had a lot of stairways and small portals.

The mildew smell vanished. The air suddenly changed from humid and dank to crisp and cool. I heard the whine of motors overhead and glanced above me. There, in key places, I could make out whirling ceiling fans that drew the heated air up and out of the building.

Then I heard the voices.

I stopped.

Kohl?

I looked but couldn't see anyone. They were still ahead of me, somewhere off in the grayish dark. I kept moving.

And then saw some red light spilling out of another doorway.

I slowed.

And drew my pistol.

After all, better safe than sorry. I'd rather have to apologize for the presence of a gun than not have it ready if I needed it in a real big hurry.

I drew up next to the doorway and got down on my knees. I poked my nose around the corner and followed with my eyes.

Red light bulbs kept the room well lit. I wondered why they'd chosen red instead of normal lighting. But then I remembered. Red certainly wouldn't spoil the need for night vision, which you'd need to negotiate your way through these passages.

The voices grew louder in the room, but I still couldn't see anyone. I spotted another open doorway branching off the red room. The voices must have been coming from there.

I eased through the doorway, gun at ready, and moved to the other doorway.

I repeated the observation process. And this time, I didn't like what I saw.

Not one bit.

The room looked like someone had transplanted a Manhattan penthouse apartment into the bowels of a dreary building. And while the light was still red, I could make out enough details to know this must have cost a helluva lot of green money.

Paintings adorned the walls. Most of them looked like oils but a few could have been acrylics plus a watercolor or two. Rugs that looked like they'd been imported straight from Afghanistan covered the floor.

Kohl leaned back on a huge leather couch. He propped his feet up on a table in front of him. He looked completely at home.

Off near the back of the room, a huge desk occupied the center position, imposing its sheer weight on the rest of the room.

Behind the desk, a large high-backed leather chair sat. Its back was toward Kohl so I couldn't see who might have been there.

But I could hear their voices better now.

I heard Kohl speak. "Would you relax? Nothing is wrong. There are no problems."

Whoever sat behind the desk didn't sound like he was buying into it. "Don't tell me to relax, Kohl. In fact, don't ever tell me to do anything. You aren't the one with so much invested in this venture. The risks are not yours. They're mine."

Kohl kicked his feet off the table. "I'm assuming most of the risk right now, not you. If they don't buy my act, then all of this is for nothing."

"And is he buying your act?"

Kohl shrugged. "Seems to be. But then he called this morning. And that's why I'm here now."

I guessed the "he" was me. I always get such goose bumps when folks talk about me behind my back.

"What did he say?"

"Something about something falling out of the trees he's been shaking."

The chair stayed quiet for a time. Then I heard him clear his throat. "There are only so many trees he can shake. It's not as though we are a forest, after all."

"You think we have a leak?"

"I don't think it's anything quite so elementary as that. If this Fixer is as accomplished as his record leads us to believe, it's not at all surprising he'd be able to discern some measure of what's occurring."

"This wouldn't have happened if—"

"Yes. I know. If our man had finished his job yesterday, the great Lawson would be no more than a memory."

"He'll be on guard now, you know. He'll be tougher to take down."

"Was he ever easy? I think not."

I frowned. I didn't like the way this sounded.

Kohl picked up a glass I hadn't noticed before. I knew it was blood—what I like to call juice since the prospect of drinking blood doesn't always thrill me.

Kohl drained his glass and set it back down on the table. "I'm supposed to meet with him tonight to discuss whatever it is he thinks he's figured out."

"You know what to do."

"Sure, make him think he's got nothing."

"You don't sound convinced that it will work."

"You haven't had the pleasure of meeting him yet. There's something about him. Something different."

I heard a sharp intake of air. "All Fixers are different. They're freaks of nature, somehow singled out for this rubbish destiny force-fed them by the Council. No one knows how it happens, how they're seemingly divinely chosen for their work. But whatever they are, they are all different. If you are convincing, he'll swallow whatever you put in front of him."

"Lawson is different from other Fixers. It will be tougher than that."

Again the chair stayed quiet for a moment. "Well, if you can't convince him, then simply kill him."

"Killing him might unleash a storm of attention we can't afford right now. If he's been in touch with his Control, and there's every reason to believe he would be since it's standard protocol, they might know what he's got figured out so far. If there's even a hint of our involvement, the Council would send a team down here to finish us all off."

"We've dealt with the Council before. They're more interested in leaving us alone than meddling in our business. The few times there have been problems in the past, we've been able to keep them from shutting us down."

"Not for a lack of trying."

"There are always back channels that can be exploited if handled properly. For example, this Lawson character may be a very formidable Fixer, but he's about as well liked as old socks."

Well. Gee whiz.

I frowned. I knew I wasn't going to win any personality awards, but hearing someone I couldn't even see say it kind of set me back a second. Who the hell was this clown anyway? And how the hell did he have that kind of intelligence on me?

It seemed obvious then that this group must have been somehow connected to the Syndicate. Maybe this was the Syndicate. I'd only had limited involvement with them in the past. I'd never found their headquarters.

But one thing made sense: the Syndicate were the only ones down here with the kind of power to buy that sort of information.

And they'd obviously been buying quite a bit.

There was some movement on either side of the chair and for the first time I could make out two incredibly large bodyguards looming in the shadows. They looked like former East German steroid-laden athletes capable of crushing heads with their pinkie fingers.

The chair seemed oblivious to their presence. He

kept talking to Kohl. "This entire program is remarkably simple. It's up to you to make sure it works out to our advantage. Is that understood?"

"Yeah, I know the game plan. That's not what's got me worried."

"What then?"

"Lawson came to town looking for his cousin. He won't quietly go away until he finds her."

"Didn't I cover this already? If he looks troublesome, like he won't go away, then you are to kill him."

"What about that so-called incredible shooter you hired to do him? Why not have him do the job?"

"He failed yesterday."

"Yeah. So what?"

A chuckle wafted out from behind the chair. It reminded me of some of the maniacal voices you might hear in old horror flicks. "He seems to have suffered an unfortunate accident in the hours following his failed attempts yesterday."

"You killed him?"

"Well, it's not as though he was one of us, Kohl. Goodness. He was a human. Who really cares what happens to him?"

"Did he know what his target was?"

"We simply gave him the gun and the bullets. We showed him a picture and that was it. He knew what he had to do."

"And you killed him for failing."

"This isn't the sort of country club organization where failure is readily accepted. You might even do well to remember that."

"I know it."

"Would you like another glass?"

Kohl looked at the empty glass in front of him and

considered it. "No. To be honest, it wasn't all that good."

"It's fresh, though. That counts for something, doesn't it?"

"I guess. Where'd you get it from?"

The chair swiveled slightly and I craned my head for a look. But all I saw was a misshapen hand reach out of the gloom and push a button in the desk. I heard a whining grind and the wall to Kohl's right suddenly shifted and opened.

Another room came into view.

And suspended upside down from a length of chain, still twisting and swaying, was the body of a human man. Naked. I could make out surgical incisions at his neck, wrists, and groin. Dark crimson dribbled out of the wounds, snaking down his flesh toward the giant basin underneath him.

Now I knew what I'd smelled earlier: death.

Kohl gasped.

"You weren't kidding about an unfortunate accident."

"Well, it seemed silly to waste such a perfectly good human. And you see? In the end, he actually did manage to serve some useful purpose."

I'd heard, and seen, enough for now. I needed some fresh air.

I backed out of my observation post and backtracked to the entryway.

Outside, even the fresh air didn't do me much good.

Fourteen

My prospects for getting back to flirting with Teresa looked dismal. I had to reason out who was calling the shots behind a huge desk in a shitty looking building just north of the Fulton Fish Market.

Kohl was dirty. Of course, he might never have been clean. I needed a lot of personal time with him to pry out what exactly he was doing in New York. I also wanted to know where D'Angelo was. And most importantly, where the hell Marilyn was.

Outside the building, I walked back to my car and sat in the front seat trying to figure out what I'd accomplished in the short space of time since my arrival. Aside from pissing off some people who had the ability to hire and fire shooters, not much.

I started the car. I headed for FDR Drive before I could develop an inferiority complex about my job performance.

On a whim, I phoned Teresa's apartment. Surprisingly, she answered.

"It's Lawson."

"I was just thinking about you."

Good news. "Yeah?"

"Yeah. Raoul says he won't be able to find me any work as long as you're around making things difficult."

"What'd I do?"

"And I didn't make the cut on that music video, either. So now I'm back to pounding the pavement, finding my own auditions, and all that crap. Who knows—if you hadn't shown up at my door and started making friends all over town, I might have the lead spot on a heavy rotation video on MTV. Thanks a lot, Lawson."

The phone crashed down in my ear.

A Toyota cut me off on FDR Drive and I had to jerk the car to the right to avoid hitting it.

I grabbed the next exit and slid the Mercedes off the highway and onto another street. Farther on I hopped Broadway and slid down that until I found my way back to the dance studio in Little Italy.

I parked in the same space I had yesterday and hopped out of the car. I wish I could say that I was approaching this whole thing levelheadedly.

I wasn't.

At the top of the stairs, the same music and sweat smells greeted me. I could hear him before I saw him.

Lucky me.

Raoul didn't notice me until I'd already grabbed him by the scruff of the neck, exerting pressure on a vital point near the base of his skull. His shoulders jumped up reflexively and I moved him into his office using my body weight.

I steered him toward a chair in front of his desk. Then I shut the door and locked it. Outside, several dancers had gone wide-eyed while I made my move, but it happened so fast they likely weren't even sure they'd seen it.

Raoul groaned and rubbed his neck. "Lawson, how absolutely wonderful to see you again."

I slapped him across the face.

Point of fact: a slap across the face usually hurts a helluva lot more than a punch. It's also less damaging to the hand. And it has the added benefit of shocking and embarrassing the person you're slapping.

"You're a piece of shit."

He smiled. "Flattery from the likes of you—"

I slapped him again on the other side of his face. Now he looked like he'd fallen asleep in the sun. Red welts blossomed on both cheeks.

This time he stayed quiet. Maybe you could at least teach a stupid dog new tricks.

I leaned against his desk. Papers and pens dropped to the floor. Oh well.

I leveled a finger at him. "Why are you fucking with Teresa?"

"I'm not fucking Teresa."

I smacked him again, this time square on the nose. A thin trail of blood dribbled out of his left nostril. He sniffed.

"Don't be cute with me. Why are you giving her a hard time? What's the deal, Raoul?"

He sniffed some more. "You may not have much appreciation for this, but in this business you get judged a lot by the company you keep. It just so happens that the . . . company Teresa is choosing to keep right now does not jive well with the rest of the dance community."

"That company being me, of course."

He pinched his nostril shut with one hand. "Of course."

"And so you're going to make her life hell until I'm gone, is that it?"

"Maybe even after you're gone. She needs to be punished for her lack of judgment."

"Maybe she didn't have a choice."

"We all have a choice."

"You didn't have a choice when I just grabbed your scrawny neck and wheeled you in here, did you?"

"Perhaps I appreciate your persuasiveness. Maybe I wanted to even talk to you about her."

"About Teresa?"

"About Marilyn."

I frowned. "You've got something to say, you'd sure as hell better start talking."

Raoul smiled and crossed his legs. "So, you see, there is something I have that you want."

I sighed. "Listen, I don't know how much plainer I can make this. If you're jerking my chain, there's not much that's going to keep me from beating the living shit out of you. So, I'd strongly suggest that you forego any dramatics and just let that tongue of yours start forming words and sentences."

"You'd do that, Lawson? You'd beat the shit out of me?"

"Not right now."

He looked out the window. "Did you know she was a hooker?"

"I heard you pimped some of your girls out."

"It takes two to tango."

"You trying to shelve some of the guilt?"

"I'm not feeling guilty at all. I merely provided a service for these girls. In some ways, you could almost say I was helping them."

"Bullshit."

"It's not that at all." He shifted. "Look at it this way: do you know how many women come to New York with dreams of becoming a dancer? Thousands. Tens of thousands. The numbers are truly staggering."

"Like actors in Los Angeles. So what?"

"So, the fact of life is that these women, and some-times men, have little recourse in their lives. They have dreams. Wide eyes full of hope and daring. And then they get here and reality bitch-slaps them—much the way you just did me—in the face."

He meant the rents and the cost of living. I knew it. But it didn't stop him from running down the extensive list of obstacles facing society's dreamers when they came to the Big Apple. Funny how much of his speech sounded similar to what I'd heard from Rebecca.

"And you provide them a way out of some of those obstacles? Is that how you see it?"

"It's not just how I see it. It's how it truly is. If it wasn't for me and what I'm able to do for them, these girls would have nothing jobs that taxed their strength and agility, leaving them dried out husks unfit for dance of any type except for what passes as erotic entertainment nowadays."

"But you're just herding them into another form of erotic entertainment, aren't you?"

Raoul's slimy grin wandered out across his face again. "Well, everyone has to sleep, don't they?"

"You aren't paying them to sleep."

"True. But that's sometimes an added benefit." He shifted again. I wondered if he had a problem with he-morrhoids. "Look at it this way: if they work for me, they earn a helluva lot more money than they would serving tables or sliding up and down poles. They get home at a fairly decent hour—no later than if they'd gone out dancing with their girlfriends—and with sev-eral hundred dollars to boot. They're able to eat and support themselves while chasing after their dreams."

"Unless they supposedly cross you. In which case

you make their lives a living hell and stomp all over those same dreams."

"I have to protect myself."

"You aren't interested in protecting yourself. You just want the control your little side gig gives you."

He said nothing so I continued. "Let me tell you how I see this whole thing: you're a washed-up woulda-been-coulda-been who knows he hasn't got a chance in hell of making it anymore. You run a crappy little dance studio where you espouse the path to success even though you wouldn't know the right road if it smacked you in the face. You put on a real good show and the ladies fall for it. But it's nowhere near the truth and you know it. You take advantage of these young women. You hear their sob stories and you handpick some pretty nifty talent. Then you pimp them out to old-time geezers and other walking heart conditions. In turn, you make some money, feed your ego *ad infinitum,* and believe that you're helping these women, when, in fact, you're not."

"That's not a very fair assessment."

"Fair doesn't even enter into it. At best, you've been responsible for emotionally scarring a lot of young women—"

"You think they're emotionally scarred? Lawson, no one holds a gun up to their heads and orders them to fuck these guys. They do it willingly."

"Bullshit. You don't need a gun to make them do what you want. Your ability to stonewall their careers is enough incentive to play between the sheets." I slid off the desk. "And at worst, you've been responsible for at least one death."

"Death?"

"My cousin Marilyn."

"No one ever said she was dead."

"I haven't heard anything that convinces me she's alive, either."

"Maybe you haven't been listening well enough."

I leaned in close to him and narrowed my eyes. "Maybe you haven't been telling me everything you know, either."

"Maybe I haven't." He smiled again and I found myself growing weary of this repartee.

So I balled up my fist and hit him in the side of his head, high up on his jaw close to his orbital socket. I heard the crack and knew I'd scored. Raoul's screech reinforced that notion.

I left him sitting there and walked out of the office just as the first girls were running toward the door.

One of them looked at me. "What happened?"

I shrugged. "The consequences of his actions caught up with him I guess."

I walked out of the dance studio. Maybe going there and roughing him up like that wasn't the smartest thing I could've done. Maybe I should have spoken with him more about easing off Teresa and letting her get on with her dancing. Maybe I should have let him do some more talking.

I shook my head. He wouldn't talk. Raoul wasn't the kind of idiot who spills his guts at the first sign of trouble. He'd hold out on the information, whatever bit he had, until the last possible second. He was the kind of asshole who doesn't mind seeing people die as long as he feels he's important.

I hate people like that.

And truthfully, it felt damned good smacking him upside the head.

As far as Teresa went, she'd be mad at me for a

while. I doubted very much Raoul would ease off her any time soon. Of course, he might actually smarten up and do the right thing.

But I doubted it.

After all, if you've been around this planet as long as I have, you start to see trends in people. Behavioral psychologists and all that psycho-nut talk not withstanding, there are two classes of people in this world: those who deserve to live and those who deserve to die.

I was pretty sure I knew which class Raoul would fall into.

Now it was just a matter of time before he did.

Fifteen

I had a little time before my meeting with Kohl. And I had a lot of questions about everything that had happened in the last forty-eight hours. In that short span of time, I'd managed to piss off of a lot of people, including a woman I would have rather not pissed off.

I phoned Niles. He answered on the third ring. I could hear music in the background. Loud music.

"Where the hell are you?"

"A bar. This had better be good"

"You busy?"

"I wasn't sitting around waiting for your call."

"What do we know about the Syndicate?"

There was a pause and then the music volume got lower. I heard a door close in the background then Niles's voice came back on. "Okay, we can talk now."

"Where are you now?"

"My friend runs the bar. I'm in his office."

"What bar?"

"I don't think you'd frequent it, Lawson."

"What's that supposed to mean?"

"Did you suddenly decide you like sleeping with guys?"

"No."

"There you go."

"Gotcha."

"Truth is, we don't know all that much about the Syndicate. What I've seen in the files, the Council has only had to step in and discipline them twice. Once back in the eighteen hundreds and then again around 1950."

"Why?"

"I forget the reasons. Probably not that important if you think about. I don't think they were anything too earth-shattering, that's for sure. Just a normal criminal organization trying to expand where it shouldn't have expanded."

"What about after the last time the Council intervened?"

"Things have been rosy. The Syndicate went back to minding its business. Although, since you're down there now and given what you told me yesterday, I'd doubt that the rosiness will last much longer."

"Thanks for the vote of confidence."

"Well, I am your Control. Now, if you don't mind, there's someone I'd very much like to get back to."

"I didn't screw things up for you by calling, did I?"

"I told him I was a secret agent anyway. I think your phone call might have increased the dramatics some."

"Glad to help."

"Go away now, Lawson."

I disconnected and didn't feel a single bit better, even if I had helped Niles. I pressed another series of numbers into the phone and waited while it rang.

"What?"

I almost laughed. "Helluva way to answer the phone."

"I'm not known for my phone manners. What can I do for you, Lawson?"

"I need some information."

"You always need information. Clothes, money, a place to sleep, a shoulder to cry on, a good swift kick in the ass. Jesus, how many times have I bailed your ass out of confusing situations in the past?"

"Too many."

"Damned straight." Wirek, the recently reformed alcoholic Elder, sighed. "Well, what is it this time?"

"Am I interrupting?" I was batting a thousand today, it seemed.

"My private nurse was about to give me a sponge bath and a massage."

"I didn't know you were sick."

"Who said anything about being sick?"

"That usually goes along with the nurse."

"The hell it does. I get a nurse over at my apartment, you can be damned sure I'm not going to screw up the opportunity by being sick. Now what do you want?"

"Information on the Syndicate. Ever hear of them?"

"What—are you trying to insult me now? Helluva way to start a conversation. I mean, I'm only an ungodly old fart. Not like I'm eight hundred years old or something and have been around this planet twice. By foot."

"By foot?"

"What—you never walked anywhere before?"

"Forget it. Okay, so obviously you know a little something."

"Sure. I know some things. Not the kind of stuff you'd find in a case file, though. My stuff comes from firsthand experience."

"I could use some help, pal."

"I'll bet. The Syndicate's been around as long as any law-abiding aspect of our society has been."

"I thought they were a recent invention—maybe two hundred years or so."

"Who told you that?"

I grimaced. "The case files."

"Shut up now, okay?"

"Yeah."

"You know anything about the Triads?"

"Chinese gangs. What about 'em?"

"Calling the Triads 'Chinese gangs' is like saying Einstein's theory of relativity was just another science experiment. The Triads have a history over a thousand years old. They're not just a gang per se. They're a society within a society. They have their own values, their own codes of honor, their own everything. You think the Italians are badasses with their La Cosa Nostra bullshit? Maybe the Japanese with their Yakuza think they're pretty badass as well. Lemme tell you something: they all took their cues from the Triads."

"And the Syndicate's the same way?"

"You bet."

"How come we don't hear all that much about them?"

"Are you listening to me? For the same reason you don't hear that much about the Triads. They're very good at keeping a low profile. You'll only hear about them or see them if they want you to. Or if they're up to something big."

"I think the Syndicate might be up to something big then."

"You're in New York?"

"How'd you know?"

"The Syndicate's seat of power has always been rumored to be in the Big Apple. If you're investigating them—"

"It didn't start out that way."

"Never does with you."

"You mentioned firsthand information."

"Before I became the Elder you know me as, I went off for a number of years. We called it missionary work, helping spread word of our society's traditions to the various centers of vampire activity throughout the world." He paused. "Anyway, I eventually found my way to New York. I was doing some counseling with some vamps on the down-and-out. Poverty was rampant back then."

"Back when?"

"Early 1800s."

"Okay."

"Anyway, it seemed that a lot of the troubles the vampires in New York were going through were the result of this band of criminals. I investigated it some and it turned out that I'd run into the Syndicate."

"What happened?"

"They roughed me up pretty good. Told me to keep my nose out of their business. I backed off but did some research on them. I wouldn't be in too much of a rush to mess about with them if I was you, buddy."

"I don't ever seem to have a choice in these things. You know that."

"That's what I thought you'd say. Oh well, can't blame a friend for trying."

"Who runs the Syndicate?"

"As far as I know, no one's ever really known. From what I gathered about them, the identity of what they call the 'Dangul'—"

"'Dangul'?"

"It means 'elevated one.'"

"In Taluk?"

"No way. The Syndicate doesn't speak the normal Taluk. They have their own subdialect."

Great, another dialect. Taluk has more dialects that any language on the planet. Each generation has put their own spin on it. Over the years, Taluk has grown to resemble an onion more than a language.

"So, who's the Dangul?"

"It's a closely guarded secret. None of the members of the Syndicate would ever admit to knowing it. And that's supposing that they even know who it is."

"They have that many cutouts?"

"Can you blame them? After all, if word got out about who ran the show, what would stop the Council from dispatching one of their Fixers to put a permanent end to the show?"

"I don't know. What's kept the Council from doing anything so far?"

"Near as I can figure, it's the usual between-the-sheets political fucking that goes on no matter who's in power. Human, vampire, lycanthrope, it doesn't matter. Bureaucracies all function the same."

"You're such an optimist."

"Tell me about it. So, what have you run into so far?"

I ran it down for him. I left Teresa out of the equation. Deliberately. Unfortunately, I didn't fool Wirek for a second.

"There's a woman, isn't there?"

"What?"

"A woman. A babe. I know you, Lawson. I know human chicks make your head spin and your crotch swell."

"Mister Colorful strikes again."

"You're not denying it."

"Okay, there might be a woman."

"She hot?"

"She's a dancer."

"Ouch!"

"Yeah. But she's pissed at me."

"That's only because she hasn't slept with you yet."

"Or the fact that I might have ruined her career."

"Yeah? Way to go, Fixer man. Hope your tongue is in good working condition."

I started to say something but stopped. Sometimes it was better not to feed too much into Wirek's randy speech.

"So, what's her name?"

"Who?"

"The woman, you idiot. What's her name?"

"We were discussing the Syndicate, weren't we?"

"We're done with them. I told you what I know. Now you give me some dirt and then let me go horizontally assault my nurse."

"Her name's Teresa."

Wirek sighed into the phone. I could feel his longing from 212 miles away. "What is it with you and women who have T and A in their name?"

I smirked. "I really have to answer that?"

He paused. "Jesus Christ, Lawson. I should have known if anyone would construe it that way, it'd be you."

"You should talk. I just had to listen to you wax on and whack off over the phone."

"Did you apologize yet?"

"No."

"You might want to."

"I might want to do a lot of things. I don't think I've got time to do any of them tonight."

"What's going on?"

"I've got a meeting with someone claiming to be a Fixer down here."

"Someone's impersonating a Fixer?"

"Seems that way. The Academy's got no record of any agent with his name."

"That's got to be a first for me. I've never heard of such a thing."

"Well, he's remarkably well informed about our customs and greetings, that's for sure."

"If he's connected to the Syndicate, I guess he would be. The Syndicate has inroads into every aspect of our society. I once thought of them as insular, but they're widespread. Remember that."

"I will."

"Who was supposedly stationed down there?"

"Guy named D'Angelo. He's missing now. I've got to find him, too."

"And to think, you just went down there to find your missing cousin."

"Yeah."

"Ain't life grand?"

"She's something. I'm not sure if grand is the word I'd choose just now."

"Good luck, pal."

I rang off and checked my watch. I really did want to swing by Teresa's apartment and make amends. It was my fault that Raoul had stomped all over her. I didn't like that much. Even me stomping Raoul didn't buoy my spirits that much.

But my watch read seven-thirty and that meant it was time to go. Daylight savings time was in full effect and the sun had already vanished. I swung the car around and shot back toward midtown.

There's something magical about watching a city come alive at night. I don't care what city you're in, there's something innately cool about watching the night come on.

Of course, thousands of years ago my kind was born to the night. Back then, it was survival that mandated we hunt at night. Hunting humans during the daylight wasn't the best prescription for the survival of my species.

Maybe it was something instinctive in my soul that always made my heart beat a little stronger when the sun began its westward retreat. I could feel the adrenaline dripping into my veins and arteries.

Around me, New York's nightlife started to emerge.

Well-dressed couples in expensive cars set out for dinner. Street performers put on their acts hoping to scare up a living. The human predators emerged and went to work. The glow of a million neon lights poked their way through the increasing darkness, with promises of perfect bodies, hip music, and hipper drinks. Lights came on all over town. People threw off their daytime garb and got funky.

At night, it's always a great time to be alive.

If this had been anything other than a job, I might have even joined the crowds. Maybe I'd find my way to a nightclub even. I don't usually do the nightclub scene, but I've found there's something about New York City that can make a dancer out of even the most stalwart wallflower.

But I was working.

So even as the night blossomed all around me. Even as the pretty women came out in search of vapid sex and smoky lungs, even as everyone else got ready to have one helluva fun night . . . Even then . . .

I was getting ready to go meet with Kohl.

Hopefully, I wasn't going to walk straight into an ambush.

Sixteen

I stashed the Mercedes around the corner from the Fixer building and waited. Nothing seemed unusual. I got out of the car and then took my time walking over. More specifically, I walked a wide box around the building on parallel streets, drawing closer and closer each time I walked around it. I wanted to make sure there wasn't some sort of kill team waiting to take me out as soon as I rang the doorbell.

There didn't seem to be.

Finally, at about eight-fifteen, I rang the buzzer. Kohl answered it two minutes later with a big bright smile plastered across his mug. He looked like a bad toothpaste commercial.

"Good to see you, Lawson." He extended his hand. As much as I didn't want to, I shook it anyway. He pumped it twice and then let it go.

"Come inside."

I followed him in. He led me into the same sitting room we'd had our first discussion in. I sat with my back to the wall this time. He faced me on the couch, leaned forward, and clasped his hands together.

"So."

"So."

"You want a beer?"

"No thanks."

He kept smiling. "You mentioned something 'big' this morning when I spoke with you. Said it might have to do with the Syndicate, right? What gives?"

"I think," I said slowly, "that the Syndicate is getting ready to do something."

"What exactly?"

"I don't know." That was the truth. I think part of me was hoping Kohl would spill his guts and let me in on everything.

"I thought you came down here to find your missing cousin."

"I did."

"Doesn't sound to me like that's what you're doing. Is this a black bag job? Are you really investigating the Syndicate?"

"I think the two things are connected."

"Your cousin and the Syndicate? How so?"

"I haven't confirmed it, yet."

He eyed me. "You said this morning you were going to shake some trees and see what fell out. Anything?"

"Not much. Just a low-life dance instructor who took a few shots this afternoon in the name of decency, that's about it." I filled him in on Raoul and waited for his expression to change.

Whoever Kohl was, he'd obviously been schooled pretty well. He kept his composure in check. But I caught a slight discoloration near the base of his neck. Of course, he knew Raoul. They'd been here together last night.

But Kohl chose to skip past that item. "So, how's the Syndicate involved?"

"I heard they were neck deep in the entertainment scene down here. Dancing, which my cousin had a passion for, is considered entertainment."

Kohl grinned. "Especially when they slide up and down those greased poles in the clubs, huh?"

"Not that kind of dancing."

He leaned back. "Sorry. I forgot it's family."

"And the thing is," I said, "I've got the distinct impression that everyone I've been talking to hasn't exactly been forthright with me, you know?"

"Everyone?"

I didn't answer. "I feel like I'm missing out on a joke here. Everyone else knows the punchline and I look like a fool."

"Maybe you don't have a very good sense of humor."

"My sense of humor's fine, thanks. I can appreciate humor most people wouldn't even dream about."

"Is that so?"

I leaned forward. "Why don't you try me?"

Kohl stretched and pressed his spine into the couch. "All right." He took out a cigarette and lit it. Now I knew for sure he wasn't a Fixer. Smoking's illegal unless it's necessary for the operational parameters. Kohl wasn't on operations just then. Lighting up gave him away.

I watched him suck a lungful of toxins in and then exhale a stream of smoke with a heavy sigh. "What would you say if I told you there were some very powerful people here in town who'd love to have you working for them?"

"I've already got a job."

"And you wouldn't have to give it up, either." He let the cigarette loll through his fingers and then pointed the stupid thing at me. "Think of it more as a sideline type of thing that would score you some big points and a lot of cool perks."

"What kind of cool perks?"

"How about the freshest blood money can't buy?"

"I can get blood anywhere. You'd have to do better than that."

Kohl nodded and sucked down some more smoke. "Yeah, I heard blood doesn't do much for you."

I said nothing. When I was finished with Kohl, I was going to know exactly who had supplied him with such detailed information on yours truly. I don't like knowing my personal issues are a part of the collective consciousness of scumbags everywhere. Not cool. Not by a long shot. But even with his excellent information, he didn't seem to know that smoking was illegal. How did he manage to miss that?

"How about human women?"

"What about 'em?"

"You like them."

"So do a lot of us. So what?"

"Sure, we all like 'em just fine. But you really like them."

"I really like good Chinese food, too, but that doesn't mean I can be tempted with it. If you've got a point to make, do it already."

Kohl narrowed his eyes. "What about Talya?"

Part of me had known that was coming. When he'd mentioned my dislike of having to drink blood, part of me thought briefly his information might even include Talya. But I'd hoped I was wrong. So much for hope.

"Talya's not part of the equation any more. The Council saw to that."

"They didn't kill her."

"No, of course not. But they told me I wasn't to see her ever again. Otherwise they might pass down two termination orders."

"What if I could make it so it was perfectly okay for you to see Talya again. As much as you want, in fact. Hell, you could get married for all I care."

"How you gonna do that, Kohl? Are you going to rewrite thousands of years of our history just so I can shack up with a human chick?"

"Maybe not something quite so spectacular as that, no. But I can make it okay for you to get with her. I could arrange it so the Council stays off your back."

"I'm still listening."

"I have some friends here in town who could pull some strings. They could get the Council to look the other way. With your service record, a request like that shouldn't be too difficult to pull off."

"You know about my service record?"

"I know a lot about you, Lawson."

No shit. The kind of information Kohl was pulling out of his hat could have only come from someone on the inside. And the thought of someone in or near the Council selling information about Fixers just sickened me.

"You must have some very good sources."

"We do."

"Who's we?"

"Me," said Kohl. "And the Syndicate."

"You're in bed with them?"

"This is New York City. Everyone's in bed with everyone else. It's what makes the city go 'round."

"I thought Los Angeles was where everyone fucked everyone else."

"New York, too."

"So, when you and the Syndicate get busy, who bends over and lets the other one drive?"

"I don't understand the question."

"Never mind. You just answered it anyway."

"What do you say about my business proposition?"

"I didn't hear any proposition."

Kohl smiled. "You're going to make me spell it out?"

"I'm a bit of an idiot. I have trouble reading between the lines. So, yeah, I'm going to make you come right out and say it."

"The Syndicate is, as you suspected, getting ready to make a move."

"What kind of move?"

"They're unhappy with their allotment in life. They want a bigger piece of the action."

"How much action do they have now?"

"They control New York City."

"That's a pretty big piece already."

"They want more."

"Greedy, huh?"

"They want Los Angeles, Tokyo, Paris, and London as well."

Inside, something didn't seem right. Considering what Wirek had told me before his rendezvous with Florence Nightingale, if the Syndicate was as old as he said, they should have already been well entrenched in those cities. And the fact was, they probably were. Kohl was playing me. That was fine with me. I'd go along with it for right now.

"Can they handle all that action?"

Kohl beamed. "There's very little they can't handle. Trust me on that one."

"You been working with them for long?"

"They approached me when I got to town."

"You mean when you replaced D'Angelo?"

"Yes."

"All right, how do I fit into this equation? I'm just a Fixer. I don't know how much I can do."

"You can do plenty, Lawson, believe me. All it takes is just a little creative blindness on your part."

"Meaning?"

"You look the other way when some things happen. Maybe you don't really care about a shipment or two coming into Boston."

"Shipment? What does that have to do with the entertainment business in those cities you mentioned."

"In order to finance the move into those cities, the Syndicate has to engage in some creative marketing schemes. They'll be moving a lot of narcotics around the country in preparation for the big jump."

"What kind of drugs are we talking about here? The standard fare of cocaine, heroin?"

"No. Something much better."

"What?"

"Have you ever heard of Saber?"

"Rumors only. Supposed to be a designer drug. I don't have the stats on it, if that's what you're asking."

Kohl lit a fresh cigarette. I was gagging for an open window. He paced around the room. "Saber is specifically designed to interact with neuro transmitters and give a combination outstanding high and vivid hallucination to the user. The comedown is minimal, and the addiction rate is a whopping ninety-nine percent."

"Impressive. What happens to the other one percent?"

"Usually," said Kohl, "they die."

"Doesn't that kind of publicity tend to hurt product sales? After all, the risk of death doesn't always sit well with people."

"Believe it or not, it's actually helped us."

Kohl was using the word "us" a helluva lot more than I would have liked. And it wasn't doing much for his shoddy disguise of being a Fixer on the take. Kohl was speaking like he was part of the organization—which of course he was.

"How has the possibility of death helped?"

"You know how humans are nowadays—always looking for the next exclusive thing to become a part of. They're all so locked into their pathetic nine-to-five routines that they lose every aspect of their personality. They become cogs in the great Corporate machine. And that machine routinely shits on them and their retirement funds with no retribution. Humans know they're powerless to stop the influence of big business so they go looking for their identity in other ways."

"Go on."

"Well, think about it. They all want to go from being that tiny no-name cog, to a member of an exclusive group. It used to be what schools they'd gone to or who their parents were that determined their individuality."

He actually grinned as he was saying this. "Nowadays, it's addiction to designer drugs that gives them a sense of personality."

"You're sure about that?"

"Of course, I'm sure."

"And this Saber is the drug that gives humans back their individuality, is that it?"

"Yes."

"Pardon my ignorance, but if the addiction rate is ninety-nine percent, then where's the exclusivity in that? If everyone's addicted to the same drug, isn't that just as bad as being part of Corporate America?"

"If the drug was as public as big business, sure. But it's

not. Drug use has never been all the way out. Cocaine almost made it in the 1980s, but even that got reined in. So the illusion, if you want to use that term—"

"Seems applicable."

"—is that the users will think they are part of an exclusive group, when in reality they are not. But all around the country there will be pockets of people enjoying their own 'exclusive' designer drug."

"You've released it already then?"

"Only in very small amounts. We needed to see what the effects were on the mass populace." Kohl smiled. "Are you familiar with buzz?"

"The sound?"

"The concept. Specifically in marketing."

"Not really."

"Buzz is something that happens when people experience something and then tell everyone about it. They start talking and more people start talking and before you know it, you've got a veritable gold mine brewing. Hundreds of thousands of new clients are lining up to use your product."

"Again, doesn't that go against the whole exclusivity idea?"

"Not at all."

It didn't seem level to me, but that wasn't the point. Kohl could spew whatever he wanted and I was going to agree to it tonight. I had goals to accomplish.

"Okay, I'm in. But on one condition."

"What's that?"

"I want to meet him."

"Who?"

"The guy who runs the Syndicate."

"Who said it was a 'him'?"

"I'm generalizing. Whatever it is, I want to meet it."

"I don't know if that's possible."

"If that's not possible, then I'm not possible either. I jump into this thing and it's my career and my life on the line. No offense, but for that kind of action, I'm going to need to speak with the head honcho, not the middle man."

"You think I'm the middle man?"

"You as much said you were earlier."

He sighed. "All right, I'll see if we can arrange something for tomorrow, okay?"

"That'll be fine."

He nodded. "Well, good night, Lawson."

I stopped him. "One more thing."

"Yeah?"

"My cousin."

He frowned. "Like I said, I'll see what I can do."

"Do that." I walked outside and felt the October air bite into me.

Things were about to get interesting.

Seventeen

Even though it was late, I wanted a chance to talk to Teresa. I don't like loose ends and I felt pretty bad about Raoul teeing off on her and her career. Part of me hoped she might even want to go out for a late dinner.

On the way over to her apartment, I took a hit of juice from the flask I'd taken to carrying several months back. Traveling can be a problem what with my requirements for sustenance. And ever since I saw Wirek use a flask during our time over in the Himalayas almost a year ago, I'd started having one with me as well.

The problem was that the blood wasn't chilled. Warm blood tends to coagulate into a gooey molasses-like substance that grosses me out even more than the thought of drinking chilled blood does. But I needed the life-force energy it contained, so I pressed my lips to the mouth of the flask and sucked down a few quick gulps, trying hard to not let the stuff linger on my tongue any longer than necessary.

I felt the hit when it came a few seconds later. That's the great thing about the metabolism of vampires: we can draw the life-force out of blood very quickly. It doesn't have to be digested per se, just inside us. Our bodies take over and do the rest. How? Beats the hell out of me. I just drink the stuff because I have to.

I felt my strength wax and then the sudden flush of my skin as my own circulation sped up to quickly spread the infusion of energy throughout my body. Suddenly, I was a lot more optimistic about heading over to Teresa's.

At the door, I paused. How was she going to react when the doorman rang her up and told her she had a visitor at ten o'clock at night?

I didn't have to worry. Fortunately for me, the same doorman was on duty. He grinned when I walked in.

"Here to see the lady again?"

"I thought you worked the day shift."

"Grabbing a little overtime. What's your excuse for showing up this late at night?"

"No excuse, apparently. Just wanted to swing by and say hi."

"Not to me you didn't," he laughed. "You two have a fight?"

"What makes you say that?"

"You know how long I've been a doorman? Long time. You know what I've seen? Lotta stuff. Two reasons a guy stops by a beautiful young woman's apartment this time of night: maybe he thinks he can get lucky; and two, they've had a fight."

"You don't think I thought I could get lucky?"

"I'm giving you the benefit of the doubt that you're a pretty upstanding man yourself and wouldn't try to score that way."

"The benefit of the doubt? That's a first for me."

"Want me to call her up?"

"Yeah."

He spoke into the phone for two minutes. Finally he hung up. "No go."

"Didn't want to see me, huh?"

"Nope. Said to tell you you should just go home and forget about ever sleeping with her."

I frowned. "Huh?"

"What she said, pal. Guess you two had a helluva fight, huh?"

I nodded slowly. "Yeah, but certainly not about that. That hasn't even come up." I looked at him. "What are the odds that you'd let me up anyway?"

"Why?"

"I don't like the way that sounded."

"What she said?"

"Yeah. Doesn't make any sense."

"You know a lot of women who make sense when they're angry?"

"Regardless. Can you let me up?"

"I could call nine-one-one."

"And what if it's nothing? Look, if it's something, you'll know pretty fast. But if it's nothing, then there's no harm done."

"What if she gets pissed I let you up. I could be out of a job here."

"I'll take the blame and say I punched you in the head or something."

He looked at me and finally sighed. "You owe me."

"I owe a lot of people," I said rushing past him. "I'll be sure to add your name to the list."

On the elevator up I drew my pistol and eased the slide back to make sure I had a round chambered. As the doors slid open, I hugged the side of the car and then poked my head out.

I checked the hallway.

Nothing.

Hammer back and safety on, I slipped out of the

car and paused while the doors slid shut. I heard the car descend.

A stillness filled the hallway.

This time of night, I hopefully wouldn't run into any other tenants. I was sure the sight of a vampire assassin stalking down the corridor with a gun wouldn't really do much for their sleep tonight.

Teresa's apartment number was 232.

I was outside of 236. I crept down the hall, constantly checking my rear to make sure I wouldn't have any nasty surprises sneak up on me.

That was the last thing I needed.

I heard the commotion before I got close enough to her door to verify it was coming from her apartment. Muffled voices, almost shouts really, bounced off the walls from inside.

I didn't like what I was hearing.

Teresa's voice. Plaintive. Almost wailing. What she said was unintelligible, but I didn't really need to hear it to know she was in trouble.

I heard another voice. Gruff. Deeper. I wasn't sure I recognized it.

I leaned against the doorjamb and considered my options. I could stay where I was and try to eavesdrop on the conversation. Maybe I might hear something that would give me a fresh angle on the case. I could also kick the door in, storm the pad, and see what happened when I did so. That was the risky venture since I had no way of knowing how many people were inside. I could kick the door in, acquire a target in front of me and totally miss the guy to my side or back who would then drop two in my heart.

Not a good plan. Not at all.

Teresa screamed then.

Long.

She'd made my decision for me.

Risky or not, I'd heard enough.

Kicking in a door isn't necessarily as easy as it is in the movies. In a perfect situation, I would have had another guy with me armed with a shotgun. He'd fire two rounds at the hinges and then I'd kick in the door.

But I didn't have another guy with me.

I was alone. As usual.

And not having the benefit of a portable battering ram like the kind SWAT teams and crash units use to take in a door, I opted for the solitary approach.

A lot of the time you'll see folks rushing a door and trying to take it in using their shoulder. The only thing that accomplishes is a sore, possibly dislocated shoulder.

Experts will tell you that to kick in a door, you should normally aim the heel of your foot above the doorknob or lock since that's structurally where the door is weakest. That presupposes that the door is lightweight and there are no extra heavy duty locks in place on the other side.

I knew there were whole formulas for determining how much force the kick required, depending on door construction, whether it was hardwood or laminate, whether it was a solid core or not.

I didn't have the time or the will to try to figure it out.

For a human to break a door down, it might take a few kicks in the same area.

For me—because of the juice—it would only take one.

I positioned myself at the right distance across the hall.

More commotion broke out in the apartment.

I took a big step, brought my right knee up into my chest to chamber the leg, and then drove the heel of my right foot into the door.

It exploded inward, almost bouncing off the hinges. I gave a quick thanks to anyone listening for the juice I'd ingested on the way over. It certainly had helped.

I brought the pistol up.

No one was in my immediate sight line.

Teresa screamed again. I cleared the hallway, almost running now.

I rounded the corner.

And saw him.

Raoul. That worthless puke.

He had a hand around Teresa's shoulders. I could see a surprised look on his face, but that didn't stop him from trying to bring Teresa in close.

So he could bite her.

Shit.

A vampire.

Goddamnit!

His fangs were exposed. No wonder Teresa was freaking out. I almost expected her eyes to roll white and then for her to pass out, but she didn't. She just kept staring at Raoul.

Like she was mesmerized.

She was. Raoul was exerting his power over her.

He'd hypnotized her.

One of the few things the movies have gotten right over the years is the fact that we can hypnotize people. It's not an instinctive trait, however. It's learned. You have to be taught the skill to make it work. Raoul obviously had had a decent teacher.

He was breaking the law in a real big way right then. Even if I didn't have a past with him of sorts, I'd be hard-pressed not to punish him for doing what he was about to do to Teresa.

"Let her go."

He glared at me. "Stay back."

I leveled the gun on him. "You're breaking about five laws right now, you know that?"

"Do I look like I care, Fixer?"

"Let her go, Raoul. Then we can talk."

"You don't want to talk, Lawson. You want to kill me."

"Maybe."

"Put your gun down or I'll slice her neck wide open and bleed her out right in front of you." I could see the nail of his pinky finger poised over her pulsing carotid.

I'd been in a similar situation before on a rooftop back in Boston. I'd paused and given in for the sake of saving the woman who was being threatened up there at the time.

By letting Cosgrove escape that night back in Boston, I'd set myself up for an even harder chase. I sometimes wondered if I'd done the right thing.

Seeing Teresa in a similar situation did not make me feel all warm and fuzzy inside. Seeing Raoul think he had me over a barrel did even less for my previously confident mood.

But he'd been smart enough to position Teresa in front of him so I couldn't get a clean shot.

I frowned.

And lowered my gun.

He smiled.

"You're too honorable, Lawson. You should have shot me while you had the chance."

"Someone has to have some honor around here."

He smirked. Teresa still seemed to be in a trance. "You're going to let me walk out of here now."

"Not with her you aren't."

"You're not in much of a position to dictate my actions just now, are you?"

"Maybe not right now."

"So maybe I'll take her with me."

"You kill her and I'll never rest until you're deader than she is."

"As if you could."

"Try me."

"You don't really have any idea what you're dealing with here, do you? This is so much bigger than you, Lawson. So much bigger than you and those pathetic laws you uphold."

"So tell me about it."

"And ruin the surprise? Fat chance. I'll enjoy seeing the look of disbelief cloud your ugly mug when you finally understand what it is we're after here."

"Let her go, Raoul. You don't need her. She's tranced out anyway. She won't remember a damned thing about this."

"You will, though. If I take her with me, she becomes my insurance, doesn't she?"

"The problem with insurance is the premiums always go up. You can't pay and then you don't have the coverage anymore."

He frowned. "I'm tired of talking to you, Lawson. Step aside and let me by."

I moved to my left. He walked closer, still herding Teresa in front of him. "Put your gun on the table there."

"You don't want it?"

"I don't need it," he said.

I nodded and slipped the gun on the coffee table. "All right."

"Step back now."

I moved toward the window. Raoul eased closer to the door. "You know why I'm not going to kill you just now, Lawson?"

"Because the rest of your army isn't here to help?"

"Funny. No. I'm not going to kill you because we're supposed to leave you be for right now. Apparently someone thinks you're going to roll over and play for our side."

"You don't sound convinced."

"I'm not. I've known Fixers before. I know your kind."

"My kind?"

"So damned honorable. You all make me sick. The past is the past for a reason. Your pathetic loyalty to all it stands for is one reason why our society is so fucked up now."

I nodded. "You done with the soapbox routine?"

"You'll regret messing with us."

"Only thing I regret in life is not having enough time to hunt down and kill all the pieces of shit like you that contaminate our world."

"We'll meet again, Lawson." He shoved Teresa ahead of him and then turned back to smile at me.

I grinned. "Bad move."

He frowned, but I was already moving toward him, yanking my backup pistol from the small of my back holster and bringing it up point blank onto his heart. I pressed it in, using my momentum to get it flush with his body and then squeezed the trigger two times.

In the close confines of the apartment, it should have sounded like a cannon going off, but Raoul's clothing absorbed almost all of the sound. Plus, my backup's a .22 so the noise is slight anyway.

But the effect wasn't.

Raoul's eyes went wide and white.

Surprise flew across his face.

And then died there.

The same time Raoul did.

I watched him slump to the floor.

A wide pool of blood spilled out and onto the carpet. Teresa was going to kill me for staining the place.

Raoul's eyes stayed open. His canines stayed elongated.

And he stayed dead.

So much for one part of the trouble.

But how many more parts were there?

Eighteen

With unitard-boy dead, I had a more immediate problem: how the hell was I going to dispose of the body?

In the normal course of events, I'd be able to call my Control Niles. He'd arrange what's known as a cleanup team to come in and sanitize the area.

But I wasn't in Boston.

So as fun as it was going to be explaining to him what had happened, I had no choice but to call up Kohl and see what he could do. It took Kohl about five minutes to answer the phone, his voice heavy with sleep.

"You killed him?"

"He didn't leave me much choice."

"He attacked the girl?"

"He was an inch shy of tearing her neck open when I kicked the door in. Believe me, the kind of noise he was making, it would have been a miracle if someone hadn't heard the commotion and called the cops. And then we'd be a lot worse off than we are now."

"That's tough to imagine."

"Is it?"

"What do you want me to do?"

I paused. Kohl didn't know I knew he wasn't a Fixer, so I'd have to play it like he was still the man. "D'Angelo and his Control must have had cleanup

crews or contingency plans in case this happened.
Didn't he tell you about them?"

Kohl cleared his throat. "I think he said something
about his Control going over those when he got back
from vacation."

"There's got to be something. D'Angelo wouldn't
have left his station without giving you a rundown of
all the procedures. It isn't done that way."

I was forcing Kohl to improvise something, but at
this point, I didn't care. I had a dead vampire in an
apartment on the twenty-second floor of an Upper
East Side building and getting him out without anyone noticing was going to be a task in and of itself. If
Kohl could come up with something, I'd be grateful,
no matter who it was doing the cleanup.

"It's going to take some time for me to arrange
something."

I checked my watch. "It's fifteen past right now.
How much time do you need?"

"Maybe an hour."

"Okay, but don't leave me hanging here." I gave
him the address and then disconnected.

I glanced at Teresa. She was asleep on the couch
with her legs folded up under her. A damned good-
looking woman, she was.

She might be lucky and come out of tonight's events
with only a vague recollection that Raoul had paid her
a visit. As far as she'd remember, he'd left soon afterward. She'd probably be real confused when she found
out he was dead. So would a lot of dancers down at his
school. But those were the breaks. Raoul had fucked up
in a big way and I'd had to put him down.

Bring on the fallout.

The plus side was that I'd ended Raoul's little side-pimping activity. Although if you went along with Raoul's justifications, I'd just put a lot of dancers out of work.

The negative was that I'd killed a member of the Syndicate. Not that Kohl or anyone else knew I knew that. And really, I wasn't sure how deep into the organization Raoul had been. I'd only seen him meeting with Kohl after all.

But I felt sure there'd be some repercussions. It was just a matter of when they came.

As it was, Kohl took just over an hour to show up at Teresa's apartment with two men who looked as honorable as Capitol Hill lobbyists. One of them had a jagged scar running obliquely down his right cheek and the other had greased-back hair that almost dripped with slime.

I looked at Kohl. "Colorful crew you got here."

"Best I could manage on short notice."

"They aren't part of the organization, are they?"

Kohl eyed me. "Which organization are we talking about?"

"Not the one we belong to."

He thought about that. "In that case, no. Call 'em work-for-hire if you want."

"What about the other?"

"What do you think?"

"Yeah, I thought so. Must be real tough job requirements for that place."

"They'll do what's necessary and that's all that counts right now."

"How'd you get past the doorman downstairs?"

"We brought a small container of Saber gas."

"What the hell is that?"

"Saber in an aerosol form. Colorless and odorless,

it delivers a knockout punch with very vivid dreams. The doorman's asleep downstairs having some wild shit floating through his skull. He'll probably wake up with some crazy memories."

"How long does it last?"

"Well," said Kohl, "I wouldn't want to stand here and chew the fat with you all evening. But it'll last long enough for us to get the body and get the hell out of here." He looked at the two men and nodded.

They slid a heavy duty body bag open and then got Raoul's corpse into it. Kohl stopped them and bent down to examine the body. He looked up at me.

"Contact shots?"

"Had to use my backup piece."

"How'd that happen?"

"He had the girl and threatened to bleed her out unless I dropped my gun."

"So you did?" Surprise flooded his face. "Why not just shoot him through the girl?"

"I need the girl alive."

"Why?"

"She might know something about where Marilyn is."

"You don't need her for that."

"I'm not exactly receiving oodles of information from any other sources right now, am I? I have to keep my options open."

"I wouldn't worry too much about that." He thumbed at Teresa. "Keep her around, sure. Play with her. Sleep with her. Take a drink, I don't care. But don't think she's going to know what happened to your cousin. Because she doesn't have a clue."

"And you do."

He shrugged. "I know more than she does."

"And exactly when will you be sharing this information with me?"

Kohl looked at his watch. "Tomorrow. You have an appointment."

"With who?"

"You know where the Fulton Fish Market is?"

"I can find it."

"Sorta close to the South Street Seaport. Parking's a bitch but you'll manage."

"What time?"

"Eleven. Should give you enough opportunity to rest up after your fight tonight and then maybe even get some quality bed time in with the little hottie here."

"Damned considerate of you."

He straightened and adjusted his jacket. "You know, I heard that you chose to lay your weapon down another time a year or so back. Rumor was you had some really bad dude in your sights and then let him go." He smiled. "All because of a human woman."

"You trying to make a point here or what?"

"You got a real soft spot for human broads, huh?"

"I have a real soft spot for trying to make sure innocents don't get hurt by our business."

"Can't be helped sometimes."

"I'm not insisting it can. But if I can do something then I will. The same as I'd expect any other Fixer to do."

Kohl frowned. "Some of those traditions belong in the past, Lawson. You know that?"

"And some of them need to stick around."

"If you say so."

"Doesn't matter what I say. Matters what I do."

Kohl looked at the two guys who were zippering up the body bag. "You all set?"

Neither said a word, but they nodded. Kohl turned to me. "We're out of here. Don't forget about your appointment tomorrow, okay?"

"I won't."

"And don't be late. They don't like tardiness."

"I'm not a big fan of it myself."

Kohl took a final look at Teresa on the couch and then winked at me. "Have fun."

I hate it when grown men wink at each other. I frowned. "Get the hell out of here, Kohl."

He shut the door behind him. I was left alone in the apartment with Teresa. I could already hear her soft breathing.

I walked to the living room window. Up here on the twenty-second floor, she had a helluva view. Skyline blossomed before me, yellow and red lights blinking on and off far below. It was tough to imagine how much life this city held.

And it was tough to imagine how much evil it held as well.

I glanced back at Teresa but she was still out of it. I could bring her around if I wanted to, the way I had with Talya all those months ago up on that shitty rooftop.

But I chose not to.

For one thing, I didn't want to have to explain things right now when I wasn't even sure how best to do so. And I wasn't sure I wanted the pressure of suddenly having to make conversation.

I had a lot of crap to figure out. There didn't seem to be too much of anything working in my favor. It was too late to call Niles and let him know what I'd found. That would have to wait until the morning when I'd be heading down to the same building I was in earlier today—yesterday.

It was after midnight now. That meant my appointment was even closer than I wanted it to be.

I'd be answering for Raoul's death soon enough.

Lucky me.

Nineteen

Time always seems to speed up when you've got something awful to do that you don't want to do. The next morning sure as hell arrived a lot sooner than I would have preferred. I dragged myself out of bed and hopped into the shower, hoping I'd impale myself on a bedpost along the way.

I'd left Teresa's apartment only after making sure that she seemed okay. And then I went downstairs and checked on the friendly doorman. I hated the idea of Kohl's men having slipped him some weird sort of designer drug.

But sometimes that's just the way things work out.

His breath came in long drawn-out gasps, but otherwise he seemed okay. I started to bring him around but then stopped. The last thing I wanted was a bunch of questions thrown at me that wouldn't get honest answers.

Somehow, I managed to evade the bedposts and got dressed. Since this meeting would involve some potentially powerful vamps, I chose my power look: black slacks, charcoal turtleneck, and a black blazer. I caught a glimpse in the mirror and almost smiled, imagining some accented voice calling out a description over the microphone of a runway show. "Nothing says death and mayhem like Lawson—dressed to kill in only the best gabardine." I can get a real chuckle out of myself.

I had a hit of juice from the flask, washed it down with some freshly squeezed orange juice and then had a couple of eggs and wheat toast on top of that. By the time I left the hotel, I almost felt ready for my so-called appointment.

The fish market area was dead silent this time of morning. And since the corporate financial types were still plotting ways to lose more money for the average American, the streets were almost empty. I parked in a metered space but discovered I'd left my change at the hotel.

I stepped out of the Mercedes and glanced around. The only thing on the street were puddles of smelly fish gut water. I broke the meter with a well-placed shot. The digital display went tilt. Free parking in New York City. How about that? I walked toward the building.

I'd seen Kohl as soon as I drove into the area. He loitered in the darkened recesses of some building. His cigarette ash gave him away. As I drew closer, he stepped out of the shadows.

"Public vandalism from a Fixer?" He shook his head. "I never would have thought it possible."

No shit. I shrugged. "What the hell do I care any-more?"

"You're in a great mood."

"Lack of sleep. I get cranky without my teddy bear."

"Well, teddy ain't here right now, but we are. You all set for this?"

"Why wouldn't I be? I requested it, didn't I?"

He nodded. "Yes. You sure did. I just want to make sure you have some inkling of what you asked for."

"Does it matter?"

"Might."

I stopped him. "Look, you guys approached me, right? I don't see why I should feel like I'm stepping into hot water here. As far as I'm concerned, this is just another business meeting. I've had plenty of them before."

"Not like this."

"What makes this so special?"

"Who are you used to meeting with?"

"You name it. Scumbags, high-class society, stock-brokers, delivery boys, harlots, go-go dancers, blue collar, white collar, and everyone in between."

"Yeah," said Kohl. "Well trust me: you haven't met anybody like this before."

"And that's just how you're going to leave it, too, isn't it? Just keep me dangling off that bullshit baited line."

Kohl grinned. "I have to take my entertainment where I can find it."

"Get a Gameboy. Let's do this."

We walked up the same steel steps I'd traversed the previous day. Kohl led and I came up behind him. We were about to go into the belly of the beast.

Yet again.

Kohl held the door for me. "Go in, but do not move one inch farther until I get in there with you. Got it?"

"Sure."

I walked inside and then waited for Kohl to join me. As the door closed, we were surrounded by that absolute darkness again. It seemed even more impenetrable than the day before.

Kohl cleared his voice. "Take two steps forward."

I did.

"Put your hand out."

I did and Kohl guided it to the ladder railing. He

directed me the rest of the way down until we were at last beneath that ebon cloud. I glanced back up.

"What the hell was that?"

"The dark."

"No shit."

"I wasn't being funny," said Kohl. "That was the embodiment of darkness and evil. It's some type of magical security thing they have on this building."

"And what's it supposed to do to intruders?"

"Confuse them so they fall off of that very steep precipice up there. It's a disorienting cloud that fogs the mind and willpower."

"You get many vagrants here who suddenly fall and die?"

"We had a few when we first moved here. Not so many lately. Word must have gotten around."

I didn't want to tell him that his magic cloud hadn't worked on me. I'd been engulfed by it, true, but I'd managed to find my way just fine. Still, I gasped and muttered an appreciative "wow."

Kohl's skin glowed crimson under the red light bulbs. "This way."

I followed him down several corridors of steel skeleton framework. Again, the same sounds I'd heard the other day—the pings, clicks, and drips—all echoed back with a resounding familiarity.

"Fun little place you all have here. You rent this out to Shriners?"

"I'd keep the jokes in check for the next few minutes, Lawson."

"Party-pooper."

At last we came to the doorway where I'd spied Kohl and the chair talking. Kohl turned to me. "Last chance to bail."

"I'll go down with the plane."

He nodded. "Inside."

I ducked in through the doorway and stood in front of the huge desk. The chair behind still had the back facing out. I couldn't see who sat there. The two bodyguards who'd been there before were still standing like robots. I could see they wore sunglasses as well.

"Welcome, Lawson."

The voice seemed to drip like ooze slinking down a wall. I found it a bit weird speaking to the back of a chair. "Hi."

"Sit down."

I looked around.

"On the couch please."

I sat on the couch. Kohl sat next to me.

"Kohl here has told us so much about you."

I grinned. "How nice of him."

"He says you're thinking about joining our effort. Is that true?"

"I haven't exactly heard much of what your effort is about. I'd be a fool to just up and agree to something I wasn't fully aware of."

"Indeed." The voice paused. "We've done a great deal of research into your past, do you know that?"

"Find anything interesting?"

"We got your training record from the Fixer Academy. It was most impressive. We had no idea you were trained for STA-F." There was a vague chuckle of sorts. "What does that stand for, anyway?"

There didn't seem to be much point in trying to bullshit him. After all, their information was top-drawer stuff. "Special Tactics and Assault—Fixer."

"Yes. A sort of elite unit within your organization, is that it?"

"Something like that."

"But you aren't always together. Just sort of called upon when you're needed by the Council. What do they do—save you all for the especially bad cases?"

"We haven't been called out much in the past decade or so. But yeah, that's the idea. If things get really hairy, we go in."

"And kill everyone."

"Something like that."

"There's not really any other way to phrase it, Lawson. That's what you do."

"We've done rescues in the past. Hostage rescues. Some covert intelligence gathering."

"Hostage rescues? Are you serious? With our people?"

"It's a dangerous world out there. Human terrorists don't know who they're kidnapping. One of our kind gets nabbed, it's even more imperative that we get them back without the humans discovering the true nature of what their hostages are."

"And you've been on these . . . what do you call them, 'ops'?"

"A few, yes. And 'ops' is fine."

"And how did you find them?"

"A challenge. But no more of a challenge than anything else I do."

"Once these operations are concluded, the team members dissolve back into their roles as Fixers?"

"Yes."

"And you get together and train every once in a while."

"We have scheduled activities. Since we can't train together all the time, the unit suffers a bit from lack of team unity and integration, but our training activities tend to bring it back together fairly quick."

"How many STA-F teams are there?"

"I don't know."

"You don't know?"

"It's classified. They keep that hidden, even from STA-F members. I don't know. We could be the only team—the guys on my unit and me. Or there could be two dozen other teams scattered across the globe. It's on a need-to-know basis only. We don't need to know anything but the other guys on the team and what our mission is."

"Nice and simple."

"Cutouts. It keeps things safe."

"So you can't spill the beans and give away all your dirty little secrets if you're captured and interrogated, more likely."

"Probably. Doesn't matter much to me."

"You don't care that our government thinks you're expendable?"

"I'm in the line of work. I've made my peace with it. Not much I can do about it, is there?"

"You're referring to your divine calling?"

"Call it what you want. I don't ever see myself being an accountant or a stock broker."

"And even though you're in love with a human woman named Talya, your expendable status doesn't bother you any more?"

"It might bother me a little more than it did. But I do a week's work and take a week's pay off the Council. The expendable thing is part of my life."

"You're being honest with me."

"Sure."

"That's good."

I shrugged. Kohl nodded approvingly. I wanted to tell him to shove it up his ass. "Well, this is a business meeting, right? Can't be much business going on if we aren't completely frank with each other."

"I'm glad you think that way. I can see Kohl may well have been right about you."

I grinned. "Oh, Kohl's a shrewd judge of character."

"Perhaps."

I waited. I had an idea what was coming next.

"Would you mind if I asked you some questions?"

"Aren't we already playing that game?"

"Of a sort."

"What sort of questions do you have in mind?"

"Would you be willing to betray everything that you've worked for, for the last four decades?"

"You don't waste any time, do you?"

"You requested this meeting. Besides, there's time better spent doing other things than circumventing the true aspects of your future relationship with us."

I looked at Kohl who nodded again. I looked back at the rear of the chair. "I have to be honest with you. I'm not used to making business deals without knowing who I'm talking to. I mean, we haven't even been properly introduced. So I can't really answer that question unless we have a bit of *quid pro quo* going on here."

Kohl looked like I'd just suggested the guy go make the beast with two backs with a dead pigeon. I shrugged.

There was a pause. "You want some *quid pro quo*?"

"Be nice, yeah."

"All right then, Lawson. You'll have it."

In the murky reddish gloom, I heard a creak and saw the back of the chair begin to swing around. The two bodyguards never moved. Their positions must have been far enough away that they didn't risk bumping into the chair when it moved around.

The chair creaked into view.
I swallowed.
And then knew why Kohl had said what he'd said earlier.

Twenty

"Jesus."

Kohl whispered. "Told you."

And the thing seated in the chair merely looked at me. "I would hazard a guess that judging from your reaction, I'm not at all what you expected. Am I?"

"You could say that, yeah. No offense or anything."

"None taken. I'm quite aware that my very appearance is rather disturbing to the vast majority of people I meet—be they human or vampire."

"And you seem very comfortable with it." It was a lame comment but it was the best I could do given that I was still reeling from the visual impact.

He—because I guess it really was a he—measured all of three and a half feet tall. His legs dangled from the chair, unable to even reach the floor. I could see the undersides of his shoes, for crying out loud.

But it wasn't his height that had made me blanch when he'd turned around. It was the fact that his face was entirely a misshapen mess. Things were not where they were supposed to be.

His eyes, which on a normal person would be situated higher than his nose, were actually lower on his face. They drooped at the outer edges, and tilted up closer to his nose. His mouth sagged on one side. It reminded me of the way some stroke patients lose muscle control over one-half of their face.

A melange of translucent albino hairy moles pockmarked the skin of his face.

He looked like a melon rotting in the sun.

I had no idea what might have caused him to look like such a sideshow freak, unless someone had force-fed his mother some heinous narcotics while she was pregnant.

"Don't try to figure out what went wrong with me. I was born this way a very long time ago, before our medicine had evolved to the point it is at now. I have no recollection as to the cause, nor does it truly matter. I am an ugly creature, but I am still very very capable of living an extraordinary life. And that is exactly what I do."

I didn't say anything. I didn't think this was a good moment to inject levity.

"My name," he continued, "is Yang-Jul Cho. Most of my associates simply call me Cho."

"Korean?"

He nodded. "Yes, and you're no doubt thinking to yourself how very un-Korean I appear."

"Well . . ." Napalmed to hell didn't even come close to describing it.

"As I said, my appearance truly isn't of much concern. If you're able to get past it, we can do a great deal of business, you and I."

Easier said than done. I kept looking at him and thinking I could hear a carny shouting "step right up and see the grossest creature ever born to a man and a woman—fifty cents!"

But instead, I nodded. "Tell me about your organization, Mr. Cho."

"The 'mister' isn't necessary. In fact, I prefer Cho."

"Okay."

"I asked you before if you'd be willing to forsake your past and what you work for. That question still remains unanswered."

"I have my own questions about what you're doing here. And those haven't been answered yet, either."

He eyed me and I saw one of his hands—I noticed how pudgy they were—reach for a glass that had suddenly materialized on the desk. He held it up to his lips and took a long drag. I guessed it was blood.

He set it down and wiped his mouth on the back of his hand. It came away dark against the white of his skin.

"You've heard of us before, yes? We are the Syndicate."

"I've heard of you."

"And you know what we do." He wasn't asking, just confirming my knowledge.

"I know you are largely responsible for controlling the entertainment that goes on in New York. You run the shows and the dancers and the plays and everything else that goes on down here."

"Covertly, of course. On the surface, everything seems legitimate and, in fact, it truly is. But you're right, we are involved. We have a hand in everything that goes on. We take a piece of the pie as it were."

I waited for him to continue. He seemed to be waiting, almost considering if he should give out more of his puzzle to me.

"We're bored with what we have here. There are no more challenges. No more fruits to be plucked from ripening trees." He leaned forward. "We want . . . more."

"More meaning what?"

"More cities. We want to expand our area of control. We want a lot more." He leaned back. "In the past, we would not have risked such a move due to reprisals from the Council. With their antiquated laws, they unreasonably fear that our endeavors would expose us to humanity. But we know better."

"Do you?"

He smiled. "You know as well as I do that unless you jump up and down in front of humans and rip their necks open in public, they are largely unaware of the world around them."

In fact, I knew plenty of humans who were pretty aware, but this wasn't the time or the place to insert my opinions.

"Besides," said Cho, "we have years and years of experience. It's not as though we're simpletons at this type of activity. We know how to work our magic and get what we need."

"What do you need from me?"

"You're the head Fixer for the Northeast, aren't you?"

"I'm the Fixer in charge of Boston. That's it."

Cho smiled. "Ah, you don't know yet."

"Know what?"

Cho looked at Kohl. "Tell him."

Kohl smiled. "You've been promoted."

"Promoted?" What the hell was this bullshit?

"Obviously, the Council didn't tell you yet. But apparently, in light of your efforts during the past year, the Council has been sufficiently impressed with your job performance. They've decided to appoint you as the overseer of the Northeast. Fixers from Washington to Maine and out to Pennsylvania will report to you. You'll have operational control apparently. It's quite a big promotion."

I sighed. On one hand, I had no way of knowing if they were just feeding me a load of crap. On the other hand, it would be nice. And it would be nice to know that all the shit I'd been through and all the friends I'd seen buried hadn't been for nothing.

But like my mentor Zero always said, "First we verify, then we trust," and it was a lesson I took to heart. So if Cho and Kohl wanted to feed me that line, that was cool with me. When I heard confirmation from the Council or from Niles, I'd believe it.

Cho wasn't waiting for that, however. "As I was saying, since you are in charge of the Northeast, we would need you to look the other way about some of our activities."

"Tell me about Saber."

That stopped him. He looked at Kohl. Kohl nodded. Cho smiled. "All right. Imagine the most potent narcotic you can. Now multiply that by a hundred."

"I suck at math. Sorry."

He ignored me, which was probably a good thing. "What we've done is figure out how to synthesize a revolutionary new addictive substance that delivers a hundred times the high, a thousand times the addictive qualities, and very little in terms of bad side effects. It has a whopping addiction rate. And the buzz around it is amazing. It's sucking up converts from dance clubs to art gallery openings. No one is immune to it; it's a veritable black hole of desire. It bridges demographics easily and it's making us tons of money."

"How much?"

"What would you say if I told you on the order of three hundred million in the last year alone?"

I whistled. It seemed like the appropriate gesture.

Cho smiled. "Exactly. We could use that money to muscle our way into the organized crime families of London, Frankfurt, Milan, Paris, Tokyo, Seoul, and Manila."

"And that's what you want."

"Yes."

"You're going to need to buy off a lot more Fixers than just me."

"We aren't concerned about that."

"Why not?"

"Because we'll be moving all of our Saber out of the Northeast. There's no need to involve any other Fixers." He smiled. I almost gagged. Brown, plaque-encrusted teeth jutted out of his gums at odd angles. "We only need concern ourselves with you, Lawson."

"Pardon me for saying so, but I'm not much impressed with how you're winning me over."

"How do you mean?"

"Well, my cousin's missing. And since she was a dancer, there's good reason to suspect that the Syndicate had something to do with her disappearance."

Cho sucked in a gulp of air and it sounded like a wet, raspy breath. "Well, honestly, we had everything to do with her disappearance, Lawson."

"I don't follow."

"Of course, you don't." He smiled. "Oh, that wasn't an insult. Not at all. I'm just always amused by how much people miss."

"So, clue me in."

"Your cousin, Lawson, was the bait. To get you down here so we could talk business with you. Don't you see?"

"You could have approached me up in Boston."

Cho's claim of baiting me didn't really fly given the fact that they'd put a shooter on my ass yesterday. Then again, maybe they did that because it was part of the plan. My head swam. I hate conspiracies.

He laughed. "We most certainly could not have. You would have shot the messenger. And besides, what incentive would you have to help our cause?"

The word incentive made me nervous. When people start tossing that word around, it generally means something bad is coming next.

Cho made a barely perceptible gesture and one of the bodyguards stepped forward and pressed a button on the wall. The heavy red velvet curtain started to slide back. As it did, Cho looked at me.

"You see, we had to have some reason to get you down here. We had to make it seem like you were urgently needed. Only then could we initiate contact. Away from your Control—away from your home base—you would be more open to our invitation."

The open curtain exposed a wall of glass. But it was dark on the other side. I couldn't see what might be there. But I had a sinking feeling I knew what was.

"Show him."

A light popped on somewhere on the other side of the glass.

Marilyn.

She was sitting in something that looked like a jail cell. Her face had a lot of bruising around the eyes. They'd roughed her up. I felt my pulse quicken. I fought to control it.

Cho didn't seem to notice. "She gave us a very courageous fight, this cousin of yours. Did you train her in martial arts by any chance?"

"My uncle sent her to Judo and boxing when she was younger."

"Indeed. I thought I noticed an attempted *Harai Goshi* when my men intercepted her. Too bad for her my men have all been extensively trained."

"By who?"

Cho grinned. "Why, by me of course."

Looking at Cho, it seemed about as possible that he was some sort of martial arts master as it was that Dan Quayle could muster a coherent thought. Some things just do not go together.

Cho must have noticed. "You think my size and ugliness preclude me from having any degree of skill in fighting?"

"I didn't say that."

"You didn't have to. Your left eyebrow quivered slightly when I made my remark a moment ago." He waved his hand. "Don't worry about it. You certainly aren't the first to think that. Most likely, you won't be the last, either."

Kohl had slipped down in his seat next to me. I wondered why. Cho pushed his chair back and hopped down from his seat. He came around the desk moving with some sort of weird waddle.

"You'll also notice that one of my legs is shorter than the other. That's why I limp."

"Oh." Cripes this guy was a walking mess of genetic malfunction.

Cho gestured to his bodyguards. They came around the desk on cue. Cho looked at me. "Perhaps something of a demonstration would be in order."

"I don't really see what that has to do with our discussion of business or the well-being of my cousin there."

"It has quite a lot to do with it, actually." Cho moved closer. "I need to know that we understand each other absolutely and completely before we begin our arrangement."

"Seems to me I'm being strong-armed into this whether I like it or not."

"You can always say no," said Cho. "Of course, then your pretty little cousin there will die a truly horrific death. But not before I rape her mercilessly and send enough of my deformed sperm into her uterus to ensure that another evolutionary blasphemy like myself comes out nine months later. Only then will she die. But then again, perhaps the mere sight of our commingled genetics will make her die of fright before I have the chance to do so." He smiled. "Such things to ponder."

"You have a point to make, Cho?"

"Stand up, Lawson," he said. "And let's have some fun."

Twenty-one

The last thing I wanted to do was fight a dwarf with an attitude problem.

But Cho didn't seem to be in the mood for excuses. Part of me suspected he had something he wanted to prove—some sort of inferiority complex that needed soothing.

And now I had a big problem.

If I fought to the best of my ability, I might actually kill the pint-sized son-of-a-bitch. And if I threw the fight, that might be just as bad. Cho might suspect me of being a rollover and therefore no good to his organization.

The goal, I had to keep reminding myself, was to be able to penetrate the Syndicate, see what it was truly up to, and then bring about its downfall. Because even if the Council liked sleeping with these bastards, I'd already decided that they didn't deserve to exist.

Cho stepped around his desk. His bodyguards moved around the desk as well.

I grinned. "Three against one?"

Cho looked back and waved off the guards. They stepped back. "You'll have to forgive my associates. They take their duties very seriously."

"Lucky me."

"Lucky me, actually," said Cho. "I would have died a long time ago if not for their intervention."

"Assassination attempts?"

"Absolutely."

"I wasn't aware such action had been sanctioned by the Council."

"Oh, it wasn't a Fixer trying to get me. We've had competition in the past."

I stood up. "So, how do you want to do this? We fight now and the winner does what?"

"There's no real winner or loser here. I just want you to know what type of man I am. Even with my apparent weaknesses."

"I try to never judge a book by its cover. Your apparent weaknesses don't matter much to me."

"I'm not entirely sure I believe that," said Cho.

"Trust is always such a good way for us to start our relationship."

"Besides, I just showed you your cousin. Imprisoned and not very comfortable. I'm sure you must feel some anger toward me. Wouldn't you like to take out some of that frustration?"

"Oh sure, I get lucky with a punch and your goons there come over and stomp my ass into next week. That makes good sense."

Cho smiled. "You have my word. If you do indeed 'get lucky,' my men will not harm you."

"I'd prefer to hear that from them."

"Impossible."

I frowned. "Why's that impossible."

"Because they are unable to speak. They had their tongues cut out some years ago."

"Who th—?"

"I did," said Cho. "My bodyguards are my most

trusted men. And they are always around me. They hear everything. I needed to make sure they would never repeat anything they'd heard come out of my mouth."

I pointed. "What about writing? You forgot to cut off their hands."

Cho chuckled. "No. I didn't." He glanced over his shoulder and said simply, "Show him."

One of the bodyguards rolled up his sleeves and I saw that he didn't have hands at all, just large, round lumps of metal where his wrists ended. They looked like giant clubs.

I cocked an eyebrow. "Good thing you didn't think they were telepathic."

"I have attendants take care of my bodyguards, in case you're wondering how they get their clothes changed or take baths."

"Or eat or drink," I said. "Do you think you might have been a little . . . overzealous in your security precautions?"

"They volunteered."

"You explained to them what it would mean?"

"Of course."

"And they still volunteered."

Cho smiled. "You haven't had the benefit of seeing how I operate, Lawson. To some of these men, I am a god. They would gladly lay down their lives for me if I asked them to. Or even if I did not. The chance to serve as my personal protectors was deemed a tremendous honor."

"I see."

"They were more than willing to put up with the minor discomforts of what the role entailed."

I took my sport coat off. "Well, let's get into this."

Cho chose not to remove the red blazer he wore. He walked with a definite limp and I soon pinpointed his left leg as being the shorter of the two.

There wasn't much room to move for a guy my size and I realized that Cho had ingeniously set the room up so it favored his size and abilities.

He smiled when he saw that I realized this. "Yes, you are a bit more aware than some of the others who have tried this."

I circled right, keeping the coffee table between us. "How many others have you had to prove yourself to?"

"I unfortunately have to prove myself to everyone I meet. The world does not look kindly upon men with my peculiar attributes."

"Attributes?"

"I prefer to view my abnormalities that way." He hopped across the coffee table and sent a sidekick at my left knee. I lifted the leg and he missed.

But it had been a feint; he'd only used it to break down the distance. Even as I withdrew, he doubled his attack and caught me with a high hook punch to my left floating rib. It hurt like a bastard and I fell over the armchair, rolling when I touched the floor.

I came up in time to see him rushing me. I pivoted and sent him flying into the wall. He hit it face first, which I didn't think would make him look any worse than he already did.

He spun and smiled. "Not bad."

I threw a low kick and it nailed him in his solar plexus, but he grabbed my foot above the ankle and turned then, affecting a leg lock. I went with the twist, flipped over and caught him off the jaw with my other heel.

I heard a dull crack and wondered if I'd broken it.

I saw a dribble of blood appear at the corner of his mouth but Cho remained unfazed by it.

He kept moving and darted left this time. I crossed his centerline about six feet out and then threw a series of punches at him. The right jab set up the left rear cross and then I came back with the right hook. He blocked the first two successfully but I caught him again in the gut with the hook. He grunted and back-flipped out of range.

There was a frown on his face. Then I heard an audible click.

The little bastard had pulled a knife.

"You're quite good, Lawson."

"You're bringing a knife into this? That seems even less fair."

"You haven't been properly schooled yet."

"This is bullshit." But I kept as many pieces of furniture between us. Knife fights are bad news. And no matter what supposed martial arts experts tell you, there is an almost guaranteed chance that you will get cut during one. It doesn't matter if the blade is ten inches long or pocket folder. In the hands of someone who knows how to use it, that knife will cut you.

The preference therefore is to try to take any slashes and cuts across the areas of your body that won't be mortally wounded. Protect the face and the vital organs and let the back of your arms take any cuts if possible.

Distancing is also vital to knife defense. Try to close on a knife-wielding attacker too soon and he will find your gut before you know it.

If any of this gives you the impression that knife fighting isn't the glamorous bout of fun that some folks make it out to be, that's because it isn't. I hate dealing with knives.

Cho was no slouch. I could tell from the way he moved that he knew some sort of martial style. And the way he held the knife seemed another good indicator.

He threw a high roundhouse kick first and then followed that by coming in with a straight left punch and then a stab with the knife. The kick missed but it was supposed to. The punch was the setup, and the stab was the follow-through.

I backpedaled away from the punch, deflecting the arm down and across his centerline, hoping to take his momentum in that direction. Cho was good, though. He'd anticipated my move and righted himself so the stab cut in toward my belly.

I felt the front of my shirt tear open.

And then sharp pain across my abdomen even as I was pulling myself farther back.

No time to assess the damage, I felt for his knife hand and grabbed him around the wrist then drove a punch into the back of his hand. The knife clattered away, hopefully underneath some of the furniture. I heard another dull snap and wondered if I'd broken any of the bones in Cho's pudgy hand.

He grunted, clutched his hand, and then spun away. He walked back toward his desk.

"Well, that was fun."

I guessed the festivities were over. I glanced down at my midsection and saw the score line from the blade—a red jagged line of dribbling blood across my stomach.

That cut a bit too close for my comfort.

Cho sat down with a heavy sigh. "I didn't realize you were quite so good."

"I'm not that good," I said. "I got cut."

"You're a pro. You know the inherent probabilities in knife fighting."

"I do. Makes me wonder why you even pulled a blade out in the first place."

"You were obviously doing better than I anticipated in the unarmed combat. I wanted to see what you'd do if I escalated it."

"What would you have done if I'd disarmed you right off—brought out a Howitzer?"

He laughed. "Isn't it good now, though? You and I, we can look at each other with some degree of respect now. We know a little bit more about each other."

I knew I didn't want to fight the little freak again.

"Why, you're lucky to have me here. You know that?"

"How so?"

"Now, you have some experience fighting a midget."

Great. The next time I got roughed up at a circus, I'd be all set.

He took another sip of blood from his glass. "You know, there's something incredibly honest about a fight. When two people enter into combat, everything reveals itself through the movements of the two players. There is no dishonesty, no ulterior motive. Just the simple task of attacking and defending."

"That's not always such a simple task, Cho."

"Indeed. As I think we have both shown today. But you must admit there's some truth to my statement."

"Sure." I wasn't going to tell him about the whole schools of thought that are out there on using deceptive strategy in the course of a fight to disrupt the opponent. Let Cho think every fighter in the world operated honestly. That was fine with me.

"And what do you think of me now that we've had a chance to tangle some?"

"Impressive. It's obvious you've studied a martial style. Perhaps more than one."

"What would you guess?"

"Tae Kwon Do is too much of a sport—"

"Not necessarily. True, most of the schools here in the U.S. and even in my beloved Korea exist solely for the stupidity of competition. But there are some schools of Tae Kwon Do more suited to combat."

"You didn't study Tae Kwon Do, though. I'm familiar with the style and I saw very little in your movement."

"What did you see?"

"Looked like Han Pul."

His eyes narrowed and he looked even more bizarre. "You do know your styles, that's for sure. I am impressed once again with you, Lawson."

"My lucky day." In more ways than one. I had little doubt that Cho had made a very concerted effort to splay my guts open with his knife. If I'd been any slower in moving, I would have had a hard time eating and shitting for a while.

"So, we once again come to the inevitable question of whether we can count on you to help us."

I glanced at Marilyn. She hadn't moved much. I frowned. "I help you and she goes free?"

"Eventually."

"What's eventually?"

"Well, we can't let her go just on the basis of you saying that yes, you'll work for us. We need to hold on to her to make sure you live up to your word."

"My word is good."

"Not for me it isn't. You're a Fixer. You might be lying."

"All right. I want a cut of the profits."

Cho sniffed. "How much of a cut?"

"You said you cleared three hundred million last year? I want twenty million for selling out."

Cho's eyebrows jumped. "Twenty million is a ridiculously exorbitant sum of money, Lawson. What would you do with so much cash?"

"Not your concern. Just pay me and then let me do my job."

"Twenty million." Cho sighed. "You realize that the money we earn from Saber is to go toward our expansion into other cities?"

"You can part with a measly twenty million."

"Perhaps." He turned around in his chair, still massaging the back of his hand. "All right, Lawson. We'll try you out. Your cousin stays with us, and you get twenty million. If everything works out well, you'll have her back soon enough as well."

I nodded. "Good."

"There's just one other thing," said Cho.

"What's that?"

"Kohl here tells me you killed Raoul last night."

"Was he somebody important?"

Cho turned back around. "He was my adopted son."

Uh oh.

"He was about to kill a woman. I had no choice but to stop him."

"We all have a choice in life, Lawson. Sometimes, they just aren't all that apparent. It's up to us to spot them for what they really are."

"Pardon my saying so, but you don't seem all that broken up about Raoul's passing."

Cho shrugged. "I'm a pragmatic man. I know Raoul had impulses that made him likely to encounter misfortune. That doesn't mean I didn't love him dearly. Nor that I won't miss him now that he's gone."

"I see."

"After all, his death, in a way, brought us together. And I think that that alone is more than enough to justify his murder."

I looked at the back of the chair, but damned if I understood that sentiment.

"You can go, Lawson. Be careful on your way out."

"How so?"

Cho looked at me. "The dark cloud, remember?"

I nodded. "Kohl says that's magic."

"It is."

"Really?"

"Absolutely." Cho smiled. "We aren't just involved in worldly things in the Syndicate, Lawson. We dabble in every area of creation. You'd do well to remember that on your drive back to Boston."

Twenty-two

But I didn't head for Boston.

I needed to check in on Teresa—make sure she wasn't suffering from any lasting results of the hypnosis. Having her neurons scrambled by a nutjob like Raoul was bound to leave her with some type of residual effects.

The doorman frowned long and hard when he saw me.

"I do something wrong?"

"I fell asleep after you came in here last night."

"Oh yeah?"

The frown never wavered. "I never fall asleep on the job."

"First time for everything."

"Not this. Not me."

"You think I had something to do with it?"

"I think there's more to you than meets the eye."

No shit. I nodded at the door. "Going to let me up?"

He buzzed the door. I walked to the elevator with his eyes boring holes in my back the entire way. I'd have to mention to Kohl that the Saber gas wasn't exactly the top-notch stuff they'd made it out to be.

The hallway outside Teresa's apartment showed no signs of last night's visit. Even Teresa's door had been fixed. Whoever Kohl had used for his cleanup team, they'd done a decent job.

Teresa opened the door wearing a short, light blue cotton kimono-style robe that showed a lot of cleavage and an ample amount of thigh. Neither one of those sights did much for my sense of self-control.

I redirected my gaze. "Are you okay?"

She looked like she'd just spent the last twelve hours being run over by a steamroller. But she still looked damned good. Her eyes stayed half-closed and the effect on me was fairly substantial.

"Were you here last night, Lawson?"

I glanced around. A hallway wasn't the best place for the conversation we were going to have. "I should come in."

She stepped back and I entered the apartment. She closed the door and then walked past me to the couch. "You don't mind, do you? I'm bone tired."

I sat at one end of the couch. She plopped down on the other. The light material of her robe fluttered from the movement and exposed the white cotton panties she wore. Teresa didn't even seem to care.

"I was here last night," I said when I regained some measure of control over my pulse.

"I thought so. But all I can remember is some weird dream about . . . Raoul?"

"Yeah."

"He was here?"

"Unfortunately."

"And then you showed up."

"Yep."

"What happened?"

Raoul must not have been particularly proficient with his hypnosis, after all. My mistake. Judging from how he looked during the process, it had seemed decent. But sometimes appearances are deceiving. Regardless, in another minute, Teresa was going to remember everything. Bad hypnosis doesn't block out the memories. It only keeps them at bay for a little while.

Her face clouded on cue. "Oh, my God."

I waited for it. There wasn't much point in saying anything until she did. I could see her eyes dancing in their sockets. She was accessing her memory cues.

And then it happened. "He's dead."

"He is now. Yes."

She looked at me. "You killed him."

"I did."

A cloud passed over her face. "Why?"

"He was going to kill you."

"Me? Why?"

I shrugged. "Who knows? I've only known him a few days and from what I saw, I could see he had some serious issues."

"You . . . showed up last night—"

"—just in time, by the look of things."

"I remember . . . his teeth?"

I paused. "I'd forget about that. Probably just a symptom of posttraumatic stress disorder or something. Raoul had a knife on you. He was going to open you up in a bad way."

"I remember . . . a gun. You shot him."

"Yes."

"You never told me you had a gun."

"Didn't seem to be much point in it."

"It sure came in handy."

"Last night it did." If only she knew how many times my piece has saved my ass.

"What about the police?"

I smiled. "The cops weren't involved."

"They have to be."

I leaned closer. "Teresa, I work for some very powerful people. They're well above the level of the police, do you understand?"

"Like what . . . the CIA?"

"Something like that. Anyway, there's no use involving the police because it will raise too many questions and focus too much attention on you. You don't need that. And neither does anyone else. So, for the sake of the students down at his studio, let's just pretend that Raoul left the country and he's never coming back, okay?"

"He never had any family."

Tell that to Cho. "Exactly. So there won't be any questions coming from that angle. As long as you stick to the story, everything will be fine."

"Rebecca knew a lot about Raoul, though."

Good point. I'd forgotten about the chunky agent. I'd have to deal with Rebecca at some point. I wasn't sure yet where she fit into this mess. But a big part of me knew that she did somehow.

"You just let me worry about Rebecca, okay?"

"Okay. Any luck finding Marilyn?"

"No."

"What's your connection to her? Were you close? I mean, in terms of being her cousin."

"I never really hung out with her, no. She's far younger than I am."

"But you seem so invested in this pursuit."

"Probably more for her family than for her. As bad as that sounds."

"I don't understand."

I leaned back. "Marilyn's father—my uncle—he

never really approved of my life. When my father died, it left my mother and I alone for a while. I went off to college. Was busy. School. That sort of thing. Then my mother died unexpectedly. I couldn't come home for the funeral."

"You couldn't?"

"It's tough to explain."

"That must have left quite an impression on your uncle."

"A bad one, yeah. I explained it to him later on, but you know, the damage gets done pretty hard and pretty fast in those situations. I've often felt he's never gotten over holding some type of grudge against me."

She nodded. "So you see this as a way of getting back on even footing?"

"I'm hopeful, yeah. Probably a bit naïve on my part, but what the hell."

"And if you save Marilyn's life . . ."

"Would be a good thing."

She sat up then. The robe slipped higher up her thighs. Her eyes were wide and wet. Moist.

"You saved *my* life last night."

"Yeah."

"My hero."

There was a funny word. I'm about as unheroic as they come. I'm born to a job that demands I do what I do. There's little reason to think of me as a hero, but every now and again, someone seems to think so. Usually, it's a beautiful woman. A beautiful human woman. This is about where my life gets complicated.

I frowned. "Heroes end up dead a lot of the time. I'm not real crazy about that word."

"How about savior?" She leaned closer.

"Too religious. People will expect me to secede from the government if I go around with that title."

She smiled and licked her lips. Then she kissed me. Long, soft, and with a gentle probing tongue that made me suck in air like a vacuum cleaner set on high. After a minute, she drew away.

"Thank you."

I sighed. "I should thank you. That was some kiss."

"I was wrong about you yesterday. I knew Raoul was riding me for no reason at all, but I blamed you. I shouldn't have. You're just looking for Marilyn. If Raoul had a problem with that, it was his thing. He did what he did out of some petty power manipulation."

"Probably. But Raoul's a moot point right now. So let's forget about him, okay?"

"We could kiss again."

I leaned into her and she drew me down on the couch with her. I could feel her nipples pressing through the fabric of the robe into my chest. I kissed her neck, sliding down to her breasts, suckling her lightly. She arched her back and moaned softly.

I started to dive deeper and she pulled away then. A very fast, smooth motion and she was up and out from underneath me, clutching her robe to her.

She smiled. Shy. "I should shower."

I was caught off guard. She saw it and grinned. "I've been asleep for hours. I don't feel very . . . fresh. Why don't you sit down and make yourself comfortable while I take a quick dip."

"All right. We'll go out for a late lunch afterward."

Teresa vanished around the corner and I leaned back into the couch. If I'd been in her position, I might have gone for the shower as well. Still, the memory of her kisses made me want her more.

A lot more.

My cell phone rang. I slid it out of the inside breast pocket of my jacket and flipped it on.

"Yeah?"

"Well, well, well. You're still here."

Kohl sounded particularly smug. "Yeah. I had an errand to do first before I left."

"You're at the woman's house again, aren't you?"

"What if I am?"

I could hear rustling in the background. Then a new voice came on the phone. "Lawson."

"Cho."

"Why are you still in my city?"

His city, huh? We'd see about that. "I had an errand to do before I left."

"You have more important things to do than sleep with Marilyn's roommate. You're supposed to be on the road right now heading home to Boston."

"I will be soon enough."

"Did you already forget the pledge you made? Not only to me, Lawson. But also to your cousin? You don't want to disappoint her do you?"

"Of course not."

"And you certainly don't want to disappoint me, either."

"I told you I'll be leaving soon enough."

"Make it now and I might even still spare your cousin's life."

"You kill her and our deal's off. You know that."

"I know you'd try to avenge her death. So what? You think I haven't dealt with tough people before?"

"What I think is, you haven't dealt with anyone like me before."

There was a pause on the other end of the phone.

"Get on the road now. Forget the girl. Put yourself into that Mercedes of yours and start driving."

The line went dead and I stared at the phone. I'd never given Kohl my phone number. How had he found me? Maybe he had the caller ID function on his phone. I looked back toward the bathroom where a cascade of hot water was washing soapy bubbles off the delicate mounds and curves of Teresa's body. I licked my lips. I wanted those curves and mounds for myself.

But as much as I hated to admit it, I had work to do. And that meant the drive back to Boston.

I sighed and sat down to write a quick note to Teresa. Then I headed for home.

Leaving never hurt so bad.

Twenty-three

"It doesn't make much sense to me."

Three hours after Cho's call, I was sitting in Wirek's apartment on the backside of Beacon Hill. Even though Wirek had cleaned himself up a lot since I'd first met him a year and a half ago, he still clung to some old ways. Chief among them was living in the shitty walk-up he kept above a convenience store. The halls and stairs leading up to his apartment reeked of urine and stale booze.

Niles sat next to me on the couch. He scribbled furiously into a small spiral-bound notebook. Something about it seemed woefully antiquated in the age of PDAs. But Niles didn't trust the PDAs; he said they were potentially hack-able. I didn't know if that was true, but Niles did his job in a damned fine way, so I wasn't about to mess with his technique.

"It didn't make much sense to me, either," I said. "And I was there."

"They kidnapped Marilyn just to get you down there and then talk you into working for them?" Niles frowned. "No offense to you or anything, but it seems to me they wouldn't really need to buy you off in order to ship this Saber thing out of the northeast."

"What about the promotion? Is that true?"

Niles shrugged. "First I've heard of it. Sorry."

Wirek chimed in. "Although, if it does come to pass, that'd be a pretty sure indicator that someone on the inside is dirty."

"I think that's pretty much a given at this point. Those guys down there had information on me that couldn't have been found anywhere but inside my personnel file. Someone's definitely on the take. But how deep inside they are is another question we'll have to answer."

"More traitors," said Niles. "Do any of you think that there's just been much too much of that happening lately? I can't recall there having been so much treasonous activity in years past."

I nodded. "Time was I'd go off hunting down private citizens for breaking the law. The last year it's been all about people on the Council, or close to it, trying to wrest power away for themselves."

"Makes me wonder if we're missing something." Niles glanced at Wirek. But Wirek had his eyes closed. He'd done that once with me and I thought he'd fallen asleep. Turns out that's how the old guy thinks.

He opened his eyes on cue and looked at us. "You're wondering if there's something written somewhere— some sort of prophecy that would explain this?"

"I think we're looking for anything that would help us understand why these events are happening."

Wirek nodded. "Give me some time and I'll look into it."

Niles ticked the incidents off on his hand. "According to Lawson's case history, he's been involved in three power-grabs so far this decade. Cosgrove and McKinley, Arvella and Petrov, Shiva and Jarvis. And now, there's the potential for another one here dealing with the Syndicate."

"What's the common denominator?"

Niles looked at me. "What?"

"If there's a pattern emerging, then there ought to be a common denominator. With all of those cases, there is. They all involve a vampire of immense power connected to, in some fashion, a Fixer."

"A Fixer?"

"He's right," said Wirek. "McKinley was a former Fixer, Petrov was a star Fixer back in the day, and Jarvis was a smelly noodlehead but still a Fixer."

"But where's the Fixer variable in this situation?"

"It can't be Kohl," I said. "He's not really even part of the service."

"But D'Angelo was," said Niles. "Only problem is, he's missing and we've got no clue as to his whereabouts."

"You think he might still be alive?" asked Wirek.

I frowned. "I was sure he was dead. Killed by Kohl who then assumed his position down in New York to help facilitate whatever the Syndicate's true plans are. But now I'm not so sure."

"If he's alive, he'll have some answers to these questions," said Niles. "He might just be the missing link."

"He'll be tough to find."

Wirek hacked up some phlegm. "Maybe not so tough."

"Oh?"

"There's a way we might be able to find out where he is."

I shook my head. "How's that? You got a crystal ball you can look into to ask for help?"

"Not me," said Wirek. "But you do."

"I do?"

He nodded. "Have you talked to Jack lately?"

I frowned. What did an Invoker have to do with this? "Sure. I spoke to him last month. He's doing well at school. But so what?"

"Is this the Jack I read about in the case file dealing with Arvella and Petrov?"

I nodded. "Yeah."

"According to the file he's up in Canada."

"Still is. I keep in touch with him."

Niles glanced at Wirek. "I'm afraid I don't see the connection either. How would this boy be able to help us locate D'Angelo?"

"One of the first things they teach young Invokers is to be receptive to spirit energies. What that generally entails is a lengthy course in clairvoyance and clairaudience. The Invoker trainees acquire the ability to see and hear things from the spirit world prior to learning how to harness the spirit energies."

"So, they're psychic?"

Wirek shrugged. "That's a very human way of explaining it, but yes, I suppose that fits."

"And you think he'll be able to find D'Angelo?"

Wirek smiled. "I think that kid could do anything he puts his mind to. Locating D'Angelo at this point ought to be fairly easy for him to do. Hell, he might even be insulted." He chuckled to himself.

"Well," said Niles, "that's good news."

"I suppose." I looked at them. "The problem is, the Syndicate thinks I'm up here getting things ready for them."

"What do they think you're doing?"

I shrugged. "Waiting? I don't know for sure. But they might well have someone watching Boston to make sure I'm not off doing something other than sitting tight."

"You really think they could pin a tail on you?"

"It's happened before."

Wirek grinned. "You're ruining all my preconceptions about the supposedly mighty Fixer service here, buddy."

"I thought that happened in Nepal."

"Lawson's right," said Niles. "If they think he's gone to ground, they'll kill Marilyn." He looked at me. "What do you want to do about it?"

"We've got to make sure Marilyn's safe before I go off to see Jack." I looked at Wirek. "I don't suppose if I called up the little dude, he'd be able to do it over the phone?"

Wirek shook his head. "What I know about the process, he'll need to have physical contact with you in order to tap into your own consciousness."

"What good will that do? I haven't even seen D'Angelo."

"No. But you've been in contact with the people who most likely know of his whereabouts. Jack will need to use that memory base as a starting point to locate D'Angelo. It's like taking a base reading of something."

I nodded. "Okay. I guess I'm heading off to Canada."

Niles frowned. "What about Marilyn?"

"Obviously, I want her rescued before I move. I can't risk her life on fooling any potential watchers the Syndicate will employ to watch Boston."

"Rescue, huh?" Niles looked away. "That might be tough."

"I think this case is a good enough reason to justify it, don't you?"

"Sure, I do. But I'm not the one you have to convince. The Council has to sanction it before I can order the team into position."

"And what if there's a mole on the Council?" I asked. "We'd be compromised before we could even stage the damn op. We'd be walking into an ambush."

"You might be walking into an ambush anyway," said Niles. "Especially if the Syndicate thinks this is how you'll proceed."

"What are the chances the Syndicate doesn't know about Jack?" asked Wirek.

"Not good," I said. "If they knew all that other stuff about my record, there's a very good chance they know all about Jack and his abilities as well. My file's a track record of every case I've been involved with."

"True," said Wirek, "but they may not know much about Jack beyond his power to conjure spirits. They may not know that he'd be able to locate D'Angelo."

"Are you sure?"

"Hell no."

"Great."

"Look," said Niles. "This isn't going to be easy. You know I like to do things by the book."

"I know it."

He sighed. "But there's also a time when the book has to go out the window. And as much as I hate admitting it, that seems to happen more times than not when it comes to you, Lawson."

I grinned. "Guess the rules and I don't necessarily get along so good."

"Maybe not, but there's no arguing with your record of success."

"So, you'll hold off going to the Council?"

"Just until after the operation begins. If I wait much longer they'll fire my ass and get you another Control.

And probably it won't be someone nearly as cool as I am."

"And we wouldn't want that."

He grinned. "You need any other resources?"

"Just my team," I said. "They should still be pretty fresh after our last bout of training."

Wirek chuckled. "Fixer commandos. What a concept."

"I'm surprised you didn't know about them," I said. "Considering you seem to know almost everything about everything else."

"Nobody's perfect. There are a few things I don't know that much about. Storming buildings and rescuing hostages happen to be two of them."

"You did well enough that time in Newton."

Wirek sniffed. "That was luck. And a distinct lack of enemy forces as I recall."

He had a point. I stood. "All right. I've got some phone calls to make. And then I'll be heading back to New York."

"What if they do have watchers in place?"

I shook my head. "Probably don't have them yet. They couldn't be sure I'd go along with them on this. We might have a two-day window before they can get someone in place."

"Might not be that long," said Wirek.

"What other choice do we have?" I looked at Niles. "I'll call you when we're just about ready to hit the place."

"You sure they'll have her there? Wisdom would dictate that they'd move her to a new location if they even suspected you might try something like this."

Wirek nodded. "Especially since they know you were STA-F."

It was a fair point. I'm not sure why I felt sure they'd keep her in that crappy building, but I did. "Maybe it's ego," I said. "Maybe it's something else entirely. Could just be a simple power trip. Even a taunt."

"Or an ambush," said Wirek.

"Thanks for the cheerful thought."

"Devil's advocate, pal. Someone had to say it."

"Yeah."

"Whatever the case," said Niles. "You and your boys better make sure your intelligence is good before you hit the place. If they've moved her, you'll have to find out pretty damned fast. I can't dick around with the Council for too long. And your other team members will be sorely missed if they're gone from their regular duty stations for too long."

I nodded. "Good points, all of them. I'll make sure things happen as fast as possible. The sooner we're in and out, the sooner things get back to normal."

Wirek stood and Niles followed suit. "Good luck, Lawson."

I shook their hands and headed out.

Damn, did my stomach hurt.

Twenty-four

STA-F is something relatively new in terms of vampire society. Basically, it came about as a result of increasing hot spots and flashpoints across the world. The administration of the Fixer Academy recognized the potential that some of our people might be inadvertently snatched up along with human hostages. Vampires, then, needed a rapid reaction force that could do the same things a human hostage rescue team could. In order to stave off the possibility of our society being exposed.

The administrators then cajoled and bullied the Council into passing the legislation necessary to see the unit implemented. I was approached back when I went through the Academy, but everything was handled with the strictest of security.

STA-F isn't called into action all that often. And it takes a lot to get a deployment call. I was damned close a little over a year ago to calling them up when it looked like Cosgrove might have begun a mutiny. I hadn't let Zero know that.

Maybe I should have.

What I'd told Cho down in New York was the truth. I'd only recently returned from a training session with the other members of my team. STA-F is broken down into small four-man units that can get into the tight places, do the job, and then just vanish back into the shadows.

I really had no idea how many other STA-F teams there might be. All I knew about was my own. All I had to focus on was my own. And the only guys I cared anything about were my own.

The true instrument of success for a specops team isn't due to awesome technology or incredible fire-power. What it comes down to is team members having the ultimate trust in each other. Each guy knows the others have his back. These are the men you'll walk into the depths of hell with.

It takes a lot to bond a unit so tightly. But bonding is what it's all about. We practiced over and over again until, despite long periods apart, we could act as one cohesive team.

Nobody knew Gopher's real name. It didn't matter much what it was. We were all active duty Fixers drawn away from our usual duty stations to fulfill a mission and then go back to work. Most of us had nicknames.

Gopher got his because the guy could scrounge anything we needed, no matter where in the world we operated. If we couldn't fly into a location with weapons, it would only take Gopher a matter of an hour to procure what we needed. He was that good. Slight of build at five feet six inches and rail thin, Go-pher could get his wiry body into any nook and cranny that we needed him to go into. He was our chief sneak-and-peek guy.

Boxcar was aptly named for his size. A six foot six inch tall, six-foot wide Norwegian weight lifter with shockingly blond hair and white bushy eyebrows, the guy had muscles bulging on top of his muscles. On room clearing, Boxcar went first a lot of the time because the image of such a giant coming through the door with a weapon drawing down on you had as much psychological impact as the bullet. Plus, Boxcar could put six rounds from his submachine gun inside a circle only two inches across in under two seconds—from a distance of three hundred feet.

Boxcar and I went way back. Way back. All the way to our days at the Fixer Academy. During the first few weeks when we'd learned the basics of hand-to-hand combat, Boxcar was the first guy I'd gone up against. He'd demolished me. Back then his name was Samuelson. But we all called him "The Truck." It took me a few months before I could hold my own against him. From there on out, we'd been friends.

Pinkie Johnson hailed from Kingston, Jamaica, originally. A thick Jamaican accent blanketed his speech, but it was an act. Pinkie enjoyed speaking like a Rastafarian more than anything else. He said it helped get him laid. Who were we to argue? Especially since he handled demolitions. Pinkie could make anything under the sun go boom. He knew roughly ten thousand shirt sleeve formulas for making improvised explosive devices. Years ago, Pinkie'd lost a finger when one of the charges he'd made detonated ahead of schedule—right when he was placing the charge. Considering it was a shaped explosive full of wood fragmentation designed to kill the vampires in a house, Pinkie was damned lucky that his finger was all he'd lost.

And then there was me.

We rendezvoused at the McDonald's at a rest stop on the Massachusetts Turnpike. I drove out from Boston with Boxcar who'd caught a flight over from London after humping jets from Oslo. Pinkie came up from South Beach, Miami, where he'd somehow managed to score an incredibly cushy assignment. Every time we got together, we had to listen to Pinkie regale us with tales of hot-blooded and tan-skinned babes who had shown him new sexual feats down in the sand of South Beach.

Gopher just showed up. No one knew where he came in from. Whenever we had to get together, Gopher would just appear. Almost as if the guy materialized out of thin air. Rumor was he worked on special assignments for the Fixer Academy. That explained a lot if you considered Gopher's inherent ability to find things all over the world.

Not that it mattered much. What mattered was that we were together and we were going to do a job. We'd do it, get it done, and then go back to our separate lives.

The McDonald's was crowded and noisy. Thousands of drivers and passengers surged through, using the bathrooms and ordering food. The environment was perfect for discussing the upcoming job. I cued them in on the target, the mission (to rescue Marilyn), and the potential for trouble.

Boxcar sat there absorbing everything. "This Syndicate, all they're into is organized crime?"

"Apparently not," I said. "They're taking hostages now and trying to force me into betraying the Council."

"Must be a big move they're planning," said Pinkie. "Wouldn't make sense otherwise."

"You said they know that you're STA-F?" asked Gopher.

"Yeah."

"That said, won't they be expecting us?"

"I doubt it. As far as they know, I'm up in Boston

waiting to turn my head and not notice them shipping drugs out of the ports up there."

Boxcar sighed. "It's dangerous this thing."

I nodded. "Yeah. It is. We could be walking into an ambush. I don't know how to try to convince you guys otherwise."

"Can't convince us if it ain't there to begin with," said Gopher. "Don't matter much anyhow. We'll do what we're gonna do, regardless of whether it's an ambush or not. This Syndicate can't go around just hoiking hostages and demanding people obey them. No way, no how."

Boxcar looked at Gopher. "'Hoiking'?"

Gopher shrugged. "I heard it somewhere. I forget where."

"Right."

Pinkie finished off his french fries. "What's the window for the op?"

"I'd like this done in under two days, if possible. Any longer than that and there's a chance they might know we're coming."

"Why so?"

"They might start looking for me in Boston. If I'm not there . . ."

They all nodded. I kept going. "We hit the ground tonight. Do an insertion and make sure the hostage is still where I said she was. If she is, we hit them tomorrow night, make the rescue, and kill anyone who gets in the way."

Pinkie used his teeth to open a fresh packet of ketchup. "What kinds of demos we need?"

"Steel door at the top of the stairs leading into the building might be locked."

Boxcar frowned. "Might be?"

"It's not usually."

"Who keeps a door unlocked in New York City?" asked Gopher.

"There's some sort of magical darkness cloud inside. Damned thing apparently disorients intruders who fall and break their necks upon entering the building."

Pinkie's eyes shot off his head. "Magic?"

Boxcar sighed. "Oh, great."

Gopher shook his head. "What do they do with the intruders that fall and die?"

I frowned. "I don't know."

"Lay you ten to one odds that they bleed 'em dry for a fresh drink."

He had a point. "Guess that's another law we can add to the others they're breaking, huh?"

"I guess so."

Pinkie sucked on his soda. "I do not like dealing with magic. It's bad news. Very, very bad."

"Come on, Pinkie," said Boxcar. "We've dealt with it before. Just get a handle on yourself and you'll be fine."

Pinkie shook his head. "I ever tell you guys about the time my grandmother cursed this guy and did some real bad voodoo on him?"

"You've told us about ten times since the team came together," said Gopher. "We all know how it ends, so do us a favor and can it, okay?"

I redirected the team. "Gopher's got the easy job this time out. No need to scrounge weapons. Boxcar and I hit the armory before we left Boston and got everything we could possibly need. We've just got to stay to the speed limit going down because I don't want some state cop yanking us over and discovering the veritable arsenal in the back of my Mercedes."

Gopher knew what his job was. "You want me inside checking the place out?"

I nodded. "We'll be backing you off scene. On comms. Boxcar's got a secure radio network in place, so we'll hear everything that you tell us. But it's up to you to get in there and make sure the hostage is still in place."

"You got a map?"

"I'll draw you one, yeah."

"How you want me to play it?"

"Black BDUs are out. They catch you in that and the gig will be up before we get started. Go in civvies. Look like the intruder they're trying to keep out. Just get lucky."

He nodded. I knew he'd have no problems. Gopher had been in some of the tightest, nastiest situations I'd ever heard about. And somehow, he always managed to get out of them with very few problems.

It didn't make sense for me to do the sneak-and-peek in case the Syndicate got wind about it. I was supposed to be in Boston. Gopher could do that job ten times better than I could, even though I'd been there twice before.

Boxcar leaned back and pushed the remnants of his Big Mac away. "Can we stop at a real restaurant the next time?"

Pinkie tore into what was left on Boxcar's tray. "Hey, this is good stuff."

Boxcar looked at him. "What if I told you I had the flu last week?"

Pinkie grinned. "Doesn't matter. We don't get sick."

Boxcar frowned but shoved the rest of his uneaten food Pinkie's way. Gopher was still wearing a frown.

"What's the matter?"

Gopher shook his head. "Just trying to figure it. This Syndicate sounds either wicked stupid or wicked smart."

"I'd rather go up against the wicked stupid," said Boxcar.

"Wouldn't we all," said Pinkie. "But what if Gopher's right and they're smart about this whole setup."

"We'll just have to adapt and overcome."

Boxcar leaned forward. "One thing you haven't mentioned yet, Lawson."

"What's that?"

"Who's the hostage?"

I'd kept Marilyn out of it for as long as possible. I didn't want the team getting the feeling that this was a personal vendetta I was waging.

But the time to tell them had arrived. "My cousin. She was living in New York when she got snatched."

"Cripes, this is a family thing?" said Gopher.

Boxcar stopped him. "I didn't know you had any family left, Lawson."

"Yeah, well, I don't talk about it all that much. I don't have a lot. My dad died young, my mother a few years later under some very weird circumstances. No brothers or sisters to speak of. Just a few aunts and uncles. My uncle has a daughter and now the Syndicate has her."

"Lemme guess," said Pinkie. "He called you up."

"Yeah."

"And you agreed to look into it."

"What choice did I have?"

"None," said Boxcar. "And any of us would have done the exact same thing. The point is not that she's your cousin. The point is that we've got to stop the Syndicate before whatever they're planning gets way out of control."

I appreciated the comment. "Thanks, big guy."

Pinkie finished Boxcar's food and took a long drink of his soda. "Where are we staging down in New York?"

"I don't have any place in mind," I said. "As far as we know, the Fixer down there isn't a Fixer at all and the guy he might have replaced might just be a traitor."

"We can't stage out of your Mercedes, Lawson," said Boxcar. "Gopher—"

"—I'm on it. I got a few friends I can call who won't mind letting us use their pads for a few days."

Boxcar nodded. "Pinkie, you can get the dems done up fast? We need to be ready to go within a few hours of arrival."

"Sure. No sweat." He looked at me. "What about interior doors, Lawson? They got any of those to worry about?"

"The chamber they're holding my cousin in looked like it might have been made out of glass or even Plexiglas."

Pinkie nodded. "Okay, we can handle that. Gopher?"

"Yeah?"

"I'm going to need a few things."

"Give me a list and I'll get 'em."

Boxcar checked his watch. "All right. Gopher, better go make your phone calls. We don't want to be rolling into the city without a place to crash at."

"We'll do the insertion tonight," I said. "We'll get eyes on the target and slip Gopher into position. The rest of us can pull back and maintain a loose outer perimeter in case the shit hits the fan unexpectedly."

Gopher sniffed. "As if."

"You never know."

He grinned. "True enough."

I looked at them all. "Thanks guys. I appreciate this. I know it's not necessarily what we normally do."

Boxcar chuckled. "Hell, we're Fixers. Nothing we do is ever normal."

Twenty-five

We hit New York around six that evening. Gopher led us into the city using a route I'd never known existed before. Eventually, after skirting alleys and one-way streets, we emerged into the Upper East Side. Ironically, the pad Gopher found was barely a spit from Teresa's apartment building.

Boxcar whistled when he stepped out of the car. "A converted loft?"

Pinkie murmured his approval. I looked at Gopher. "Doorman?"

He shook his head. "Nah. Sophisticated alarm system."

"How sophisticated?"

"Well," he grinned, "not enough to stop us since we've got the code, but it ought to stop anyone else from bothering us." He punched a few numbers into an alarm box at the front door and then opened it. An old-style elevator grumbled its way up three floors. When the door slid back, the view was superb.

The loft had vaulted ceilings and lots of room. Long sofas adorned the entranceway. Huge windows looked out over the neighborhood. Pinkie dropped his gear bag and folded his arms. "Who the hell owns this place, man?"

Gopher frowned. "What's the difference? Guy's outta

town, we're not. Here we be. What more do you need to know? The place'll serve our purposes perfectly."

"We won't be here that long," I said.

"Unless, of course, our little research gathering expedition hits a snag tonight," said Pinkie.

He said what we were all feeling. The chances the Syndicate had moved Marilyn were high. But I had nothing else to go on. There were no other leads. Aside from what D'Angelo might have to say. But I had to try and get to Marilyn first. And this was the best way I knew how.

Gopher went out for about an hour. While he was gone, Boxcar and I hauled the weapons up to the loft and set about breaking them down, checking them over, and putting them back together.

"Wish we could zero 'em," said Boxcar. "I hate the idea of not test-firing a piece before I use it."

"Makes two of us," I said. "But we can't risk it. On the plus side, the place we're hitting is pretty in-close anyway. Shouldn't affect the accuracy much at all."

Gopher reappeared laden down with duffel bags full of stuff. Pinkie opened one of them and got a huge grin on his face. "Looks like Christmas came early this year."

Gopher pointed. "You know how much that stuff cost me?"

"I would have brought it with me if I could have," said Pinkie. "But since security's been stepped up and that lame fool tried to blow up his shoe, I can't get anything past the checkpoints."

"We're on the Council's tab anyway," I said. "This has been cleared as far up as it goes." They didn't need to know Niles was the "top" right now.

Boxcar nodded. Pinkie got started making his

charges. He was busy molding the plastic explosive to bits of Styrofoam and wood. Somehow, he knew what he was doing. The rest of us would just have to trust that his explosives would do what they needed to.

Gopher went up onto the roof. I glanced at Boxcar. "Where's he going?"

"Don't you remember? Gopher always meditates before he goes into a hairy situation. Since he's the guy we use for recon, he's out there on the tip of the spear. So he gets into himself as his way of calming down and focusing on the task at hand."

"Always so interesting to see a street-tough guy like that deep into the meditative side of things."

Pinkie snorted. "He ain't meditating on peace. He's thinking about ways to kill the enemy better, I expect."

"Long as it calms him down," said Boxcar. "He can meditate on salt water taffy for all I care."

I slid the receiver back into the MP5 I was assembling. "What time do you want to go forward to the target?"

"You're the experienced one on this," said Boxcar. "You make the call."

I thought about how active the building was likely to be at night and figured the later we went, the better.

"What about midnight?"

Boxcar shrugged. "Poetic. Seems fine to me."

Pinkie looked up from molding the plastic explosive. "Someone better tell Gopher we aren't going for a while yet. He might want to take a nap before we head out."

"And a hit of juice," said Boxcar. "I'll tell him."

I watched him go to the roof and leaned back. The

team was a meritocracy. Everyone was welcome to contribute to the mission plan. No one held rank over anyone else here. We were all experienced Fixers and we'd all gotten a lot of experience working on STA-F. Ideas bounced off of walls during the planning phase and nothing was ever dismissed as downright silly. That's just how it went.

Boxcar came back down with Gopher and we sat on the floor amid a pile of weapons and explosives. Boxcar got out a big sheet of paper and handed me a pen.

"Wanna draw it out for us, best you can remember?"

I started drawing from memory, rattling off facts as I went. We covered the entryway. I pointed out the location of the handrails, the number of ladder rungs to reach the lower level below the magic cloud, the path to Cho's office and what sort of resistance we were likely to encounter.

"What about the area around the building?" asked Pinkie.

"Fish market area," I said. "Place stinks to high heaven. A lot of old corrugated steel buildings and warehouses. At night, it's not active until the place comes alive at around three in the morning."

"A three-hour window," said Boxcar. "If Gopher waves us on in, we'll want to hit it hard and fast, then get the hell out." He looked at me. "How long do you think it'll take us from the word go?"

"If we stack outside the main entrance, we can hit and clear within three minutes, I'd expect. The biggest initial threat is that magic cloud. Once we're through that, we're all set. Make the grab and then scram."

"We'll have to deal with that cloud of darkness on the way out, yeah?" asked Gopher.

"Yeah, but for some reason, it's not as bad going out as it is coming in."

"Noted."

Pinkie held up some angular pieces of Styrofoam. "Charges are set. This one's good for taking Plexiglas off at the molding. It'll blow and cause the glass to come off the shelf it sits on in the frame."

"It won't implode into the room and take out my cousin will it?"

Pinkie grinned. "Hey, trust me, would you?"

Boxcar looked at Gopher. "How long you figure it'll take you to make your approach and work your way inside?"

Gopher eyed the map. "If no one's looking I can be inside in under a minute. Once I clear the first hurdle, I'll be moving quickly. You listen on the comm gear and when I signal you, come running."

"You're the only one who'll be in civvies," I said. "We'll have to watch that when we link up."

"Yeah, fer cryin' out loud don't fucking shoot me," said Gopher. He was serious but he said it with a grin.

"That's it then," said Boxcar. "Midnight." He glanced at his watch. "Time hack in fifteen seconds."

We all checked our watches.

Boxcar rattled it off. "That's seven-thirty in five . . . four . . . three . . . two . . . one. Hack."

We all got our watches synchronized and that was it. The rest of it would unfold when it needed to. There wasn't much point in getting worked up about all the what-ifs that went along with a mission. If something came up, we'd handle it. We'd trained for what was coming. We knew each other's strengths and weaknesses. We could operate as one.

It was, after all, just another job. And while it might

have been something more for me since my cousin was involved, it was still a job I'd been trained for. And I'd do it the best I knew how. It was that simple.

Boxcar stood. "Let's get the weapons ready to go. Pinkie, can you rustle up some food for us? I say we eat and then get our heads down for a quick nap. It could be a long night."

I nodded. "Here's to quick endings."

At eleven-fifteen, we moved out.

Boxcar and I drove in my Mercedes. Gopher rode with Pinkie who would drop him out of his minivan two blocks from the building and then cruise around to another prearranged point on the perimeter.

Boxcar and I took up a position a block closer to the South Street Seaport.

Gopher's walkie-talkie, a miniature earpiece that was also a microphone, came alive in the confines of my car.

"That's Alpha going foxtrot."

I clicked the radio key switch. "Bravo and Charlie roger that."

Pinkie's voice sounded. "Delta has that."

Gopher would give us a running commentary as he approached the building. The way he was talking, he sounded slightly drunk, but we knew it was part of his act.

"One hundred meters out. No one home by the look of it. Moving closer."

Boxcar looked at me. "What's he carrying?"

"He took the MP5K. It's small enough to fit under his jacket on the swivel rig. It doesn't have a suppressor though so if he gets in the shit, we're going to have to bail his ass pretty fast. Those shots will bring everyone running."

"Spectacular."

"Fifty meters," said Gopher.

Pinkie's voice sounded. "Alpha, Delta. Hold position. You've got a blue boy rolling into your vicinity."

We knew Gopher would disappear into the shadows. He'd have to do it convincingly in case there was any type of lookout on the Syndicate building.

"Alpha has the blue. He's still rolling. Past the building now. Looks clear. I'm continuing on."

We affirmed his statement and then kept waiting. The hard part was coming up.

"At the stairs." Gopher's voice was quieter now. "Moving up."

In my mind, I knew he'd have the MP5K out. This was the biggest obstacle right now. He had to get inside quickly without alerting anyone to his presence. Once inside, he could give us commentary on who was there and if he needed backup.

Boxcar sighed. "I hate the waiting."

"Me, too."

Pinkie must have been sweating it, too. We all did when we couldn't be right on the target with the point man. But Gopher's skill at getting into places like this was legendary. If anyone could handle it, he could.

"At the door." We could barely hear him.

"Door is open."

"Watch the cloud, Alpha," I said into the microphone.

"Roger that."

There was a pause. "Cripes, can't see a damned thing."

"Remember the route," I said.

"Proceeding."

Boxcar cracked the window and cool air rushed in over us. Sitting there in our black uniforms we looked ridiculous. We had balaclavas to go on over our faces but they were curled around our necks right now, ready to pull on with a second's notice.

Not that they were really necessary, but they helped achieve a shock effect that was useful when it came to controlling the inside of a room or building in as little time as possible. We needed shock value. We needed noise and confusion over our enemies in order to win the day. If we didn't, we died.

We each wore battle vests as well. I had a shock trauma plate in mine that covered my heart and was supposedly good at stopping bullets. Especially wooden-tipped bullets that could kill vampires.

We had extra magazines of ammunition in the vests as well as a trauma kit in case of injury. If we took a serious shot, there wouldn't be much we could do. But if we were grazed, we could reverse the injury if we got to it fast enough.

My sidearm was my trusty SIG Sauer pistol that went everywhere with me on my regular Fixer operations. I'd had it for years and I never got tired of it. Boxcar was using a Heckler & Koch USP that had been modified—like all our weaponry—to fire Fixer bullets.

He nudged me now.

"Yeah?"

"Want some?"

I looked down and saw the flask. Juice. We'd had some earlier with dinner, but there was always room for a little bit more. Especially since we were about to get into some potentially nasty stuff.

"Yeah. Thanks."

I took a hit and then handed him back the flask. He drank long and deep. He wiped his mouth on the back of his leather glove and smiled. "Wish Pinkie was with us so he could have some, too."

"Probably got his own, anyway."

"Yeah."

"Gopher ought to be clear of that cloud by now." I keyed the microphone. "Alpha, this is Bravo, status check, over."

Silence.

I tried again.

Nothing.

I heard Pinkie try.

Nothing again.

Boxcar looked at me. "What do you think?"

I tried the microphone one more time. We got no response. I chewed my lip. "I think Gopher might be in trouble."

Boxcar nodded. "Better let Pinkie know."

"Delta, Bravo."

"Delta."

"We've lost Alpha."

"Copy that."

"We're rolling. Meet us at the target."

"Roger."

I glanced at Boxcar. "Does going in ever get easier?'

Boxcar's face looked grim. His hands curled around the stock of his MP5SD. "I've never found it to, no."

I gunned the engine, slipped the Mercedes into drive and shot out of the space. "Well, here's to raising a little hell before we die."

Twenty-six

We hit it hard.

And as fast as possible.

I didn't care if someone saw the Mercedes. I jerked the car to a screeching halt and immediately, Boxcar was out, covering my exit.

Pinkie hurtled around the corner fast and skidded by the Mercedes. He came out with a couple of small objects I knew would be shaped charges for taking in doors.

Boxcar nodded and I moved up the stairs. Behind me, I knew the muzzle of Boxcar's MP5SD would be aimed just over my right shoulder. Behind him, Pinkie had another MP5K that he could shoot with one hand like a pistol if he needed to take out anyone behind us.

The door at the top of the stairs was unlocked.

Boxcar held the door handle and eyed me. I looked at Pinkie who nodded. Boxcar yanked the door open and we went in.

Then the door shut and we were inside. In total darkness.

We paused.

Listened.

We couldn't see anything.

Vampires have naturally good vision at night, but the black cloud obscured everything.

I knew from how we'd entered that Pinkie was be-hind me. I turned to him and taking one of his hands, I signaled how we would proceed. Then he turned and did the same to Boxcar. When he squeezed my right shoulder, I knew we were all ready to go.

I felt forward for the ladder railing. *Found it.* I let my MP5SD swing back on the rig I wore so I could use both hands. Just as I'd done the other day, I grabbed for the rungs and then found my way to the edge. Be-hind me, Pinkie and Boxcar made no noise as they progressed the way I had.

That was the great thing about working with pro-fessionals. They knew their jobs and they did them the very best they knew how.

I swung out over the steep drop.

Paused.

Listened.

Nothing.

I let my hands and feet carry me down the ladder. The darkness started to dissipate. I knew this would be the most vulnerable we'd be during the operation.

On the ladder, we were exposed.

And we had no way of knowing who was waiting for us down below or farther inside. Gopher was supposed to have figured out that part of the equation.

But something had gone wrong.

Now we were going to have to put everything on the line.

I could see Pinkie's boots above my head. He was coming down the ladder fast. I didn't blame him—the less time exposed, the better.

I dropped the last few feet and landed quietly. I swung my MP5SD up into my shoulder, covering the likely attack points while Pinkie came down. Boxcar swooped in a few seconds behind him.

Pinkie huddled a meter away, hugging wall. He had the hardest job right now of having to protect the delicate framework his shaped charges used, while still having to maintain the same level of silence and cover that Boxcar and I were using.

Boxcar covered our rear. Since I'd been here before, the natural assumption that I'd take point came into play.

I let the suppressed muzzle of the MP5 drop just off the imaginary horizon in front of me—into the low-ready stance—and crept forward. Pinkie came off the wall, one hand clutching the demolitions, and one keeping his stubby machine pistol at the ready. Boxcar melted into our wake, watching out for anyone trying to surprise us from behind.

We ducked through the portals, our rubber-soled boots making very little noise on the skeletal steel framework. The red light bulbs cast their same sinister crimson glow about the entire plant. Far off, pings and clinks sounded in the night.

But nothing else did.

It was a little surreal creeping through the building.

Fact is, any time you do an insertion, you always get the feeling that someone's watching you. Like they're just waiting to drop the big axe and kill you in one fell blow.

We took another doorway the same as the others, stacking first and then clearing it. Still, we found no resistance.

We didn't find Gopher, either.

Instead, he found us.

His hand snaked out of a shadowy recess in the wall

and tapped me on the shoulder as I crept by. I nearly shit myself and shot him at the same time. But I saw the hand signal and sucked wind instead. When you're operating as we were, you get high strung very easily. A hand poking you from out of nowhere isn't the best prescription for relaxation.

I cupped my hand over his ear. "What the hell happened to you?"

He pointed at his radio. "I couldn't hear you guys either. I figured I had a malfunction. Better to just keep on checking the place out."

"We thought you got nailed or something."

He shook his head. "Haven't seen anything that could nail me in here. What I've seen, the place is a ghost town."

I thought about the cloud. Could it have done something to our transmissions? Could it have somehow affected things? There wasn't much time to think about whether it did or not. We had work to do.

I motioned for Gopher to take his place in line. We switched the order. Boxcar went behind me, then Pinkie and then Gopher. I took point again and we resumed our stalk.

We reached the entryway to Cho's office.

I wanted to hit the office if possible, so we stacked again. This time Boxcar would be the number one man. Like I said before, his sheer presence can have a profound impact on an enemy. And I wanted as much impact as possible with Cho.

I was playing in part on Cho's likely insecurity about his height. Boxcar's sheer magnitude might overwhelm the little bastard.

I sure hoped it would.

Pinkie readied some of his charges. There wasn't

much to do with them aside from slapping them into place and initiating the explosion. But he got them sorted out anyway. Just in case.

Gopher covered our six.

Boxcar, me, and Pinkie stacked. Pinkie squeezed my shoulder to let me know he was ready. I squeezed Boxcar's shoulder to signal the same. I could see Boxcar's head nod.

One.

Two.

Three—

We rushed the room.

Boxcar cut left immediately while I went right. Pinkie would come in behind us.

My vision was trying to tunnel itself now. It was the natural reaction to the extreme stress of taking down a room. Your thoughts and senses become so concentrated on the narrow field of vision ahead of you that you naturally close down to just that area. The problem lies in the fact that doing so means you miss a helluva lot of other potential threats.

"Clear!" I had no targets to engage.

I heard Boxcar say the same thing.

The room was empty.

Boxcar let his balaclava come off his face. His skin shone with sweat in the red light. "I don't like this. The place is deserted."

I didn't like it, either, and told them so. Gopher nosed his way into the room and then set up shop, keeping watch over the corridor from the safety of the portalway.

Pinkie looked around. "Where's the cell?"

I motioned toward the curtain. "Should be a button

over there that releases the curtain so you can see the Plexiglas."

Pinkie rooted around. "Nothing here, Lawson."

"What? There has to be. I saw her the other day myself."

I walked over and looked. Pinkie was right. Whatever switch I'd seen one of Cho's dimwit bullet catchers hit the other day, it was gone.

How would we get to Marilyn's cage?

"This doesn't make sense."

Boxcar frowned. "Are you saying we don't have a cage here?"

I shook my head. "I don't know. It was here. I saw it. It was right behind the curtain. I saw Marilyn there. She was right there."

"You sure it was her?"

"Of course, I'm sure. I know what my cousin looks like."

Pinkie poked the wall. "This thing seems pretty damned solid. Even if we wanted to blow it, I don't know if I have the necessary stuff to take it down. I came expecting Plexiglas. Ain't no Plexiglas here."

"This is not making me feel all warm and fuzzy," said Boxcar. He looked at me. "What do you want to do, Lawson? We can't stand here all night waiting for someone to come back here."

I looked at the wall. I'd seen her. I knew I had. But there was nothing there now. Nothing at all. She was gone. The cage, the room, the Plexiglas—all of it— gone.

I glanced at Gopher. "Any other rooms in here besides this one?"

"Checked 'em all. Empty as this one."

Shit.

"Let's clear," I said.

Boxcar nodded. "We'll find her, Lawson. Don't you worry about it."

Yeah. Easier said than done. We reversed order and headed back toward the ladder. This time Gopher took point. I brought up the rear. It wasn't a good position for me, because the temptation was incredibly strong to go back and try to figure out what the hell had gone wrong.

But there was nothing I could do about it now.

Marilyn was apparently gone.

And I had a bad feeling Cho had played me for a big time fool.

I just hoped it didn't cost Marilyn her life.

Twenty-seven

I left Boxcar, Gopher, and Pinkie down in New York and drove back to Boston. I called Niles en route and told him how things had gone.

"What we need to do," said Niles, "is find D'Angelo and see if he can make sense out of this situation. You need to be in Canada."

"I'm coming home to get a few things and then I'm headed straight there."

"What about the rest of your team? Can I send them home yet or what?"

"Not just yet. I need them in New York."

"I can't keep their activation a secret from the Council for too long, Lawson."

"I know it. But I gave them a few things to run down and I think they'll probably set up surveillance on the Syndicate's building, trying to track them down and see if they hole up anywhere else."

"You think they do?"

"They have to," I said. "It's the only thing that makes sense. I know I saw my cousin there and then she was gone. If she isn't in that building, she's got to be somewhere else."

"How do you account for being able to see her then?"

"Video, hologram, hell I don't know. I saw her but

so what? She wasn't there when we came calling so they've got her stashed elsewhere."

"Makes your life a lot harder, pal."

"Funny thing about that, I can't remember my life ever being easy."

"If I didn't know you, I'd say you were just being melodramatic."

"Yeah, like I don't have enough drama in my life that I have to go out and cook up something like this."

Niles paused. "Let me know how it goes in the Great White North. Good luck."

"Yeah," I said to the empty phone. I hung up and kept driving.

Miles later, I still wasn't feeling at ease.

The town of Harriet in British Columbia is as small as they come. Sequestered on the side of a big mountain with lots of caves and large old homes, it's the sort of picturesque village that most people who visit Canada have in mind, but never actually see.

In this case, it was better that way. Harriet was home to the Invoker School. The location was new for the school. They'd moved it over to the Canadian Rockies a few years back, from its old location in the snowy Himalayas.

But the Canadian Rockies had plenty of snow as well. The Council had moved the school, I later found out, because the prevailing opinion was that the Himalayas were just a speck too volatile. Having a million Chinese troops squatting a few miles away just looking for the slightest excuse to swoop in and crush the last vestiges of some incredibly archaic and powerful religions made the Council worry about its Invokers.

So the school moved.

Canada was, after all, a helluva lot more stable than most of the rest of the world was.

They chose Harriet for several reasons. First off, vampires had controlled the town for over a hundred years. It was located on a mountain and the school could be built inside its caverns and catacombs without attracting too much attention.

The premise was much the same for the Fixer Academy I'd gone to in the Northeast Kingdom of Vermont. Located by a vampire town, the community surrounding the school could act as a level of security for the institution. It worked with the Fixer Academy, so the Council reasoned it would work again with the Invoker School.

So far it had.

I used the Council's Gulfstream to head up North. We flew out of Hanscom Field in Bedford, Massachusetts. Hanscom Field is a lot easier to drive to than Logan International Airport in East Boston. Hanscom Field sits next door to Hanscom Air Force Base. I always enjoyed watching military planes come and go. A C-130 dropped in as we taxied out onto the runway.

Hanscom Field was being used as an alternative to Logan nowadays, especially by the smaller commuter airlines. The Council had kept their Gulfstream at Hanscom for a few years now. They had one at Logan, too, just in case.

I flew alone on the flight, except for the crew. I frowned and saw the Council still had not implemented my suggestion of hiring beautiful flight attendants with short skirts.

Idiots.

The pilot and copilot were Loyalists.

I was still getting used to the idea of any human knowing about our existence. When I'd found out a year or so back about Loyalists, I'd been told there were only maybe a dozen in total. I'd since realized that number was probably closer to several hundred.

That was an awful lot of potential leakage dripping around.

I had nothing against humans. But my sole purpose for existing was to protect the Balance—that line between humans and vampires that had to be guarded at all costs. Knowing that there were humans fully aware of the existence of vampires could mean one of two things for me: that humans would eventually embrace us, thus putting me out of a job; or that they'd hunt us down, meaning my job would get a lot busier.

We touched down in British Columbia some five hours later at a small mom-and-pop airfield. I grabbed a rental car at the end of the small terminal and headed west out of the airport. Up here, the air felt even cooler. I was sure there'd be frost on the leaves and branches tomorrow morning when I woke up.

The highway didn't have much traffic on it. Trees lined part of the roadway, stretching their withered limbs out over the lanes. I cracked the window and smelled the moldy scent of bark after a cold rain. It hadn't snowed up here yet so far this year, but it probably would soon.

Reaching Harriet took me another hour after I left the airport. Off the highway, it was a thirty-minute drive through some pretty rough country. I was glad I'd shelled out the extra hundred Canadian dollars for the four-wheel drive SUV. I engaged the traction and felt the wheels grip the gravely roads a bit better.

I passed a farmhouse on the right side of the road and slowed down.

It wasn't really just a farmhouse.

I pulled ten feet into the drive and then got out of my car, and waited.

They emerged five seconds later.

And I never saw them until they surrounded me.

Exotic camouflage covered each from head to foot. Grease paint streaked their faces. They held some pretty ominous looking rifles.

There were four in total. A squad. The one I took to be their leader approached.

I smiled, held up my left hand and said, "*Khal ju arang.*"

The three others had weapons trained on me. The leader didn't smile. He didn't take a hand off of his weapon. He didn't have to. They weren't paid to be polite.

"*Yessham.*"

That was all he was required to say. Instantly the four of them eased back and away from me. Their eyes and muzzles never left me until they once again vanished into the landscape.

I got back into my car and backed out of the driveway, turned back onto the main drag and kept driving.

I took a breath and exhaled slowly. As many times as I'd run into them, those guys still freaked me out.

The farmhouse was a security checkpoint.

And it was manned by some of the fiercest vampires I'd ever heard of or seen. They were called Specters. Think of them as a subset of Fixers in some bastardized way and it wouldn't be paying them enough respect.

Specters were the security force used by the Council to protect certain vampire enclaves from encroachment. Whereas Fixers are trained in all manner of military and covert techniques for operating in the stream of everyday life, Specters were trained to be an outright military force capable of doling out a lot of pain and suffering if the occasion called for it.

The four guarding the farmhouse were part of a slightly larger force that would be in the town itself. If I hadn't stopped at the farmhouse to check in, I would have been met farther down the road with a rocket in my engine block.

Specters didn't take any chances. They didn't talk unless they absolutely had to. And they didn't give a rat's ass what the locals—or anyone else—thought of them.

They called them Specters because of their ability to blend in so absolutely with their surrounding landscape. They seemed almost invisible. They spent hours laying out in the fields, the rain, the snow, and the muck. They didn't much care if they were uncomfortable or not. They were doing what they were paid to do.

If I thought my life was a harsh one, those guys had it even rougher.

And the female Specters were even more dangerous than the males.

Since I'd checked in at the farmhouse, I'd be all set driving into the town itself. The Specters at the farmhouse didn't know who I was. They didn't even care. But I'd given the appropriate recognition code so I was cleared to proceed.

I saw a few more houses now as I drove on. Most of them looked like they did double-duty as farms. I made out horses and some cattle. Harriet was like a lot of other far-out vampire towns in that they relied as little on the outside world as possible. The less questions asked about them, the better.

The closest place they'd go hunting was a village some fifteen miles away, or a bigger town forty miles away from Harriet. It was an awful long way to go for a drink of juice, but that's how they lived up here.

Then I thought about it. Maybe they didn't have to do that at all. Since the village shielded the existence of the Invoker School, the Council probably kept them supplied with their blood requirements. That way, there'd be no chance of attracting unnecessary attention.

That made better sense.

More houses crowded the streets. I saw my first glimpse of Harriet's residents. Most of them looked like you'd expect: rustic, a lot of flannel, hiking boots, jackets. It was, after all, a rural farming town.

They gave the truck a good look over. I guessed they didn't get much in the way of visitors up here unless you counted the new classes of Invokers that came here to attend the school.

I drove another mile into the town center and then parked outside the building with the word "Sheriff" written above the door.

The man sitting behind the desk was no more of a sheriff than I was. I smiled as I walked in. "*Fyar Chuldoc Erim.*"

He got up. "*Malang dol hachvem.*"

I held out my hand. "Lawson."

"Kjeld." He grinned. "I heard we might have a visitor stopping by."

"You heard?"

He nodded. "Your Control called to let me know. Said to extend you all the courtesies we could."

"That's some group you got out at the farmhouse."

"Yep. Sure is. Ornery sonsabitches, too." He slumped back into his seat. "Well, we don't have to like 'em, do we? Just so long as they do their job."

Kjeld was the Fixer for the town. The Council didn't trust Specters to the extent that they'd let them run the town, so Fixers looking for a somewhat easier assignment opted for a stint handling towns like Harriet. The best part was that they functioned as their own Controls, too. For some of these guys, it was like a long-overdue vacation.

"What happened to Russell?"

"Got transferred to Warsaw. I just got here a few months back."

"Where'd you work before this?"

Kjeld let his boots climb onto the top of his desk. "Lessee, I had a spell of action in Johannesburg, then got transferred to Bosnia."

"Yow."

He nodded. "This place is like heaven next to those."

"I'd guess."

"You're here to see a student at the school, yeah?"

"Yeah."

"Anyone I might know?"

I shrugged. "You know all the students?"

"Oh sure, I go over each year and give a lecture on safety in the surrounding areas. The kids all know me. I'm the big uncle kinda guy, always looking out for them."

"His name's Jack Watterson."

Kjeld nodded. "Oh sure, I know Jack. Good kid, that one." His eyes narrowed. "He hasn't done anything wrong has he? I'd hate to hear a kid like that went wrong."

"Not at all. I need his help."

Kjeld's eyebrows jumped. "You . . . need . . . his . . . help?"

I saw the mixture of amusement and confusion. "We worked together a year or so ago on something very delicate. His assistance came in handy back then. I thought I'd bounce my current problem off him and see if he might help me with it."

"That's an awful lot of faith to be placing in a kid who's only fourteen years old."

"Yep. Sure is."

"Well." He took his feet off the desk and slid into a jacket. "You'll be wanting to see him as soon as you can, I expect."

"Time's short, yes."

"Always is."

We took his truck and wound our way through the village. "Place is a real throwback to the years gone by, isn't she?"

"Seems like we're back a hundred years or more."

He nodded. "I kinda like it this way. At least I don't have humans shooting and bombing each other to shit around me, you know?"

"Bosnia must have been hell."

"It was."

We slid down a side street and then up a long winding road that had at first appeared to be a dirt road running into the back of someone's farm.

Kjeld gestured at the trail. "Access road is a little tough to find."

I glanced out the window. No one paid any attention to Kjeld's vehicle.

The dirt road kicked up bits of mud in our wake. "You're gonna need to hose this thing down when we're through."

Kjeld shook his head. "Be raining soon enough. Then it'll snow. Weather's like that up here. Getting colder, too."

We stopped.

"Here we are."

I got out of the truck and looked.

The road had ended. In front of us stood a huge rockface. Towering above that was a huge mountain. It didn't stop. It just went on and on. If I hadn't seen the Himalayas, I would have thought this was the largest mountain I'd ever laid eyes on.

"Pretty nice, huh?"

I nodded. "Sure is."

"Come on. It's getting late."

I started after him and then stopped abruptly. Kjeld had just walked right through the rock blocking our path.

He was gone.

Twenty-eight

I discovered how soon enough.

Some sort of hologram was projected in front of the true rockface. I walked through the rock illusion and found myself in a wide opening carved out of the stone. Ahead of me, Kjeld waited by a large door that looked like it had been made out of the mountain itself.

"Got to ring the bell."

He leaned on one side of the door and two minutes later the door slowly swung open with a massive groan and a vague hydraulic hiss. Old World and New World technology living in harmony, I supposed.

A man stood in front of us. He didn't look like a Specter. Then I remembered Jack mentioning something about Invokers that acted as security inside the school itself. Specters weren't allowed inside the school grounds. In fact, not many people were, aside from the teachers and students.

"Yes?"

Kjeld spoke. "A Fixer named Lawson is here to see Jack Watterson."

The man's eyes seemed vacant. He nodded. "Wait here."

Kjeld turned back to me. "He's blind. Don't mind the eyes."

Five minutes later, I smiled a whole lot because Jack

came through the doorway with a spring in his step
and a self-assured teenage grin plastered on his mug.
He'd gotten taller lately. A big growth spurt brought
him up to my shoulders. He was older than fourteen,
but vampires live much longer than humans, so
mostly we all convert our age to human years to keep
things simpler.

"Hey, slick."

He gave me a rough hug. "Hi, Lawson. Great to see
you."

"What happened to your glasses?"

Jack frowned. "I got contacts. They look better."

"Oh yeah?"

He shrugged. "Girls don't like the glasses."

"You've got some girls in there do you?"

"Oh, yeah."

I laughed. "This is Kjeld."

Jack glanced at him. "Kell? Is that spelled like it
sounds?"

"No. It's Danish." Kjeld rattled off how to spell it.
"You don't remember me from the safety talk I gave
at the school earlier this year?"

Jack got a shy grin. "Oh . . . well, I heard that before. I was sort of goofing around with my friends."

"No harm done."

Jack looked at me. "What brings you here?"

"I need your help, pal."

"We're not going anywhere, are we?"

"Why?"

"Uh . . . I sort of have something to do this weekend."

"Yeah?"

He nodded.

I couldn't help myself. I was smiling. Jack was a

great kid. In the time since we'd met in the wake of my mistakenly killing his father, Jack had really grown into his own man. I loved spending time with him. In a way, sometimes he felt like my own son. Other times we were just friends, and that was pretty cool, too.

"We're not going anywhere."

"Okay."

"I'm looking for someone."

"A man?"

"Yeah."

"You heard about what I was taught to do?"

"Wirek mentioned it. He said you'd have no problems doing it. Said it was one of the first things they teach you here."

"It is."

Kjeld cleared his throat. "Do what, exactly?"

I nodded at Jack. "He can locate people anywhere in the world. Some aspect of his training, where he develops some type of clairvoyance or clairaudience."

"It can be both or either," said Jack. "It depends on the individual."

"So can you do it?"

He nodded. "I need to hold your hand while I do it, though. You've got the information—the memories perhaps—that will enable me to locate him."

"Can we do this inside the school?"

Jack looked back at the entranceway and then back at me. "Not really. It's against the rules for outsiders to come into the school."

It dawned on me then that each time I'd come here, I'd never actually seen the school. Jack had neatly arranged to meet me somewhere in town. He was a smooth operator, even if he didn't really know it yet.

"Okay, well you choose the location."

Jack pointed outside. "Fresh air's always helpful to the process."

We walked outside. Kjeld wandered over to his truck. Jack and I found a reasonably comfortable boulder to sit down on.

Jack breathed heavily. "I've only done this a few times, so it takes me a moment to get into where I need to be."

"Wirek said this would be a piece of cake for you."

"Was he drunk when he said it?"

We laughed. The Wirek drinking thing was our own personal joke of sorts.

When Jack had first met him, Wirek had been sauced out of his skull. Then he'd cleaned himself up and now he was as sharp as he had ever been. But we still took it out on him any chance we got.

Overhead, dark gray clouds sidled in from the Northwest. They looked bloated and misshapen. Jack noticed them and nodded. "Supposed to snow here before too long."

"Snow's good."

"Better than rain."

I looked at him. "I've missed you, pal."

"Me, too."

There was that awkward moment. I wanted to hug him again but it didn't seem right. Jack sat down next to me.

"Okay. Let's get this done."

He closed his eyes and I saw his breathing instantly go shallow and then switch into a very deep abdominal cycle. I could hear the intake of air and the slow release as it exited his nostrils.

Jack remained very still for several minutes and then I felt his hand close over mine. I heard some words in Taluk come out of his mouth, but they were whispered so quietly, I couldn't make them out. I wasn't sure I wanted to know what they meant, anyhow.

I felt a strange desire to close my own eyes. My lids felt heavy. I let them droop. My mind exploded with images that flew past my eyes in quick succession. I saw New York from the air, I saw the streets, the cars, the people. I felt a surge of strange emotions—fear, anger, happiness, lust, anxiety. I could smell the exhaust from cars; I could smell the fish guts near Fulton Street; I could sniff the peculiar smells that made a city a city.

All of it came crashing back through my mind as Jack sat next to me, seemingly manipulating my entire memory process. I wondered what he was searching for.

I felt hot. I felt sweaty. It must have been about forty degrees outside, but it felt like it was closer to eighty. My jacket and sweater felt hot and heavy, like I was suffocating under a layer of woolen death.

Jack's hand felt cool, though. It was the one point I tried to concentrate on while he worked his magic, so to speak.

I heard more words in Taluk. They sounded a bit more like a singsong pattern than the straight mantra he'd murmured a minute earlier.

I felt lighter now, and the temperature suddenly dropped back down to its actual status. A cool breeze washed over me, drying the sweat that had broken out along my hairline.

Jack's hand lifted from mine. I no longer felt tired.

I opened my eyes.

Jack opened his.

I grinned. "Wow, that was something."

But Jack's eyes weren't smiling at all. There was something in them I hadn't seen for a very long time.

Fear.

"Hey, pal, what's the matter?"

"Lawson—"

"Everything go okay?"

I turned. Kjeld had stopped fiddling with his truck and was watching us. I shrugged. "I guess so."

He nodded and looked at Jack. "Find out what you needed to know?"

I glanced back at Jack. Jack's head was nodding slowly.

Very slowly.

"Jack."

He looked at me.

"What the hell is wrong with you?"

"I found the man you're looking for. D'Angelo is his name, right?"

"Yes."

Jack gulped. "I found him."

"So, where is he? It's very important that I talk to him."

Jack's mouth was tight, like someone had dragged a piece of elastic across his teeth. "He's right behind you."

What? I whirled around.

Kjeld? He was D'Angelo?

It didn't make any sense. Unless . . .

Then I saw the gun in Kjeld's hand.

It was aimed at Jack and me.

And suddenly things made a lot more sense.

I remembered then that stupid saying that people always love to crap out at inopportune times: ignorance is bliss.

Twenty-nine

Unlike Jack's face, which showed only fear, D'Angelo's face showed only smug happiness. Cripes, I hate it when people are smug.

"Surprised, Lawson?"

"Yep."

"We knew you would be."

"Who's this 'we'?"

"Your friends back in New York. Cho said you'd come here eventually. It was the only route you could have taken."

"What happened to the real Kjeld?"

D'Angelo shrugged. "He's dead, of course. I got here a few days ago. I paid him a visit and that was that."

"You killed a fellow Fixer?"

"Yes. And I sold out as well, so what—that makes me guilty of how many wonderful crimes now?"

"Too many to count."

He smiled. "It's a pleasure to see the look on your face, Lawson. It truly is. Surprise really becomes you."

Jack cleared his throat. "But you look exactly like the real Kjeld, if I remember right."

I looked at D'Angelo. He certainly didn't look like his family had come from Italy. "Kid's got a good

point. How'd you manage to keep the locals from sus-
pecting you?"

"It's a neat trick," said D'Angelo. "Something my family passed on to me without even knowing about it."

And then he began to change. His face literally mor-
phed into a darker complexion. His hair color turned
dark. His eyebrows fleshed out and his eyes grew
darker. There was something innately sinister about
him now.

And it made my stomach lurch when I realized
what he was.

Another goddamned lycanthrope.

"You know, with few exceptions, the lycanthropes I
run into all seem to have long overdue appointments
with death."

"I read your file, Lawson. I know you killed Shiva."

"Don't forget Jarvis."

"I wasn't."

"And now that hat trick."

"You won't kill me."

"We'll see."

"I've got the gun, Lawson." He gestured with it.
"Speaking of which, why don't you remove your pistol
very slowly with the thumb and index finger of your
left hand. If I even smell an attempt to get cute with
me, I'll kill you both right here and now. Oh, and put
a leash on the kid. If it gets even two degrees warmer,
I'll shoot."

I glanced at Jack and nodded. He frowned but understood he wasn't to try anything.

"Tell me something: just how many lycanthropes
have gone through the Fixer Academy?"

"Why? Are you worried about keeping the race
pure?"

"That's not something I'm concerned about. I'm concerned that every one of you who manages to get through comes out ready to betray our society."

"Not my society."

"You're half vampire, though, aren't you?"

"No. Not me. I'm fully lycanthrope."

That didn't make sense. How had he gotten past the Council during his centennial? The Council would have known he wasn't a vampire. Wouldn't they?

He seemed to know my thoughts. "The Council isn't as omnipotent as they would have you believe, Lawson. They can be fooled just as easily as anyone else. Sometimes, even easier."

That did a lot to restore my faith in them. "So, now what?"

"Well, we can do this two ways. My orders are to stop you. Following that I am preferably required to cart your ass back to New York where your friend Cho would like a few words with both you and the kid there."

"What's option two?"

"I kill you both right here, right now. No travel time, no muss—no fuss. Just two dead bodies on the ground."

"And you'd prefer it that way."

"Hell yes. I've seen your record. I transport you and the whole thing can go to pot if you get any crazy ideas. Killing you is so much easier."

"Well then, I guess we'll opt for number one. If only to continue to annoy you."

D'Angelo frowned but there wasn't much he could do. If Cho wanted us back in New York, he was going to have to see that we got there. Or else come up with a damned good reason why we weren't.

"What's Cho want the boy for anyway?"

"I'm not a boy anymore."

I glanced at Jack. "Sorry," I said apologetically.

D'Angelo grinned. "Hasn't he clued you in on the whole shebang yet?"

"Only bits and pieces. And to be honest with you—if I can—the whole thing doesn't make a damned bit of sense to me."

"Cho's got the hottest drug on the planet right now."

"Saber. Yeah, he told us."

"He tell you it's a designer narcotic?"

"Yeah."

"And the addiction rate?"

"Yeah."

"He wants to move a horrendous amount of that stuff. His goal is to get roughly twenty percent of the human population addicted to Saber."

"Twenty percent? That's insane. He'll never make it."

"Sure he will. He just has to make sure his lines of distribution are open and fully exploitable."

"That's where I come in."

"Sure. You got promoted. You head up the northeast now and everything flows past your watchful eye."

I hadn't been promoted yet. I wasn't so sure this whole thing wasn't some bullshit story conjured up to get me to cooperate.

"So, I'm supposed to turn a blind eye to all the drugs flowing past me."

"Yeah."

"And the b— young man?"

"Cho wants him around for when it comes time to go and discuss the future with the Council."

"What future?"

"The Syndicate's future, of course. Cho is talking about dismantling vampire society altogether. He says it's no longer needed. This isolationism that has preserved you all for so long is a thing of the past. Already, Cho's got some very powerful folks in the lycanthrope society ready to sign on with him."

"Is that how you got involved?"

"I've been involved for a long time. Just not with Cho. You've heard of sleeper agents in human terms, right?"

"Sure. They get activated when they're needed but they're usually inserted long before then so as not to arouse suspicion. Spycraft 101, what about it?"

"Bingo. I was inserted into vampire society a long time ago. When the time came for me to proceed with my centennial, I contacted another one of our sleeper agents who got me past the Council successfully."

He must have seen the frown on my face. "It wasn't difficult. Not in the least. I would have expected it to be tougher."

I'd been expecting a lot of things in my life lately and so far not one of them had come along when I needed it.

"Drugs, secession, an interracial conspiracy, organized crime." I sighed. "This has all the makings of a cheap Hollywood hit."

"Sell the rights to your story, then. Don't matter a damned bit to me. It's time to leave."

"You don't really think you'll get out of this town alive, do you?"

"Sure, why not?"

"The Specters will see you coming."

"If I was concerned about those robotic idiots, I

wouldn't have taken you here right now. I would have waited."

"Specters don't intimidate you?"

"I'm sure I can be quite convincing. And they already know you're here on behalf of the Council and your Control to help out on a matter of utmost importance. I doubt they'll mind very much if you and the boy accompany me out of here."

"Who briefed them on my arrival?"

"I did, of course. Didn't you find it odd how easy it was to get by them?"

"No. I gave the right passwords. How hard was it supposed to be?"

"Not hard at all. A brief appearance and then they let you go. All bark and no bite, I think you'll find."

That was disrespecting Specters a lot more than I personally felt comfortable with. I'd seen them in action once or twice before and they always impressed the hell out of me. Not that I was going to say anything about that, however.

Instead, I shifted my weight to my right foot. "Well, this has all been so utterly fascinating. But I suppose we should get moving soon, huh?"

D'Angelo nodded. "Yeah. The sooner the better."

He turned then, just slightly. The gun barrel was still locked onto my heart. I wanted—needed—had—to do something, but the danger was still too great to try it with Jack close by.

A cool breeze blew in from the west. I shivered slightly. "Damn."

D'Angelo shivered, too.

Jack just stood there looking annoyed. "Is this going to take very long?"

D'Angelo regarded him. "Haven't you heard a

thing I've been saying, kid? We're going to New York."
He glanced at me. "Jeez, Lawson, I thought this guy
was more on the ball than this."

I shrugged. "He's got a date, D'Angelo. And you're
going to spoil that for him. How would you feel?"

"A date?" He chuckled and looked at Jack again. "Is
that right?"

Jack frowned at me. "Thanks for spilling the beans."

"Sorry. He asked."

"You didn't have to tell him, though."

"You're the one who's upset."

Jack's mouth curled downward. D'Angelo held up
his free hand. "Okay, you two, that's enough. None of
this petty bickering. We've got miles to go before we
sleep."

"Wow," I said. "A lycanthrope who quotes poetry.
And here I was just thinking you all are just a bunch
of lazy furbags who get high on the full moon."

D'Angelo's face loomed closer. "You say the words
'moon dog' and you might just get to New York with
a few more bruises than necessary."

"You damage the goods and Cho will take it out of
your ass."

"I only pay Cho lip service. My real employers are
elsewhere."

"Wonderful."

"So, now we move."

Another breeze blew in sideways kicking up dirt
and gravel. I brought my hands up to shield my eyes
from the bits of rock and dust stinging my face.

D'Angelo grunted and a larger rock caught him off
the cheek. The pistol wavered slightly.

I moved.

My left hand guided his gun hand off the line of

attack even more and I jammed the tip of my elbow into his solar plexus. He grunted loudly. I followed up with a knee strike to his groin that lifted him an inch off the ground.

He came down hard, trying to redeploy his gun on me. "You've got a problem, Lawson."

"Yeah?"

"You've only got Fixer ammunition in this piece. Great for killing you but pretty damned useless on the likes of me."

He was right. The bullets in the gun wouldn't do a lycanthrope a lick of harm. I needed silver.

And I didn't have any.

D'Angelo swung a hard kick up toward my groin. I used my right leg to guide it away and came down with a headbutt on his orbital bone. I heard a dull crack and D'Angelo grunted again. Blood started pooling in his eye.

"Goddamnit." D'Angelo was pissed now.

There must have been a storm coming because the winds were kicking up something fierce. I grappled with D'Angelo, trying to keep control of his gun hand. He kept trying to regain control of it.

More dirt flew into our faces. I spat out a mouthful of dirt and grime and caught D'Angelo square on the eyes with my sputum.

He blanched.

I knocked the gun out of his hand with a quick chop to his wrist. His fingers shot open reflexively and the gun fell to the forest floor.

He spun around and lashed out with a kick at my midsection. I drifted back and away but still tasted some of his heel in my diaphragm.

I sucked wind.

D'Angelo scrambled for the gun.

And then screamed.

A strong gust of air lifted him off the ground. I glanced over at Jack who had his eyes open. His lips didn't move at all. And the air temperature seemed cool still. In the past, any time Jack had used his gift, the air had gotten hot and humid.

A bright burst of pink energy swirled around the base of D'Angelo's feet and then worked its way north. It began zipping around him faster and faster. It covered his head and his upper torso until nothing could be seen except for the pink energy.

D'Angelo screamed again.

And then the wind died as suddenly as it had come up. D'Angelo's body dropped to the ground. From his head to his waist, the only thing that remained was bleached pale white bones. At the waist, his innards could be seen but they'd been cauterized and any bleeding was minimal.

However he looked, D'Angelo was dead.

Jack cleared his throat.

I got to my feet and walked over. "He dead?"

"Yeah."

"What about the silver thing? Lycanthropes need to be taken down with it."

"Not in this case."

"Okay. But I kinda needed to talk to him for a few minutes."

"I thought you got everything you needed."

"Not quite."

"Sorry." He grinned. "You know, it doesn't always get hot when we summon spirits. Just sometimes in the early stages of training."

"Good to know."

"I have to report this," he said. "I used my powers outside of the school. You'll need to be my witness."

"No problem."

"Good. Hurry up then. I can still make my date if we get this over with soon."

I laughed and clapped him on the shoulder. "Thanks. I owe you one."

He looked at me. "I can't believe you told him I had a date . . ."

Thirty

"I found D'Angelo."

Niles perked up. "Hot damn! What did he say?"

"Not much. He's dead."

"Dead when you found him?"

"No. He was dirty. I saw him die."

"What the hell happened out there?"

I filled him in as best as I could, adding in the points that D'Angelo and I had discussed right before his meeting with the spirit world.

Niles sighed. "People sure do have a nasty habit of dying when they're around you, Lawson. I can't tell you how happy I am to be on the other end of this phone."

"Hey, I didn't plug this guy. He had a nasty run-in with some spirits."

"The boy did it?"

"Not really a boy anymore. He's got a date this weekend."

"I'll send a congratulatory card. Can we get back to this case?"

"What's the news on your end?"

"Word from your teammates down in New York is that nothing's changed. They've been staking out that building you targeted but nothing new seems to be happening."

I frowned. I'd been hoping the guys would have

found something. "All right, I'm going to have to go back down there."

"I know. But you'd better produce something soon. I'm going to have to run this past the Council, you know?"

"You stalled as long as you could. I appreciate it."

"What else are Controls for?"

"Talk to you soon."

I hung up and looked out the window of the plane. Clouds floated past the window. I sighed. It would have been nice to stay in Canada a few days and visit with Jack. But he was safe for the moment and that was what mattered most.

Now I had to go make sure Marilyn was safe as well.

I went forward and asked the pilot to divert to New York instead of back to Boston. Rerouting the flight plan while underway would normally have been a bit chaotic. But the pilot knew someone who knew someone outside of Newark who could guarantee us a spot at a small field owned by a local outfit who preferred money to asking questions.

And that was just fine with me.

We touched down just after eight o'clock. Darkness bled across the sky, inking out everything but the nearby lights. On the horizon I could see the permanent frosted glow of the New York skyline. It looked different now. But the resolve of the city was still as heartfelt as it had ever been. Scumbag cowardly terrorists or not, New York would always be there.

In a small way, it comforted me. The skyline had always impressed me. But knowing there were some real bad sorts running around in that city made me angry. Especially since my cousin was somehow wrapped up in all of that bullshit.

Boxcar rolled onto the tarmac a few minutes later in a Chevy TrailBlazer. I got in next to him and we headed up the Turnpike toward the Holland Tunnel.

"So, what's the status?"

"Status is that building is not being used all that much right now. We tagged a couple of what we later found out were low-level punks. Whoever you met there—"

"—Cho."

"Yeah. Well, he's gone now. Vanished it seems. We certainly haven't seen any three and a half foot tall guys running around barking orders."

"Did you go back inside?"

"Yeah. Place is cleaned out. Even that freakish cloud of darkness seems to have vanished."

"They closed up shop."

"Sure seems like a classic roll-up to me." He glanced at me. "How was Canada?"

"Worse than I expected."

"We're batting a thousand here."

"We're still in the damned dugout."

He nodded. "Any ideas?"

"If we can't find them, we've got to make them pop up. Get them interested in something."

"Like what?"

I looked out at the sidewalk jungle rushing past the window—the stores, the neon, the broken glass, the cars, the traffic, the people.

"We'll use disinformation."

"What kind of disinformation?"

"Let a rumor drop that the Council wants to set up a talk with them. To discuss their future in the vampire society."

"They'll never go for it. They'll smell a trap a mile away. You or I would. So will they."

"According to the recently deceased D'Angelo, Cho wants nothing to do with vampire society anymore. He claims it's antiquated. He wants to open up our society to the lycanthropes and humans."

"That's amusing."

"He's apparently very serious."

"Serious men have undertaken more foolish gambits."

"True."

"So you think he would approach the Council if such a message was sent?"

"We wouldn't send it."

"No?"

"I'd deliver it myself."

Boxcar looked at me. "You're supposed to be in Boston handling their affairs up there. How are they going to respond to you suddenly dropping back down into their laps?"

"Oh, they'll probably be slightly pissed."

"That doesn't bother you?"

"No. I doubt they'll kill my cousin without hearing me out first."

"And then they might kill you both."

"Possibly."

"And just how do you intend to find them anyway? We've had that building under watch since you left and not much has happened. Any tags we had faded out not too far up the pole."

"There's always the guy masquerading as the Fixer for New York."

"Kohl."

"Yeah. Is he still working out of the office?"

"Gopher says he is. He's been keeping a very normal schedule. Hours are nine-to-five and then he does very little in the evening. No visitors. No departures. No meetings."

I frowned. "Why doesn't that make me feel good?"

"Because unless all of our experience has been for naught, it means something's about to happen."

"Yeah."

"And usually that means something bad."

"Yeah."

Boxcar smiled. "Shall I deliver you to Kohl's?"

"Might as well."

We drove into the tunnel and emerged into Manhattan on the other side. We passed a few whores out hawking their bodies like cheap pewter. Boxcar shook his head. "I'll never really understand humans sometimes."

"What's to understand?"

"Could you ever go and pay money for sex?"

I shrugged. "Me? No."

"Me neither. So why do they do it?"

"You want me to theorize on why humans patronize hookers?"

"Passes the time."

"Boxcar, I've never known you to be so philosophical."

"I haven't espoused any philosophy yet."

I watched the tunnel lights flash by. "I don't know. Maybe human males feel it gives them some measure of control over a situation that by and large most men have very little control over. I mean, according to all these sex studies you hear about, most women don't have orgasms frequently enough with their partners.

Hell, some guys have to ask if the woman they were with even came. I mean, that's pretty sad."

"Agreed."

"So maybe they think if they pay for it, it takes some of the pressure off. That they don't have to deliver that knockout blow—"

"Pardon the pun."

"And they can just concentrate on themselves."

"Seems that's what they do anyway."

"Maybe."

"Oh, well."

"What—you don't like my theory?"

"Was it a theory?"

"You asked me, damn it."

"Just passing the time."

I grinned. "You might not understand humans, but sometimes I understand vampires even less."

"Ain't that the truth."

We wove into midtown and found the Fixer building. Boxcar wheeled the TrailBlazer into a space and slid the truck into park. He turned to me.

"Now what?"

"Now I go and ring the bell."

"What do you want me to do?"

"Backup?"

"You think he might try something?"

"Better safe than sorry."

I slid out and heard Boxcar duck out the other side. There was a light on in the lower level of the building. I gestured to Boxcar to disappear while I made my entrance.

Somehow in the space of a hundred feet, Boxcar managed to do just that. When I glanced back, he was gone.

I climbed the steps and thought about how going to this building time and time again was getting old. I took a final glance around, eased my pistol out of the holster, and kept it pinned against my right leg.

I rang the bell.

It took Kohl a minute to come and answer the door. The look on his face was a mixture of amusement and surprise. More amusement than surprise, though, I finally decided.

He smiled. "Good evening, Lawson."

"Kohl."

"Am I mistaken or are you supposed to be about 212 miles northeast of our present location?"

"Depends on how you see things. In my mind, I'm right where I'm supposed to be."

"That is exactly the type of thing I'd expect you to say."

I brought the gun out and leveled it on his heart. "Why don't we step inside and chat for a few minutes?"

He glanced down. "You don't need that."

"No? Forgive me for thinking otherwise."

I kept the gun trained on him. Kohl moved back into the building. I followed and made sure the lock was off the front door for Boxcar to come through a moment later.

Kohl stepped inside the hallway. "So, what is it that you want?"

"Information."

"Information costs a lot."

"You might just pay with your life if you're not careful."

He smiled. "I doubt that."

"The Council wants to talk to Cho."

"Do they?" A wide smile spread across his face. "Now, that is interesting."

"Immediately, if possible."

"And what is it they want to talk to Cho about?"

"The future of the Syndicate."

"The Syndicate's future doesn't really require much from the Council."

"They don't see it that way."

"And they sent you here as their emissary, is that it?"

"You got it."

"They sent a Fixer as a messenger boy. My, my, Lawson, your role in the service must be diminishing each day."

"Will he talk to them?"

"You don't know where he is, do you?"

"He's gone to ground obviously."

Kohl smiled. "Absolutely."

"Can you relay the message to him?"

"Oh, sure I could. But I won't."

"Why not?"

"Because the Council has no intention of speaking with Cho."

"I'm telling you that was the message I was given."

Kohl shook his head. "And I'm telling you, Lawson, that you are lying. The Council has no plans for the Syndicate. We would have heard if it was otherwise."

They had someone on the Council. That must have been it. I frowned. "Let's you and I sit in the other room, there, Kohl. I've got a few things I want to ask you about."

"I don't think that's such a good idea."

"I don't give a damn what you think is a good idea. Just do it."

Kohl chewed his upper lip. "All right." He turned

and walked through the doorway into the room I'd sat with him in a few nights previously.

I followed.

And stopped.

"Hello, Lawson."

The smile on Kohl's face would have made anyone sick just looking at it. "I told you."

But it wasn't Kohl's smile that I was staring at.

It was the person seated on the couch.

Marilyn.

Thirty-one

I didn't say anything at first.

Probably because I was more shocked than anything else. Also, I wanted to see what would happen next. I knew Boxcar would be working his way inside to back me up if anything went wrong.

Marilyn kept smiling at me. But something about her smile seemed . . . strange. I glanced at Kohl.

"What did you do to her?"

His eyebrows jumped. "Me? I haven't done anything to her, Lawson. She's the same girl she always was."

"Bullshit." I walked over to the couch and sat down next to Marilyn. "Your father's worried sick about you."

"Oh? That's nice." She leaned toward me. "My God you're a handsome man. Can I kiss you, Lawson?"

I pulled away and stood. "What the hell is this?" I turned to Kohl. "Explain it to me or we're going to have some problems."

Kohl walked to the armchair and sat. "Not much to tell, really. Your cousin there seems to have developed a peculiar desire for Cho's new drug Saber."

"You got her addicted?"

"We don't get people addicted. We simply supply the drug. What they do with it is their own business."

"You sound like a tobacco company. It's the stupidest

logic I've ever heard." I glanced back at Marilyn. "How long's she been taking the drug?"

"Long enough to get her hooked I'd say."

"You doped her up while you had her in captivity?"

"Seemed the best way to keep her under control. You have to admit the principle seems sound."

"So this drug . . . Saber . . . it works on vampires, too?"

Kohl grimaced. "Well. Sort of."

"What the hell does that mean?"

Marilyn slid off the couch and rubbed my arm. "Lawson?"

I turned. "What?"

Her eyes were deep and dark. But they looked vacant. Whatever had been behind them was gone now. I just hoped it wasn't for good.

She licked her lips. "Would you like to kiss me?"

I turned back to Kohl. "Is this the 'sort-of'?"

He shrugged. "Seems that Saber produces a certain degree of, shall we say . . . sexual proclivity in vampires."

"She's damned horny is what she is."

"That's another way of putting it, yes."

I took Marilyn's hand off my arm and pushed her back on to the sofa. I looked at Kohl. "How do we bring her down?"

"Bring her down?"

"Detoxify her, you idiot. How do we get her back to normal?"

"Um . . . yeah. We're still wondering about that."

"You used her as the guinea pig."

"We needed one. Cho wanted to know what would happen to vamps if they took the drug. Remember he was after something that would affect humans and not vampires."

"But this obviously does affect our kind."

"True. But Cho felt the 'horniness' was tolerable."

"I'll bet."

"Fringe benefits, he called it."

"And why do you have Marilyn here right now? Were you getting ready to indulge in those fringe benefits?"

"Why not? Everyone else already has."

Wonderful. I sighed. "Where is the little bastard?"

"Cho? You'll never find him. He's locked away nice and safe. He's got protectors, you know."

"You know where he is."

Kohl smiled. "I know how to contact him. I don't know exactly where he is."

"You don't have any idea?"

"No. I'm clueless."

"How do I get in touch with him?"

"Why do you want to?"

"This has to be stopped."

"You know I can't let you stop him."

"You aren't in any position to stop me, Kohl. Do yourself a favor and give me the information I want. Then let me walk out of here with my cousin and we'll call it even."

"I doubt that. I know all about you Fixers. After all, I had to impersonate one of you."

"Coming clean now? It's a little too late. I was on to you a while back."

"So you say. Not that it did you much good. We were still able to get our hooks into you."

"Only because I let you think that. Now where is Cho?"

Kohl shook his head slowly. "Oh, Lawson. You are such a fool."

He lashed out then, coming out of the chair and

swinging his right leg up in a tight arc that came rushing in at my head. I stepped forward, sinking on my right knee, dropping into the inside of his arc where the kick wouldn't be as powerful.

I jabbed a right at his groin but he moved and I struck the hamstring of his right leg instead. He grunted anyway, spun away and brought both his hands up.

"I learned a lot by watching you and Cho go at it the other day."

"Did you?" I kept my hands up, but loose, relaxed, and ready.

Kohl nodded. "Yeah. I sure did." He threw a half-hearted kick at my groin and then used the kick to ride the distance in toward my face with a straight right.

I backpedaled, drawing my left arm up to the inside of his punching arm. I knocked the arm back, striking the nerve bundles that ran along the inside of his bicep.

Kohl's arm bounced away but he ignored any pain I'd caused. He immediately clamped down with his left, trying to get me in some type of headlock.

I went with the flow and found the space I needed under his arm to escape. I brought his left arm with me, pivoted and applied an armlock, dropping my weight and slamming him right into the ground.

I heard a crunch. Kohl's elbow had shattered.

He grunted. "Asshole."

I saw the object before it dawned on me what it was. Kohl thrust the wooden knife at my heart. I barely had a chance to pivot out of the way and slam the edge of my right hand down on his wrist.

He didn't drop the knife though. I moved up his arm, punching the top of his forearm, by his elbow, and then behind his shoulder as I moved past him. Each punch caused him to jump but he never dropped the knife.

I got some distance between us and considered my next move.

Kohl spun. "This one's special, Lawson. Not your typical wooden blade."

"Oh?"

He smiled a thick syrupy grin that oozed across his face like oil on water. He crouched and I heard the sudden hiss of escaping air.

I jumped.

And narrowly missed the hunk of wood as it went screaming past where my chest had been a millisecond earlier. The wood bounced of the wall behind me and clattered under a table. I'd never seen a spring-blade wooden knife before. Chalk one up for the Syndicate.

Kohl frowned. "Cho said your reflexes were good."

"You saw them in action. You should have known. Next time, don't be so stupid and warn me what you're about to do."

"I won't." He rushed me, going for a tackle about the waist. I felt him impact, his shoulder thundering into my abdomen. Wind rushed out of me and I felt Kohl heave me up and then down. We crashed into the floor.

I brought my arms up, trying to use my elbows on his bowed back. Kohl was trying to gain a superior position by bringing his knees and legs up higher into me so he could hit me in the groin. I knew it was just a matter of time before I felt his hands close on my throat. He'd either go for a blood or air choke or a combination of the two. Once he had me unconscious, he could get that wooden knife and stake me though the heart.

I couldn't let him succeed.

I slammed another elbow down on his back, high up by the base of his skull. I felt his body react ever so slightly and then I used that moment to bring my right knee into his floating ribs. I heard another crack.

And I felt a helluva lot of pain suddenly. Then heard a sickening crunch.

Kohl's fist had broken my nose.

Blood streamed down my face.

I tasted copper and felt the hot stickiness of it flowing over me. We rolled then and I could barely see anything as more blood streamed into my eyes.

This was not good.

And anytime Boxcar wanted to show up would be just fine with me.

Kohl went for the choke.

I brought both my arms up and clapped them over his arms, breaking the hold. I went for a double ear slap using the palms of my hands. I boxed his ears and heard him cry out as the trapped air inside his ears ruptured his eardrums.

He clawed at my face, trying to rake my eyeballs out.

Sweat mingled with my blood. I could barely make out Kohl in front of me. I felt him knee me in the stomach, just missing my groin. I grunted and sucked hot wind, trying to steady my breathing.

"You're too late, Lawson. You'll never find him in time."

What the hell was that supposed to mean?

Kohl kicked at me again and we broke free then. I rolled clear.

A shot exploded inside the building.

Kohl's body pitched back, I couldn't see where he'd been hit though since he was wearing my blood all over his shirt. He collapsed by the bookcase.

I wiped my eyes and looked behind me.

Boxcar.

"You sure took your time."

"Door was locked."

"I left it unlocked."

He shook his head. "Locked when I tried it. I could hear you guys fighting. I ended up breaking the pane of glass out there to get in."

I turned back. Kohl didn't look so good. I limped over to him. His left arm was draped over a shelf and his body lay crumpled at the base of the bookcase. Pink froth streamed from his ears and mouth. I could see his canines fully exposed.

Kohl wouldn't be of this earth much longer.

"What did you mean when you said that?"

"You're . . . too late."

"Yeah. That. What's that mean? What's he planning?"

Kohl's eyes simply smiled and seemed to look beyond me. "I never . . . would have . . . told."

I frowned. Kohl's arm fell into his lap. I felt for his pulse but there was nothing. He was gone.

I stood. Boxcar stayed behind me. "You get anything out of him?"

"Not a damned word. Just that I'd never make it in time."

"What's that mean?"

"I'd like to know."

Boxcar frowned. "What about her?"

I glanced at Marilyn. She'd sat completely still throughout the entire fight and subsequent gunshot. "She's doped up on the designer drug Cho's manufacturing."

"She's wasted?"

"More like horny as hell. Apparently it makes us vamps randy dogs."

"Hell, I don't need Saber to do that," said Boxcar. He handed me a piece of black cloth from his uniform. "Better wipe off. You can't go outside looking like that."

"Thanks." I wiped the blood off of my face. My nose had swollen to three times its normal size. I felt the edges of the puffed skin and then found the bone. I took a breath in and then exhaled as I straightened it.

"Shit!"

Boxcar regarded me. "I can't believe you just did that."

"No time to go to a hospital." I wiped my face again. There wasn't much need to splint the fracture. It would heal fast enough.

"You're one determined dude, Lawson."

I handed him back the cloth. "You think it's worthwhile tossing the building looking for information?"

"Honestly? No. I don't think these guys would have been silly enough to leave something important laying around."

"Yeah. You're probably right."

"Besides, you've got your cousin back now, right? That's all that matters."

I glanced at Marilyn. I had no idea how the hell I was going to detox her. Especially if I had to spend most of the time fighting off her advances. "Yeah. I've got her back. I'll drive her home to her father's place tonight."

"Okay, good. I'll round up the others and let 'em know we're all done here."

I shook my head. "Actually, we're not really done at all."

"You've got your cousin back, Lawson. Isn't that what you wanted?"

"Of course it was. But there's more to this than just Marilyn. We've got to stop Cho, before—"

"Before what? We don't know what the hell he's planning to do. We could be sitting around with our thumbs up our asses and no idea what's going on."

"We can't just sit around with our thumbs up our asses. We've got to try to stop him."

Boxcar sighed. "Okay. What do you want us to do?"

I told him.

Thirty-two

"You're such a poop."

We were on the New Jersey Turnpike, as depressing and bumpy a stretch of road as any in the U.S. I had one hand on the wheel and one hand actively engaged in warding off Marilyn's questing extremities. So far, she'd propositioned me seven times.

But who was counting?

"I'm not a poop. You're doped up on a bad drug that's making you act all sorts of weird. Now just sit tight until I can get you home."

"Home's back in New York. With Teresa." She smiled. "Have you met her?"

"I've had the pleasure, yeah."

"She's beautiful, isn't she?"

"Sure." Of course, she was. But I didn't want to feed into anything that might have been rolling through Marilyn's whacked out head.

"Do you think I'm pretty, Lawson?"

"You're a doll."

Her hands wandered up my right arm. "You're so strong. Must come from fighting all those bad guys."

Yeah, my super exercise regimen of killing bad vampires. Better than the Hollywood miracle diet. I used my right elbow to knock her arm away. "Marilyn, contain yourself, would you?"

"I'll bet if Teresa was here, you wouldn't mind if her hands were roaming all over you."

"Even if that was true, I'd rather have both hands available to drive with. In case you haven't noticed, this stretch of road sucks."

"Is it because we're cousins?"

"Uh, yeah. That might have something to do with it."

"What else?"

"Try free will."

"What?"

I glanced at her. "I have to explain this again? Your mind is filled with some narcotic goop. You don't really know what you're doing. You think you do, but you don't. And heaven forbid you actually get yourself into a situation you think you want right now. Later on you'll realize what a big mistake that was."

She frowned at me. "You're such a poop."

I grinned. "Yeah, you explained that to me already."

Moorestown sat nestled in south Jersey, sort of close to Cherry Hill. Forty minutes from Philadelphia, I wasn't all that crazy about being so far removed from New York. Part of me was really worried about Teresa. Despite the fact that we'd removed most of the threats that would naturally go after her, I couldn't help but feel she might still be in danger.

"I slept with her."

"What?"

Marilyn was running her fingers along her lips. "Teresa. She and I used to sleep with each other. Not all the time, you know, but sometimes, when the pickings were slim out in the clubs. We'd come back to the apartment and just go at it."

For some reason, my throat felt thick all of sudden.

Marilyn sighed. "The first time was so nice. She was really gentle. I think it was the first time for both of us. I'd never been with a woman before. We just spent the whole night slowly exploring each other. Nuzzling, kissing, using our tongues. It was so . . . incredible."

Swallowing suddenly became a tough chore.

"Later on, we'd get really rough. Like a real primal fuck, you know? Animal almost. We brought out the toys, the lubes, everything. She surprised me some-times with how ferocious she was in the sack."

"Marilyn . . ."

Her voice tickled my ear. "You can't tell me that doesn't turn you on."

It wasn't the thought of Marilyn that was making my head swim with nasty visions. It was the thought of Teresa. I pushed Marilyn back into the seat. "Sit still, our exit's coming up."

She slumped back into the seat. "I don't want to go home. I want to party. Party with me, Lawson."

"Not a damned chance. I told your father I'd bring you home, and that's exactly what I'm going to do."

I pulled off the exit and we wound down the off-ramp. At the lights I broke left and a few miles farther on we rolled into Moorestown. The town itself hardly had any trees over twenty feet high. They'd all been planted back when the area had been sprung for development.

Marilyn's family lived in one of these developments. Uncle Phil ran a profitable proctology practice, what he liked to call his "ass-for-cash" business. Business must have been good because the two-floor mansion stood out among the other homes in the neighbor-hood with a large circular drive, huge bay windows, and intricate marble columns. For a vampire family, the pad was pretty ostentatious. Phil wrote it off as having to look like any other rich physician. I knew better. Phil liked the glitz. Trashy glitz was even better.

I parked the Mercedes next to his jet black Bentley and walked around to Marilyn's door. She was already out by the time I got there, leaning against the door with her skirt hiked up.

"Last chance, stud."

"Put your goods away, Marilyn. I'm not buying."

She started to say it. I stopped her. "I know. I'm a poop."

I walked her up the flagstone walk and then rang the doorbell. Deep inside the house I could hear the door chime go off. It sounded like a tinny version of Gershwin. How awful.

Phil opened the door a few moments later. He was wearing a red paisley smoking jacket and a cravat. Somehow, that just didn't synch up very well with my image of New Jersey, but I didn't say anything.

He saw Marilyn and almost collapsed. He hugged her tightly and she cooed into his ear. He pulled back sharply. "What the hell?"

"She's been drugged." I stepped inside. "Some new designer stuff. It affects our kind by making us extremely . . . uh—"

"Promiscuous?"

"Horny is what I've been describing it as."

"I don't know if I feel comfortable using that word in relation to my daughter." He frowned. "She been like this long?"

"Propositioned me the entire drive down here."

"Good Lord."

"Relax. I didn't take her up on it."

"Oh, I'm so relieved. Honestly, Lawson."

I sat down on the couch in the living room. "I could use a drink."

"Gin?"

"Juice if you can spare some. It's been a long night."

"We've got some, sure." He vanished. Marilyn slid next to me on the couch.

Phil came back in the room with the glass of blood and handed it to me. He guided Marilyn, who was now looking very sleepy, over to the opposite couch.

"Is there anything we can do?"

I sipped the juice and felt the life force hit me a minute later. I sighed. "Seems like she's starting to come down from it, anyway. I wouldn't worry."

"Who did this to her?"

"It's way too complicated to get into. And it's probably a helluva lot better if you don't know."

Phil leaned forward. "This is my daughter we're talking about here. Someone harmed her. I want to know who."

"A three and a half foot midget named Cho."

"One of our kind?"

"Yeah."

He sighed. "My God, what's become of our world? Is it so unsafe nowadays that we can't even be safe from our own people?"

"It's not a friendly world out there, Phil."

"I'd guess not." He sipped what looked like bourbon. "This man, this Cho character—did you get him?"

"Not yet."

"But you will."

"Oh, yeah. I will."

"And you'll . . ." His voice trailed off.

"Yeah. I'll kill him. He's broken a lot of our laws. The sentence is absolute."

He sat there for a minute taking that in. Phil was one of those people who could never rationalize taking the life of another, no matter how grievous the crime. Most people I know who think like that find they have a change of heart when the crime affects one of their own. "I've never understood how you can do what you do."

I smirked and finished the juice. The rush of life force energy made me feel warm. "Makes you feel any better, I can't imagine looking up people's asses all day long."

"It's a job."

"Exactly."

"It's not just a job for you, though."

I shrugged. "Probably a little more to it than that. In the service, we think of it as a calling."

"A calling that ordains death?"

"We preserve the Balance, Phil. The justification of that purpose is a pretty heavy responsibility."

He finished his drink and went looking for a refill. Marilyn had slumped over to one side and was now snoring away. At least she wouldn't hit on me in front of her father.

Phil came back with a fresh glass and sipped it for a moment. "You know, after your mother died, I wanted to adopt you."

I tried to smile. It didn't take. "Don't get sentimental on me."

"I mean it. Your father died so young. It wasn't right. And then, your mother—well, she was my only sister. You know that. I felt . . . responsible for you. But you . . ."

"Yeah. I was too old."

"The choice was yours."

"I was past my centennial. I'd just entered Fixer training."

"You could have been exempted."

I shook my head. "An exemption was the last thing that would have helped me at that point. Don't you see? I didn't have anything left. Being selected to become a Fixer was the only path open to me. It felt right. It felt exactly like what I should have been doing. I felt . . . I don't know . . . honored, I guess. After everything that had happened to me, funny as it sounds, I needed it."

"But look what you've become."

"What—a killer?" I shook my head. "I don't see it that way."

"How could you not?"

"Phil, this isn't the sort of job I could simply resign from. I happen to take it very seriously. And yes, there's a lot of death involved. The risks are too many to count. But it's my life. And I happen to be pretty good at my job."

Phil set his drink down and stood. "I won't ever understand how you can do it."

"Sometimes I don't understand it myself. But at least I can be honest about that."

He nodded at Marilyn. "Thanks for bringing her back to me. Is there any way I can repay you?"

"Part of the job." I stood. "Just be nice to her when she wakes up. Hopefully she won't remember trying to seduce her cousin."

He grinned. "You're leaving?"

I nodded. "Yeah. I have to."

"You're going after him, aren't you?"

"Yes."

Phil hugged me. It felt weird. I clapped him on the

back. He pulled back and smiled. His eyes looked misty but I couldn't tell if it was from the bourbon or sincere emotion. "Be careful, okay? You get this guy, maybe you'll come back down here and visit us for a while. Be like old times."

"Uncle Phil, we never really had old times."

"Then we'll make some. Hell, I don't know. Just don't be such a damned stranger, okay?"

"Okay."

I walked outside. The air felt cool. There'd be a frost tonight. I turned back and saw Phil wave once. I waved back. He closed the door and vanished back into the safety and innocence of his world.

I got back in my car and started the engine. It churned to life. I slipped it into drive and rolled out onto the street.

In another minute I was back on the highway.

Heading back to New York.

And all the danger it contained.

Thirty-three

Driving back through northern New Jersey, I could see the skyline of New York City in the distance. Ordinarily, I'm a real sucker for a good skyline. But something felt different now. Something felt . . . wrong.

And I didn't like that.

I headed back toward the Upper East Side. At the loft Gopher had gotten for the team, I found them all waiting for me. No one said welcome back. Their faces told me something was up.

"We got a message for you," said Pinkie.

From the frowns, I could only guess how bad the message was. "From Cho?"

Boxcar nodded. "He relayed it to us through your Control Niles."

"What's he saying?"

Boxcar glanced at Pinkie. Pinkie looked away. Gopher sighed and then spoke up. "He's got that human girl Teresa, Lawson."

I sighed. Truth was, I liked Teresa. Probably more sexual than anything else, but there's not necessarily anything wrong with that. What annoyed me more than anything else was that Cho had gone and involved her in this whole mess when I'd taken great pains to try to leave her out of it. Something about getting humans involved with vampire business tends to piss me off quite a bit.

"Let me guess," I said, "he wants me to come alone some place."

"Actually, no."

Boxcar cleared his throat. "You're supposed to go wait on a corner somewhere—we have an address. You'll be picked up by someone."

"That's it?"

"That's all we know."

I looked at the piece of paper in Boxcar's hand. The address was midtown. "What time did they say?"

"As soon as you got here."

"Great." I glanced around the loft. It was only then that I noticed the three of them were fully decked out in their assault gear. "You guys going some place?"

"We're following you," said Gopher. "That way we can kill these bastards and go home."

"They said alone, guys."

"Fuck alone," said Pinkie. "Since when did we ever let the bad guys dictate our moves?"

I grinned. "You guys are too good to me."

Boxcar grinned. "Someone's got to be."

I spun on my heels and walked to the door. "See you when I see you."

Outside, a sharp wind blew me a step sideways. I steered to my left and caught a cab. I had it drop me three blocks shy of where I needed to be. I stepped out into the night again and walked. A few blocks later, I stood at the rendezvous point.

When I'd exited the building, I hadn't seen any surveillance on the loft. I doubted they knew where we were holing up, just that we were in town some place.

Still, I knew the guys would be extra careful following

me. They'd take the back alleys and side roads. They'd assume the bad guys knew our every move.

But they'd be here.

Waiting.

And ready.

I stood, looking like an idiot, on the corner. The chilly wind made standing outside for too long seem slightly crazy. I checked the time via an overhead neon sign that flashed in time to a techno beat. Staring at it made my eyes hurt like hell.

I looked back along the street. Even at the late hour of two o'clock in the morning, New York still throbbed with life. Bustling crowds of club-goers mixed with socialites, hoodlums, bums, and working stiffs.

And still no one drove by to pick me up.

Maybe I needed to shave my legs.

At two-thirty, a navy blue Lexus slid up to the curb. The passenger window came down with a low hum barely audible over the din of street noise.

Rebecca's mug greeted me. A pudgy grin poked its way across her chin-stacked countenance. "Hi, honey. Hop in."

I didn't look around. There wasn't any need to. I knew the guys would have been in position for several minutes. They would see me getting into the car and they'd know how to follow Rebecca without her noticing.

Besides, I *was* pretty surprised. I popped the door and slid inside. The black leather squeaked once before adjusting to my body.

Rebecca shot the car into the traffic and we were off.

"Surprised?"

"Possibly."

She laughed. "Bullshit. You are. I know it."

"I didn't figure you for being involved necessarily with Cho."

"Oh, Cho and I go way back. He's the one who set me up in business initially."

"That how he got you to do this tonight? Because you owe him?"

"I don't owe him anything. Anymore." She shrugged. "Time was, I did. Cho loaned me a lot of money to get the business going. After all, rents in this town are stratospheric. Unless you're a top agency, you won't be able to afford it."

"Okay. He bankrolled you. So what?"

"So nothing. I eventually paid him back. But then Cho approached me with some business ideas that would make us both a lot of money. I was skeptical, but I bought in. Then the venture went through the roof. Of course, by that time, Raoul and I were also doing business and shuffling some top-notch human female talent his way. Cho has always had a soft spot for the ladies. Especially ladies he can have his way with."

"He do that to Marilyn?"

Rebecca sighed. "Well, that's where this thing got a bit complicated. We didn't know Marilyn was one of us."

"How could you not know that?"

She glanced at me. "Give me a break, Lawson. We don't exactly walk around with signboards around our necks, do we? I don't advertise the fact that I'm one, neither did Marilyn. Raoul would have known if he'd been able to sleep with her."

"You mean he didn't?"

"Oh, not a chance. It wasn't for lack of trying but Marilyn wouldn't have anything to do with him."

"Smart girl."

"Maybe not so smart. Raoul wanted to hurt her so he got her excited about the idea of making some extra cash. Then he shuffled her over to Cho who got excited as well. Apparently, he raped her and bit her. It was only then that he realized the mistake."

She didn't have to say any more. Vampire blood tastes slightly different from human blood. Not that most people could tell, but a vamp can smell the minute shifting balances that would signal the difference.

"Cho freaked out then, right?"

"Well, obviously. He doesn't care much for vampires. He likes bleeding humans dry."

"So what happened then?"

"We all figured someone would be coming for her eventually. We tracked her name back through the connections we have and found out that you were related. Cho jumped at the chance to lure you down here."

"Lure me?" I was still having a hard time believing this whole mess had been a setup from the start.

"Sure. Your reputation's pretty impressive. All we had to do was set the table with just the right food and you'd come running."

"And I did."

"You did."

"Glad I could accommodate you."

"Don't be so glum about it."

"I'm not. I'm sorry Marilyn got herself mixed up in this."

"So was Cho. Until we found a new use for her."

"Saber."

Rebecca nodded. "Yes. Cho was able to use the drug on her to chart its effects. Quite interesting to watch."

"I'm glad you're not a nurse."

She laughed. Her belly bounced up against the steering wheel as she did so. I felt slightly nauseous. "Where are we heading?"

"Out of the city. Cho's plans for you don't involve the Big Apple anymore."

"How thoughtful of him."

"He's put a lot of thought into this that's for sure. But not necessarily in a good way."

"That's usually how it works." I watched FDR Drive flash past, with the East River on our right side. "What's he got planned for Teresa?"

"Why do you care? You still get hopped up by human chicks? Is that it? You want to marry her or something?"

I eyed Rebecca. "I want you to know something."

"What's that?"

"The reason—and it's the only reason—that you're even still alive is that I need to know where you're taking me. If it wasn't for that small fact, you'd already be dead."

"And I'm supposed to remember that for later when you kill me? Some sort of vague threat is it?"

"You found that vague?"

"Not in the least."

"Good. I can clarify it further if you need me to."

She snorted. "As if. You don't know anything about this, Lawson. No matter what your Fixer instincts might tell you."

"It's a long ride, wherever we're going. Why not clue me in then?"

She shook her head. "I wouldn't dream of doing that. Cho's waited far too long and pulled too many strings to get this exactly where it needs to be."

"Plus there's the fact that he'd kill you if you told me."

"There's that."

I glanced at the rearview mirror and somewhere behind us, Boxcar, Pinkie, and Gopher were all ready to roll at a second's notice.

"I could give you a hint."

I looked at Rebecca. "A hint? Don't bother. I never get hints anyway. That's why I'm not married."

"You're not married because you're in love with a human woman named Talya. That and your job, of course."

I frowned. "You people certainly seem to have access to the best information available, don't you?"

"We do all right."

"Who's on your bankroll?"

She laughed. "At least you're not insulting me by trying to sneak it out of me."

"I'll find out anyway. Eventually."

"Maybe not this time."

"I'm sure I will."

"Oh, come on, Lawson. Let me just give you a hint. I'm fairly busting at the seams anyway."

"I thought you weren't going to tell me."

"I'm not. I'm giving out hints."

"You don't think I'm smart enough to piece it together?"

She smiled. "How did Marilyn like being doped up on Saber?"

"She loved it, and she would have slept her way through most of humanity and vampire alike if she'd had her way."

"Interesting isn't it? Saber makes our kind so damned horny." She eyed me again. "Not that I'd need any help getting worked up, mind you. I'm horny all the time anyway."

"How wonderful for you."

"Grosses you out, does it?"

"I didn't say that."

"You didn't have to."

Her hands tightened on the wheel and she was quiet for a minute or two. I halfway hoped she'd concentrate on driving so I could concentrate on working out a plan or two that might come in handy.

Unfortunately, Rebecca must have been used to people making cracks about her weight because she was back to normal within three minutes.

"Cho's got himself a new version of Saber."

"A new version? But I thought he was happy with what he's got. After all, it completely dopes up the humans, doesn't it?"

"Saber's never been about humans, Lawson."

"What?"

"It's always been about domination. Specifically, dominance over vampires. Saber was just the means to get to where we are . . . now."

I looked at her and my stomach suddenly felt very queasy. I knew more bad news was coming.

"Your role, Lawson," said Rebecca, "is to be the first guinea pig for the new and improved version."

So much for hints.

Thirty-four

"You want domination over vampires?" I sighed. Someday I was going to write a book called "The World's Lamest Criminal Conspiracies" and then pass out a free copy to aspiring rogues.

Rebecca grinned. "It's not only about vampires, Lawson. We want it all. Vampires, lycanthropes, humans, all the other races . . . all of them. Cho's convinced it's his destiny."

I didn't mention how many times I'd heard that before, either. "And he's got the ability to pull it off?"

"You've seen some examples of his power. You should know."

"I know he's got access to things he shouldn't have."

"Oh, please." Rebecca glanced at me. "Information is one of the easiest things to come by. Anyone can be bought."

"I can't."

"No? Not even for the love of your human girlfriend?"

"Why? Are you making an offer?"

She shrugged. "Who knows? Maybe once Cho's in power, he can swing a deal for you. Maybe you could actually live with your wonderful Talya in peace. Without the Council needing to be involved."

"How's he going to do that if I'm the guinea pig in the new Saber experiment?"

She sighed. "Good point. I suppose if things go well with the test, then it won't be a big problem."

"But if things don't go well."

She smirked. "That would be a shame."

"I'm sure."

"I'd hate to see you go to waste, Lawson. I really would. Maybe if the Saber makes you a bit more . . . relaxed about your partners, we can even enjoy ourselves some."

"I think you'll find me a bit more resistant to Saber than any of your past victims."

"I doubt that."

I leaned back into the seat. I sincerely hoped the rest of my team was behind us, tailing Rebecca's car at a safe distance. I was going to need all the help I could get as soon as I figured out where we were headed.

Rebecca's car wound its way up the interstate.

North.

Upstate New York.

"Where we going? The Catskills?"

"Not even close."

"Want to let me in on our destination? Just so I have something to gnaw on. The boredom's killing me."

"New Palz."

I frowned. Something about the name sounded familiar. I couldn't quite place it. Rebecca must have noticed my expression.

"Ever hear of Mohunk?"

That was it. I'd gone rock scrambling there once. A series of large boulders bordered what was once a very stylish hotel and getaway for the Rockefeller rich at the turn of the century. The cliff house was still there. And the clientele still proved to be on the wealthy side.

"Cho got us a suite of rooms at the hotel?"

"Nope."

"I don't do well camping."

"Don't worry. He owns the hotel."

That was news. Business certainly must have been extremely good for Cho to pull down the kind of cash needed to buy the hotel and surrounding property.

"Let me guess: it's deserted."

"It's off-season anyway. Summer and winter are the big draws. Folks in the summer rock scramble through the lemon squeeze and in the winter they ski at the mountains nearby. Fall and spring are almost nothing except for foliage freaks. Cho didn't want anyone disturbing us."

"How sweet of him."

The rest of the ride took forty minutes. Rebecca eased us off the highway and onto side roads that bled into more side roads until at last we came to rest in the gravel parking lot of the Mohunk estate.

Rebecca eyed me. "Please don't do anything foolish."

"Like kill you?"

"There's that, yes."

"I can't promise anything. After all, you've broken the law."

"Forget your job, Lawson. You've got a meeting to keep and I think Cho will be very upset with you if you show up late."

"Yeah."

"I'm also supposed to ask for your gun."

"My gun?"

"The one you always carry. Your Fixer pistol."

"Tell you what: you can have it if you can take it from me."

"He said you'd say that. He told me to tell you that if you don't give it to me, Teresa gets killed very slowly and very painfully."

I reached behind my right hip and drew my gun. For just a second, I leveled it at Rebecca. Her eyes widened only slightly. She must have been a cooler customer than I thought.

"You won't do that."

I thumbed the hammer back. I hate people who are so convinced of their own righteousness. "Are you really willing to bet on that?"

"Think of Teresa."

"I am."

"You're not. If you were, you'd ease that hammer down and give me that stupid gun."

I chewed my inner lip. I really wanted to blow a hole in Rebecca's heart. Something about how smug she seemed really rubbed me the wrong way.

Instead, I let the hammer go forward slowly and then handed her the gun. She took it with an audible release of breath. Maybe she wasn't so cool after all.

"Thanks."

We got out of the car. Rebecca pointed at the cliff house. "This way."

I followed behind her. She ambled up the walkway, seemingly having difficulty maintaining her balance. I could hear her labored breathing. Cho really needed to keep his staff in better shape.

"Rebecca."

She turned.

My hands shot out, grabbing her neck and twisting. The vertebrae at the top of her spine popped and snapped like a bunch of potato chips. She gasped and fell to the ground, flopping a bit.

On a human, that would have ended her life. But vampires are different. So even though I'd just broken Rebecca's neck, she was still alive. She was hurt bad. But she was still alive.

I yanked my gun out of her hand. She squirmed on the ground moaning.

I leaned close to her. "You chose the wrong side."

"Don't do this, Lawson. You need me. You need my help."

I shook my head and placed the muzzle of my gun against her chest. "I don't need you at all."

The contact shot helped muffle the sound, but it still broke the silence of the night and announced to everyone that I was there.

I looked down at Rebecca's body. Her chest had blossomed brilliant red. Her eyes had gone wide and white. Her canines had extended to their full length.

She wouldn't be doing any more booking for dancers, that was for sure.

I could have shot her easily when I had the chance. But I wanted her as surprised as some of the young, innocent dancers she'd helped corrupt, when they realized their dreams were being dashed against reality's rocks.

Rebecca deserved exactly what she got.

I turned.

It was time to take care of Cho.

The gravel path led up to the main entrance of the house. The last thing I wanted to do was take the front door. There might be an awful big welcoming party waiting for me and I hate welcoming parties. I particularly wasn't interested in being welcomed by Cho's tongueless, handless automatons.

I worked my way around to the rear of the building. The last time I'd been in Mohunk—years ago—I'd only seen the house from across the lake on the rocks. Now, in front of it for the first time, the sheer size of it overwhelmed me. So did the realization of just how much money Cho must have had.

I found a back entrance, ostensibly used by service personnel. The simple deadbolt was easy enough to pick. But I still took my time entering the building. I've found easy-to-pick locks sometimes act as a lure to get you to rush inside. And then you rush right into more alarms. Or worse: an ambush.

But the back entrance seemed clear. I breathed a sigh of relief and entered what must have been the main kitchen's receiving area. Giant aluminum and steel shelving units held boxes of staple foodstuffs. I saw large tins of tomato sauce, huge bags of flour and sugar, cookies, pasta, and much more.

The room itself felt cold.

Darkness enveloped everything.

But I could make out my environment very well thanks to my night vision.

I saw a door leading out of the room and moved toward it.

No lock.

I eased it open. I stood in the main kitchen now. Long countertops, elaborate stoves and ranges, and huge racks of pans and pots held sway over the rest of the room. I crouched down, moving sideways through the aisles.

Two doors branched off this room. I stopped and considered my choices.

Which one?

I snuck over to the first and put my ear against it. I could hear voices. I eased back. I didn't want to enter that room yet.

I risked a look at the overhead clock and frowned. Where the hell were Boxcar and the rest of the guys? They should have been here by now.

Unless they got lost.

That prospect did not cheer me up one single bit. Having to take down Cho and his followers by myself put me at a definite disadvantage.

But Teresa's life was in danger. And I'd have to do something before too long or else Chow would get antsy and possibly kill her. I sure didn't want Teresa killed because of something she unknowingly got mixed up in.

I went to the second door.

I heard nothing.

The hinges were on the inside. I squeezed the door handle slowly, praying that it wouldn't squeak.

I turned the handle.

And heard a click.

The bolt released.

The knob turned.

Soundless.

I pulled.

The door swung open on its hinges.

The room beyond seemed darker still.

Much darker.

I could see a staircase. Armchairs. A couch. On the floor, a thin Persian carpet ran the length of the room. Bookshelves framed it.

But no one was there.

I eased into the room, my pistol held at the ready.

The door swung shut behind me.

I whirled.

How th—

The lights came on.

My eyes blinked rapidly. The explosion of light made me wince. I brought the gun up, but I couldn't see a damned thing.

I felt a rush of movement and a blow to my wrist, knocking the gun out of my hands. Another blow landed on my jaw. My head snapped to the right. I felt an immediate swelling.

A kick landed in my stomach. I retched and doubled-over, heaving and trying to get my wind back.

Now I heard voices.

And my sight came back.

I blinked again, still gasping.

A figure emerged in front of me. It reminded me of my dream. There in the middle of my vision, like he was emerging from the mist, stood Cho.

He smiled. Then he cast his arms out to his side. "You see gentlemen? I told you he would never ever go for the door with the voices behind it. Our man here likes to be cautious."

He eyed me. "Good evening, Lawson. Are you ready to usher in a new era in vampire history?"

Thirty-five

I glanced around the room.

Cho stood in front of me flanked by his two body-guards. They looked as imposing as they had the first time I'd seen them back at that awful warehouse down in the city. In the actual light of the room, I could see their bulbous metal stumps poking out of sleeves where their arms had once resided. One of them smiled at me and waggled a stump of what had once been his tongue.

Wonderful.

Cho wore a dark gray three-piece suit. Around his neck he wore a bright purple cravat that looked utterly ridiculous.

"Lovely neck décor you've got there, Cho."

He sniffed. "You're being rude."

"No, really. I've been trying to work cravats into my wardrobe, but I am just not snooty enough to make 'em work. You don't seem to have that problem."

He smiled. "I'm sure that within the space of a few minutes, my personal fashion choices will seem totally irrelevant to you, Lawson."

"Where's the girl?"

"The human?" Cho smirked. "You and I are a lot alike. Do you know that?"

"We both breathe air and drink blood. The similarities end there."

"Actually, they don't."

"Do all bad guys go through a seminar that mandates attempting to draw similarities between the forces of good and evil? Because I hear this crap an awful lot." I sighed. "You and I aren't alike. You're three-feet tall. My dick's bigger than you are."

"Juvenile barbs don't become you, Lawson."

"Probably not. But they're sure as hell fun to throw at idiots like you."

Cho nodded. "Perhaps you'd be interested to know why I said we were similar. Your personnel file, for example, makes a note of your obsession with a specific human named Talya. It actually notes that in all probability the two of you are in love of all things."

"If you're dropping that tidbit to impress me with the excellence of your information, forget it. I've been impressed for a while now."

Cho ignored me. "And now, you're here because of your silly desire to save a human woman from death. I mean, really, Lawson, when does it end?"

"When your eyes roll white and your teeth come out one last time. I thought that would have been obvious."

He smirked. "I, too, have always had a bit of an affliction for human women. Although, in truth, not in the exact same capacity as you. Myself, I prefer them bled dry. Of course, I'll indulge a wee bit in the fruits of the flesh—who wouldn't? Sex with a human is so much more satisfying than with another of our species."

"Must be like a mouse raping an elephant."

He ignored me. "But that's where it ends. I don't care a wit whether they live or die. After all, there are close to what—six billion of them on this planet? I'm sure you'd agree the herd could use some thinning."

"I think our own herd could use some thinning, too."

"Oh, I quite agree with you there. It could definitely stand to lose a few of our more colorful characters. Or at the very least, it could stand some consolidation and domination." He pointed at me. "That's where you come in."

"I heard."

"She told you, did she?" He glanced around the room. "Now wherever did that fat little hog wander off to?"

"Shouldn't joke about her weight. She took it pretty seriously. When she was still breathing."

"You killed her?"

"It's my job."

"Pity." He sighed. "I would have liked her to see what we're going to do to you."

"No doubt. You still haven't told me where the woman is."

"She's safe."

"The last time you said that, you showed me some sort of hologram with my cousin in it. Wasn't that it?"

"A spiritual hologram, but I'll give it to you."

I didn't even want to know what the hell that was. "Whatever it was, she wasn't where you said she'd be at all."

"And you should know, right? You did break into the building to rescue her. That wasn't playing by the rules."

"Since when do the rules matter any to you?"

"I admit that the rules of the Council matter very little. But even a criminal has a code he follows."

"Honor among thieves?"

"Nothing so dreadfully quaint. More like, I do what I have to do to ensure my future and success."

"And the people who disagree?"

"They die."

"Some rules."

Cho nodded at one of the bodyguards. He left the room. Cho smiled at me. "Since you are so deeply concerned about your new girlfriend—"

"She's not my girlfriend."

"You slept with her."

"That was the plan, yeah. But then you and Kohl interrupted that possibility."

"Oops." He chuckled. "Sorry about that."

"I'll bet."

Cho looked at the side door as the bodyguard returned. He had one arm stump nudged into the small of her back. Teresa staggered into the room. Cho smiled. "Ah, here she is now."

Teresa didn't look very happy. In fact, Teresa didn't look like very much was happening with her at all.

"What'd you do to her?"

"A little hypnosis. I'm sure you'd agree it's better if she does not know exactly what has kidnapped her. That would mean we'd either have to explain it all to her—and that's a no-no—or simply kill her. And you'd be liable to get all hot and bothered if we did that."

"No guarantees I won't anyway."

Cho smiled. "Actually, I think I might be able to do just that."

"How so?"

He held up a small vial filled with blue liquid. "You agree to undergo the injection and I'll release the woman."

"And I'm just supposed to take you on your word that you'd do that?"

"Remember what I said about having a code? My word is my honor, Lawson."

"Pardon me for not trusting that. It's been my experience that crooks, traitors, and the rest of you scumbags will say anything you can to get things to go your way. You won't let her go. You'll kill her. Or else use her for something else."

"I'm sorry you feel that way." He sighed. "You don't leave me much of a choice." He turned to the bodyguard who held Teresa. "Kill her."

That wasn't part of the script. "Hold on, Cho."

He looked at me. "I thought you didn't want anything to do with my deal."

"So you'll just kill her?"

"She's no good to me alive."

"What good is she to you dead?"

"A thorn in your side. I'll settle for that."

I frowned. "Let her go."

"You'll agree to the injection?"

"I don't think you'll like the results."

He grinned. "I don't care what you think, Lawson. All I want is your willingness to accept the injection."

I looked at Teresa. There were no guarantees Cho would let either of us live. But I had to stall until my team got there. Wherever the hell they were. "Fine."

"Excellent." Cho nodded at the bodyguard who poked Teresa out of the room. Cho nodded at the couch. "You may want to lay down. It might make the entire operation go a lot smoother."

"You never said anything about surgery."

"I didn't mean operation in that sense."

I walked over to the couch.

Cho looked at me. "You'll have to strip off your top at least so I can inject your arm and hook up the monitoring machines to your chest."

The second bodyguard had vanished and rematerialized pushing in what looked like a portable EKG machine.

I slid out of the turtleneck, keeping my back hidden. Cho whistled.

"No fat on you, huh?"

"I try to stay in shape."

"I guess so. I've never seen such muscular development without being too bulky and huge." He thumbed over his shoulder. "Sure I've got the freak twins here, but their muscles are artificial. Nothing so . . . natural."

I frowned. "Thanks. I guess."

Cho began hooking up leads to my chest. "You know, Lawson, this really is going to be a momentous occasion. You'll be the first vampire to test my new serum."

"And what will it do to me?"

"Hopefully, everything will go as planned."

"And if it doesn't?"

"Let's not think about that."

I sighed. Cho stuck more leads to my body. "This is the latest generation of Saber?"

"Yes."

"And you hope to use this to control vampire society?"

"That's part of it."

"And the other part?"

"If it works they way it should, I'll be able to wield power over the lycanthropes as well."

"And the other races?"

"Almost certainly. Humans, of course, are pathetically

simple to control. But there are the others . . . and I'm so looking forward to them."

"The Council will never allow this to happen."

Cho's face appeared closer to mine. "Forgive me for saying so, Lawson, but if you're the best they can field then I'm not all that much concerned."

"There will be others. And they won't be wooed by a human woman."

"They'll have other weaknesses. And I'll find them. You'd be surprised what a few well-placed dollars can do for a person's perspective."

"How in the world did you buy off a vampire?"

Cho laughed. "I never said I did buy off a vampire."

I frowned. It made no sense. Cho had gotten his information from somewhere. But who had given it to him? Was there a deeper conspiracy here than I'd seen so far? And if so, who the hell was behind it?

The bodyguard nodded at Cho then.

Cho's smiling face reappeared. "I've been informed by my assistant that we are ready to begin the procedure."

"What about the woman?"

"You have my word, Lawson. I'll set her free just as soon as the needle enters your skin."

I grabbed hold of his arm. "You'd better not be lying, Cho."

"I'm not."

"If you are, I'll come back from the depths of hell to make sure you pay. For everything."

He considered this for all of a second. "Lean back, Lawson. It's time we started."

The second bodyguard entered the room. He looked at Cho and nodded. Cho looked back at me. "There. You see? She's perfectly fine."

"I won't know that unless I see her."

"No time now. We've got to start."

I sighed and leaned back. My hopes for a quick rescue by my team were quickly diminishing. Something must have happened.

Something bad.

Cho must have seen my face. "Oh, my. You're afraid, aren't you?"

"Who wouldn't be? I've got no idea what the gunk you're going to stick me with will do to me. Looks like window cleaner for crying out loud."

Cho looked at the needle. "That's true. You're right. I actually don't know what will happen to you. I mean, I've got some idea, of course."

"But until you actually inject it, you won't know for sure."

"We were mighty surprised with how your cousin Marilyn reacted, I can tell you that. But she's no worse for the wear, is she?"

"Sexually frustrated, but overall, she's okay."

"So there's nothing to really be concerned about. It's not like I'm injecting poison into your veins. This should actually make you feel great. It will expand your awareness."

"Every drug promises that and fails to accomplish it. It's illusory. Drugs narrow the awareness while giving the impression of doing otherwise."

"Not this one. It actually does expand your awareness."

"Are you sure you want an ornery Fixer with his awareness expanded?"

"Ordinarily no. But Saber will take the edge off of you, I have little doubt. Once this stuff hits your veins, you'll be nice and mellow. I've seen it take an angry tiger down a few notches. You won't be that difficult."

"Wonderful."

"Are you ready, Lawson?"

I glanced around the room. I expected the windows to shatter at any moment. I expected my team to come pouring through the openings, shooting holes into Cho and his bodyguards.

But nothing happened.

Cho chuckled again. "If you're wondering about the team you had following Rebecca's car, I'm afraid you will be waiting a long time. You see, I had them ambushed some miles up the road. I don't think they'll be coming for you anytime soon."

Shit.

That was not the news I wanted to hear.

Cho's voice became a whisper in my ear.

"Let's begin, shall we?"

Thirty-six

The needle poked through the skin of my shoulder, plunging into the medial deltoid. I felt the dull ache I always feel whenever I get shots, which fortunately isn't all that often.

I hate needles.

I felt a cool sensation flooding my muscle. I glanced up and saw Cho's thumb press the hypodermic's plunger down until it could go no farther.

All of his evil—all of his wicked plans—now lay inside me.

He drew the needle out and smiled at me. "All done."

"How long?" My throat felt a bit thick.

"Any time now. Saber works incredibly fast . . ."

But even as the midget megalomaniac spoke, I knew the drug had started to hit me like a freight train. I heard a rush in my ears, saw my vision start to tunnel on me, and felt the realm of my awareness immediately shrink.

My breathing became labored. It wasn't that I couldn't draw a breath so much as I felt I couldn't exhale it all back out again. I started to worry about carbon dioxide poisoning or some other silly notion that I knew couldn't really harm me, and yet, I couldn't help but worry about it at the same time.

The room's walls warped and flexed. Tears flooded my eyes, streaming out and down my face.

But I wasn't crying.

I thought I could hear Cho's voice in the background, ticking off the reactions he'd expected me to exhibit and the ones that surprised him.

Like the tears.

My heart pounded against the inside of my chest cavity. I still felt like I couldn't push a used breath out of me. My mouth went dry then and it seemed a weird condition given that my face was drenched with tears. Sweat? I didn't know any more. I tried to tongue some of the moisture off to get it back into my mouth.

I must have looked like a slobbering idiot.

My right arm went into a spasm then, twitching and slapping the side of the couch. I could feel hands on me then, trying to restrain me. I thought it was the bodyguards, but then I remembered they didn't have hands. It must have been Cho.

The thought of him touching me made me feel ill.

And then for some reason, things started to calm down. I felt the coolness I'd felt at my shoulder suddenly begin to ooze throughout the rest of my body. It felt peaceful actually, like someone was pouring cool water all over my body in a very slow fashion.

I could feel the urge to relax and accept what was happening, that I'd be much better off if I did just that.

Part of me desperately wanted to. The sensation felt so good. I didn't want it to end. And the part that wanted me to relax and accept was a pretty big part.

But way off in the distance, I could feel another part of me rebel against the drug. I could hear an inner voice telling me that it was evil.

That I should fight it.

I heard another voice then.

Cho's.

It echoed and sounded like he was talking to me from inside my own skull.

"Lawson. Don't fight the drug. Let it take you over. Let it soothe you. Relax you. Accept the gifts it has to offer. You won't ever want to do anything but feel this way again. Do you understand?"

I have no idea if I nodded in the affirmative or not. It didn't really matter because Cho went right on talking.

"Everything you've stood for. Everything you've done, it's all been for the Council. They've used you for their own needs. You haven't done anything for our society. It's all been for a bunch of old fools and their own petty ambitions."

A feeling of weightlessness came over me.

I felt like I was floating through the air.

And I loved it.

"The Council needs to be abolished. Can't you see that? There are other ways to govern our people. There are other races that we need to coexist with, to learn from."

His voice became as soothing as the coolness seeping through my body. I knew that the drug was extremely powerful, but I hadn't thought it could so easily render me so weak.

"Give it up, Lawson. Reject your past. The future is now. It's yours for the making. Work with me and together we'll usher in a new dawn of vampire history."

He was getting to me. I could feel the impact of the drug. I could feel all my defenses crumbling. I loved the feelings I felt. I loved how light and airy everything appeared. All the pressure, all the burden, all the responsibility had vanished.

And I was just . . . me.

I could hear chuckling.

Cho?

No.

A new voice.

One that seemed strangely familiar.

But I couldn't place it.

"He's fighting the drug."

"No. He won't be able to."

"You're underestimating him again."

"I'm doing no such thing. I simply have faith in my drug. There's nothing wrong with that."

My head swam with confusion. Something seemed so familiar about the voice. And yet, as I tried to analyze it, the drug worked against me.

I could feel my body, my mind, and even my spirit trying to coax me into forgetting about everything. Just to accept the drug and become whatever it wanted me to become.

Life would be so easy.

So easy.

I'd never have to worry about anything else.

Ever again.

If I just surrendered myself to the drug.

To Saber.

To Cho.

To . . . Boxcar?

The voice. It had to be. My mind fought to analyze the voice. The memories of sounds, the way he formed words, the sharp intake of breath as he formed consonants.

Boxcar.

With Cho?

I was confused.

Everything felt so . . . muddled.

I remembered that faraway piece of me that had urged me not to submit. I searched myself for it, tried to stumble through the thick cobwebs that had suddenly sprung up from Saber.

Don't do it.

Give in.

Reject your past.

Stay where it feels good.

It feels good to stay with us.

Here.

Now.

No! That wasn't what I wanted. That wasn't what I was. I pushed through the cobwebs, searching.

Searching.

And lurking far off in the deep recesses of my mind, I found it.

Myself.

My true self.

I went to the little shard of me that was left and embraced it with my mind. I poured myself into that shard, into what was left of the real me.

And slowly, something changed.

The coolness began to disappear.

My throat became moist again.

My muscles relaxed.

My heartbeat slowed.

And adrenaline began dripping into my bloodstream.

I kept every physical reaction to a minimum. Now I needed absolute surprise or I'd never pull this off.

So I simply lay there.

Waiting.

"You see?" Cho's voice again. "I told you it would work. He had no power over the drug at all. He might have tried to fight it, as you observed, but in the end, he was simply no match for it."

"I'm not sure I believe that."

"You have no faith."

Anger began welling up inside me.

Boxcar.

How could he have sold out? What had Cho promised him that would make him turn? Was he the information leak? Had Cho gotten all his information about me from Boxcar? And if so, had Boxcar sold anyone else out?

"I have faith," said Boxcar, "in what I can see. I haven't yet seen any proof that Lawson is completely under your control."

"What would convince you?"

Boxcar laughed. "Wake him up and I'll think of something."

"Very well." I felt a tap on my shoulder at the injection site. It might have hurt any other time, but the anger and adrenaline in my system anesthetized me.

"Wake up, Lawson."

I shifted. I had to play this just right.

I opened my eyes.

Cho's face smiled down at me. "How do you feel?"

I used a monotone I hoped didn't sound too corny. "Cold."

"Put your shirt back on."

I slid into it, bumbling it, but managing to keep my back hidden from their eyes. That was important.

Cho smiled at me. "I have a favor to ask of you. Are you ready to help me out?"

"Yes."

Boxcar's coveralls seemed to be covered with dark stains that could only have been blood. I wondered if the other guys were dead.

It seemed probable.

Cho glanced at Boxcar. "Well?"

Boxcar grinned. "Bring the woman out here."

Cho's eyes lit up. "Ah . . . excellent."

So much for keeping his word. I watched Cho's bodyguards nudge Teresa back into the room. Her eyes were still glazed over from the hypnosis.

Boxcar stepped in front of Cho and looked at me. "Lawson, can you hear me?"

"Yes."

"Do you see the woman? The human woman?"

"Yes."

"I want you to kill her."

My heartbeat increased. Boxcar glanced at Cho with a frown. There was no time to waste. I slid off the couch and stood. I held out my hand. "Gun?"

Boxcar frowned but Cho smiled. "Give him a gun."

Boxcar started to draw his pistol, but then stopped. "No."

I looked at him trying my best to have vacant eyes. "No?"

"No gun."

"You still think he's faking?" asked Cho.

"He might be."

"You're overestimating him and underestimating what I've worked so hard to accomplish here."

"I went through Fixer training. You didn't. I know there are ways to combat narcotics. Lawson here may have discovered some himself."

"This is ridiculous."

"He can kill the girl with his hands. Lawson knows enough neck breaks that will get the job done. And we don't have to worry about him having a gun in his hands."

Cho sighed. "Very well. Get on with it."

Boxcar looked at me again. "Kill her with your bare hands, Lawson."

I walked toward Teresa. "Yes."

Her eyes were still vacant. I kept my motions a bit uncoordinated and lumbering. I must have looked like Frankenstein from the old black and white flicks. I had no idea how I was supposed to act.

But it seemed to satisfy them so I kept it up.

Teresa was close now. She stood next to one of the bodyguards who had braced her with his own body so she wouldn't fall down.

I reached out my hands.

For her neck.

Six feet.

Four.

Two.

I snapped then.

Spun and whipped the edge of my hand into the throat of the closest bodyguard. His hands came up instinctively as he started choking. While he was occupied, I spun again and dropped to one knee.

Ripped my backup pistol from the small of my back holster.

And fired center mass at the second bodyguard even as he was trying to go from an inactive state to an active one.

Too late.

Action beats reaction every time.

My three shots nailed him right in the heart.

I dropped another two into the first bodyguard.

Bright red blood erupted out of his chest as the wooden-tipped bullets fragmented and splintered his heart.

I whirled again and saw the shocked looks on both Cho's and Boxcar's faces.

Cho's mouth moved. "It can't be."

I smiled. "Here's one reaction you might not have counted on, Cho."

He didn't say anything so I continued.

"Saber leaves me awfully pissed off."

Thirty-seven

Cho moved faster than I expected him to.

I wondered if my reflexes were slowed due to the drug, but I knew they weren't. Cho just happened to be a lot faster than your average, everyday midget.

He whirled and then vanished out of the room. I squeezed off a shot that blistered the doorjamb he'd gone out of, but my attention was jerked back to the room by Boxcar advancing on me with his MP5 coming up.

I brought the pistol onto him. "Don't even."

He stopped. "You don't know what you're doing, Lawson."

"I know I'm not betraying my society. Why'd you do it? What'd he offer you? What made you sell us all out?"

"What makes you think that it was Cho?"

My head swam. "What the hell does that mean?"

Boxcar grinned. "You see? You don't even know the start of all of this. Everything you've thought you've figured out? It's all a lie. You're just on the wrong side of things. As always."

"There's someone else." It came out more as a statement than a question. Boxcar just grinned.

"It's too late. It's too late for everything. Whatever you think you know. Forget it. You'd be better off turning that gun on yourself because you're not going to like the future very much."

"I doubt that. If the future includes you, someone's got to stay around and see that you pay for your crimes."

His eyes twinkled. "You'll shoot me? That's the easy way out."

"You planned to shoot me."

"You've got the drop on me. Let's just put both our guns down and settle this the way we did in the sand ring at the Academy all those years ago."

"You beat me once."

"And you beat me twice. Let's say it's time for my revenge."

"I never knew you'd harbored a grudge about that."

"Surprised? Come on, let's get it on."

"There's no time for this now. Cho's escaping."

Boxcar shook his head. "Hardly. We have plenty of time."

"Drop your weapon."

Boxcar frowned. "You won't play with me, Lawson? I would have thought it would appeal to your natural competitive instinct. That you'd relish the chance to best me again."

"Why? I've done it twice before."

"That was before we became true Fixers."

"You're no Fixer. Not since you sold out. All you are is a traitor."

"You still aspire to those silly myths about us? All that garbage about Prince Kendrick and his quest to establish our legacy as the saviors of the vampire race? It's all bull. Silliness concocted by the old Fixers to give us a nobility—a sense of purpose."

"And who told you that?"

"It's there for anyone to see, provided you know where to look."

"I don't care what you say, Boxcar—"

"But you do. Whatever you claim, whatever you say, I know you better than perhaps anyone else. Even better than Cosgrove did."

"You're treading on dangerous ground there."

"Why? Because I brought up his name? Because he killed the one woman you loved? So what? You killed him. Didn't you?"

I searched his eyes. My dream came flooding back to me. Cosgrove's voice. His face. His smile. His mocking tonality. But I knew what I'd done. I knew I'd killed him.

He was dead.

"You know he's gone."

Boxcar grinned. "Put your gun down, Lawson. Join me in unarmed combat. Let's have a go at it. Like old times."

I looked at his MP5 on the floor. Boxcar grinned and kicked it across the room. "That better?"

I should have just shot him.

I should have.

And then gone after Cho.

But I lowered my gun instead.

Maybe I'm just a fool.

Boxcar's smile flooded the room. "Yes."

I tossed the pistol to the other end of the room. Boxcar circled me, his hands coming up in front of him. I watched the way his feet moved. Something seemed different.

He must have noticed my wrinkled brow. "Like you, Lawson, I've studied other arts. I never intended to rely on what those fools at the Academy showed us."

I brought my own hands up.

Boxcar feinted with a looping right hook to my jaw and followed up with a kick to my solar plexus. I ignored the punch and slid back and away from the kick, kicking out at the underside of his leg.

He drew the leg back and out of the way as my own kick went past. His right hand chopped down on the top of my thigh. My quadriceps exploded in pain and I reeled my leg back in just as Boxcar went for a leglock.

I pivoted and threw a left punch at his face.

I caught him on the side of his jaw. The bones in my hand throbbed but Boxcar grunted as the punch staggered him back.

I followed up with a right elbow, closing the distance Boxcar attempted to put between us. He ducked the elbow and shot a left into my right floating ribs. I heard a crack and grunted.

They'd been broken before. Nothing I could do about them now.

He came up, lifting my hands out of the way as he did so and brought his own elbows up into my solar plexus. I clapped my hands down and over his arms, pinning them and used a headbutt to bust the orbital bone over his right eye socket.

He brought a knee up into my groin and then broke away. I doubled over and felt the wind jump out of my lungs. I heaved fire and tried to get my breathing back.

Boxcar whipped his right leg over and down toward the back of my head. I saw it too late and took the axe kick off the left shoulder blade. My arm exploded in pain and I knew the shoulder was dislocated.

I spun away and turned my right side toward Boxcar. I could see the grin cross his face. "How'd that feel, buddy? Nothing like getting your shoulder popped, huh?"

I kept trying to correct my breathing. My lungs felt like I was sucking in tiny breaths. I couldn't get control.

Boxcar maneuvered his way round to my left. I stayed with him. I didn't want him exploiting my dislocated shoulder.

I needed to pop my shoulder back in, but there was no way I could do it now.

My solar plexus exploded then. Boxcar had leapt across the room and sent a flying sidekick into my chest. I stumbled and crashed back through a set of doors.

Instantly, fresh air wrapped around me. I was outside. The doors led to some type of veranda. I felt the cold air and sucked some of it into my lungs.

Boxcar came through the doors, advancing like a viper.

"You're finished, Lawson. Give it up. I'll put you down quickly. One shot is all it will take."

"What did you do to Pinkie and Gopher?"

He grinned. "Dead."

"You killed them?"

He nodded. "Of course. They weren't much good to me alive. And now I'll kill you, too."

So much death. *And for what?* I sighed. And backed up. My legs ran into the wall that bordered the veranda. I glanced over and saw nothing but water far below where I stood.

"No escape there, pal. That drop's a good hundred feet or more. You'll be so banged up by the time you hit bottom that it'll be easier for you if I shoot you."

"I'm better off staying here?"

"At least here you'll have a quick death."

I looked over the edge again. I might make it.

Boxcar chuckled. "Let me help you."

He kicked me again in the solar plexus. I heard bone crack. I felt the wall behind my thighs. I felt my upper body fall backward.

Over the edge.

My limp left arm dropped first.

And caught something.

A pole?

My fingers wrapped around it as the rest of my body went past, my arm swung up and stopped me from falling.

I screamed.

The pain!

And then I felt—heard—the pop.

And screamed some more.

The action of all my weight being supported by my left arm had popped my shoulder back in.

I hung there, under the veranda's underside.

I heard footsteps above me coming across the bricks and I tried to scoot myself farther down the pole that held me up. The closer I got to the wall, the better. I used my right arm to help and managed to almost get myself underneath the bottom of the veranda when I heard Boxcar's voice.

"Sank already did you?"

He couldn't see me. Maybe he figured I'd already vanished beneath the waves.

But Boxcar wasn't a fool. He'd go down and check to be sure. After all, the fall wouldn't have killed me. And he'd want to finish the job right.

The way he had with Gopher and Pinkie.

I frowned. I'd trained hard with those guys and I'd miss them terribly. Friends are damned tough to come by in this business and now Boxcar had gone and wiped out two more of mine.

Their deaths needed avenging.

My left arm throbbed. But at least the stupid thing was back where it was supposed to be. I waited until I heard Boxcar's steps recede back into the house and the doors shut behind him.

I looked at the pole, which I could now see was a flagpole branching off of a bedroom built beneath the veranda. I hand-over-handed my way toward the building and the bedroom.

I hoped the windows were open.

They weren't.

But there was a small ledge outside the windows and I could let myself down. I huddled on the ledge and picked the window lock. I eased the window open and looked into the room.

Empty.

I stepped down, feeling solid floor under my feet again. It felt good.

Light bled in from out in the corridor. I could see shadows go rushing past. I huddled next to the door, expecting it to burst in at any time.

I needed a weapon.

Upstairs, I'd left my pistol. And Boxcar's MP5.

I eased the door open and risked a look outside.

The corridor looked empty. I could make out the main staircase at one end of the carpeted hallway. It would lead me back upstairs.

To my gun?

I doubted Boxcar would pick it up.

But then again he might surprise me.

But I had no choice.

I let myself out into the corridor and instantly felt

too exposed. I hustled to the stairs and climbed them. Back in the room I'd just fought Boxcar in, the bodies of the two bodyguards still lay on the ground, their blood staining the carpet a deep brown.

My gun lay in the corner where I'd tossed it under the EKG machine.

Thank God.

Teresa, however, was gone.

And where had Cho vanished to?

Boxcar hadn't seemed concerned.

I heard a noise from downstairs—a woman's voice pleading.

Teresa?

I ducked out of the room and back down the main staircase. I could make out the voices clearer now.

"Give her another shot." Cho.

"No! Please, no more!" Teresa.

"I have to find him. You give her the shot yourself." Boxcar.

I checked the chamber of my pistol and saw the shiny round it contained. I'd used six so far. That left three. I'd have to be damned sure of my shots.

I slipped the safety off and crept down the stairs. From the sound of things, Cho and Boxcar were arguing.

"You can kill him later! Help me with this impetuous bitch first."

"If I don't make sure he's dead now, he'll be back for us later."

I continued creeping down the steps. I was almost at the bottom.

"Damn it, I need you to help with the girl."

I saw them. Their feet first as I descended the stairs. Then I saw their legs and chests and finally their faces.

I brought the gun up and squeezed off a shot that caught Boxcar in the right side. He spun and whirled as the round slammed into him. His eyes searched for me, trying to bring up his MP5.

I fired again.

The bullet tore into his chest over his heart.

Blood splashed out of him. His coveralls went a darker black from the blood.

Teresa screamed.

Boxcar slumped to the floor.

I came off the stairs.

Cho stayed very still but kept Teresa between us.

I stepped closer to Boxcar. I could see his canines already extended, his eyes open.

Dead.

One down.

One bullet left.

I turned my attention to Cho.

"Your turn."

His head poked out from behind Teresa's left hip. "Not so fast, Lawson."

I stopped. In his hand he held a plunger of the blue stuff. Saber.

"If I give her another injection, she'll die. Her system can't handle the drug like you do. She'll overdose and die. You wouldn't want that would you?"

I lowered the gun. "Let her go."

"No chance. Not yet. You do as I say and then maybe I will."

"What do you want?"

He told me.

Thirty-eight

"Drop your weapon."

"You'll let her go?"

"Sure. I promise."

"I've heard scumbag politicians say that more convincingly than you just did."

"You're being redundant, Lawson."

"Am I?"

"It has been my experience that all politicians are scumbags."

"While that may be true, I don't think either one of us is ready to sit down and talk that through."

"Probably not."

"Let her go, Cho. This doesn't concern her."

"You need to drop your weapon or I will most definitely fill her veins with Saber. She will not survive another dose."

I wanted to put the gun down. I wanted to. But something inside me forced me to hold on to it. I couldn't let Cho get the upper hand here. I needed to kill him. To shoot him and be done with it.

Now!

But just as I started to snap the gun up, Cho smiled.

"Fine." I saw his mouth move. Words like I'd never heard filled the air. I felt a strange tug and then my right hand snapped open. My pistol flew out of it and across the room. It clattered away into the shadows.

Cho laughed as the shock registered on my face. "Money buys a lot of things, Lawson. Information perhaps being the most important of those."

"How did you do that?"

He smirked. "What—you don't believe in magic?"

I didn't say anything. The truth was, as many times as I've run into the unexplained, I prefer to find a rational process for things. My life has a tendency to be complicated enough without involving strange phenomena.

Cho kept talking. "What about Arvella? What about your friend Jack? How do you rationalize their ability to invoke spirits?"

"Maybe I can't."

He nodded. "So, too, you will not be able to rationalize this."

"I've never heard of any of our kind having the ability to do what you just did."

"There are those of us who can."

"Is it natural?"

"Well, for those born with the power, yes. I was not. But you can be taught to wield the power in almost the same fashion."

"And you were taught."

"I was." His eyes danced. "Want to see some more of what I can do?"

I was about to say no, but my body suddenly went completely limp and I found myself flying through the air, picking up speed. The stone wall came at me fast and I barely had time to bring my hands up to cover myself when I slammed into it.

Hard.

I crumpled in a heap at the base of the wall.

Damn, that hurt.

Cho's laughter drowned out Teresa's screams. I got to my feet slowly. How the hell was he doing this? It was like he had some sort of weird spellcasting ability. Like he was a mage or a sorcerer.

And that was something I'd certainly never run into before.

Another wave of energy picked me up again and slammed me against the vaulted ceiling high overhead. I impacted and abruptly, the energy disappeared. I dropped like a stone.

The floor felt worse than the wall had.

My forehead bounced off the floor and I felt blood stream down my face. I caught the smell of my own juice and frowned.

I hate it when I bleed.

"There's really not all that much you can do against me, Fixer. I have the advantage. I have the needle full of Saber. And I have the girl. *Your* girl." He laughed again. "And who knows? I might just keep her alive long enough to penetrate every orifice she's got."

I had a witty retort ready to go, but Cho must have gotten tired of hearing my sarcastic comebacks. Another bolt of energy slammed into me and I buckled and rolled with it into a chair across the room. I barely had time to cross my legs and protect my groin.

"Just think of her, Lawson. Legs splayed wide apart and me—on top of her—grunting and wheezing and spurting my deformed seed deep inside of her."

I wanted to puke.

I got to my feet.

Stumbled.

My head hurt. There was a chance I'd gotten a concussion from hitting the wall and ceiling and floor.

My vision started to tunnel.

Cho's image danced in front of me. I saw two of him and knew things weren't going well.

His voice filled the air again with strange words.

But it sounded different.

My vision clouded again. Everything went gray. Like a mist. I couldn't see Cho at all.

And then I heard it.

"Lawson."

No.

Not the dream. Not him. Not now.

Cosgrove.

I tried to clear my eyes and see. A kick landed in my stomach and I doubled over, retching.

More laughter.

"You thought you killed me?"

"I did kill you."

"No."

Another kick caught me in the pit of my stomach again. I heaved.

"How does it feel, Fixer?"

Arvella's voice filled the room. How had she gotten here? Could Cho raise the dead?

The intense heat hit me. It knocked me over backward. I almost caught my own feet in my mouth as I rolled.

She laughed.

"Is this bringing back unpleasant memories of our last meeting?"

Another bolt of spirit energy slammed into me. I felt more like a punching bag than a vampire at that point.

I tried to stand.

Tried to.

But something knocked my legs out from underneath me. I landed hard on my ass.

I tried to clear my eyes again. I could only see gray mist.

But I could hear all right.

Especially the growl.

It came from behind my right ear.

I rolled then instinctively. A breeze tickled the skin on the back of my neck. I knew I'd only just missed getting clawed by her.

Shiva.

The half-lycanthrope half-vampire assassin I'd killed a few months back.

But how was she back now?

How were any of them?

"He can't figure it out." Cosgrove.

"He won't have time to." Arvella.

"You'll die now, Lawson." That one belonged to Petrov.

Another growl behind me and I ducked. I felt Shiva go flying over where my head had been a second earlier.

I rubbed my eyes.

I had to clear them.

Had to be able to see.

Another kick.

But I sensed it and moved just in time. I caught a glancing blow along the right side of my rib cage. I heard something snap and felt the pain. But I'd had ribs broken in the past.

I'd survive.

I hoped.

Their laughter seemed to fill the entire room. All of them. All of them laughing, taunting.

My dream.

But this was no dream.

I couldn't wake up from this.

This was the here and now.

Cosgrove's voice echoed inside my head. "Remember when you killed me? Remember what I said? I told you that you hadn't won. And you haven't."

"No!"

I didn't realize I'd shouted until I heard it bounce off the walls of the room.

A strange silence cloaked the room.

I felt hot.

But this felt different.

I wasn't confused any more. I wasn't scared.

The shout had somehow cleansed my fear.

The mist began to dissipate in front of me.

My eyes. I could see.

Cho.

He stood about ten feet away looking at me curiously. He smiled as the last of my vision cleared.

"I never would have expected it from you, Lawson."

I glanced around. Cosgrove. Arvella. Petrov. Shiva. They had all vanished.

Had they been there at all?

"My illusions are usually quite difficult for people to defeat. And yet . . ." He paused. "A *kiai* from the likes of you. Amazing."

I frowned. *Kiai* was the kind of thing you heard in bad karate movies. Students lining up to break boards and shouting "hi-ya" before they did so.

But I knew *kiai* had a deeper meaning than the silly shouts most martial artists used to psyche themselves up. Properly used, a *kiai* could immobilize an opponent for precious seconds. Or, it could refocus a person's internal spirit and cleanse away outside distractions.

Like it had just done for me.

But I hadn't done it intentionally. I felt good. Maybe the lack of desire and intention was why it had worked so well.

At least now I only had one opponent to worry about rather than four dead ones.

Cho still had an arm around Teresa's waist. "It doesn't matter much. I can kill you just as easily. In fact, it makes it all the better."

"Let her go and face me alone, Cho." Damned if I didn't feel a lot better all of a sudden. Even my ribs felt okay. Maybe those attacks were part of Cho's illusions as well. Maybe I only thought I'd been injured.

Weird.

"I will not let her go, Lawson. She's mine now. All mine. Just like all of our society shall be. When I unleash this drug—everything will fall into place."

"No!"

Teresa's turn to shout.

I saw her move—she stomped her foot down on Cho's ankle. He grunted. She spun out of his grasp and away from him.

That was the opening I needed.

I tucked myself low like I had a football cradled in one arm and rushed the midget.

He saw me coming and limped aside, flipping a kick up at my groin. I pivoted on my lead leg. The kick drifted by, catching only air. I used my left leg to kick his knee. I scored a hard hit.

Cho grunted again and flicked his wrist.

I ducked as two hypodermic needles whizzed past

me. I looked at Cho but he still had the one filled with Saber. Those must have been a few extra empties he'd been carrying.

Memories of Shiva and her shuriken throwing stars came flooding back into my head. I grabbed one of the hypodermics and threw it back at Cho.

But the small guy merely leaped to the side as it went skittering past him.

"Your aim is lousy."

"It's a tiny target I'm aiming at."

"Excuses from you?"

"I haven't practiced in a while."

"Apparently."

I wanted to rush him again but common sense dictated that I steer clear of the vial of Saber.

What would it do to me if he managed to sink it into my neck or back? I didn't want to have to fight off a second bout of it. Nor did I want to suddenly go limp in the heat of battle, leaving Cho to do what he wanted to both myself and Teresa.

I kept Teresa behind me as I circled Cho. His arm length made his effective slashing range about two and a half feet. I gave him twice that amount, especially since my arms and legs could reach him without getting nicked.

Hopefully.

"Give it up, Lawson. Even if you win this battle, you lose the war. There are too many out there waiting for this moment."

"Who?"

He smiled. "Not a chance. I wouldn't dream of ruining the surprise."

"Ruin it. I won't tell."

"I'm sure you'd love to know. But that's just not the way this one plays out."

He took a halfhearted slash at my lead arm. It missed by a mile and I almost grinned.

Then I realized he'd used the fake as a diversion. He was going for a tackle around my legs instead.

He wrapped his stubby arms around my legs just above the knees, locking them out and tripping me. I stumbled and fell backward. Cho's arms lay trapped beneath me. I looked down and Cho was already freeing his arms and moving up my body. He'd been trained well by someone who truly knew the proper way to groundfight.

Nowadays most groundfighters like working on submission holds that work well for the ring or tournaments. But the sport aspect of groundfighting masks what it was once used for.

A very wise man told me once that getting someone on the ground was just another step in the process of killing them.

To that end, trained combat groundfighters take an opponent down to the ground and then immediately start working their way up the body. They keep their bodies very close to their opponent so there's no room to maneuver. They use knees and elbows to strike vital points as they crawl up the body until they can get a neck break or stranglehold.

It's scary enough when you practice these techniques in the safety of a dojo.

It's even scarier when you're facing someone who knows what they're doing in the heat of combat.

Cho knew what he was doing.

As he came up my body, his elbows dug holes into

my thighs, hips, and ribs. His knees pinned my hips down against the stone floor.

Mounting an effective defense was going to be tough.

I could hear him breathing hard as he came for my neck. I could see the sweat breaking out along his hairline. His misshapen face came into view and I almost grimaced at the thought of being this close to him.

But I'd been in far worse and uglier situations before so I shrugged it off.

I kept my body moving.

One of the most important aspects of groundfighting is to never freeze up. It's scary as hell being wrapped up with someone down on the ground. But you never stop moving. If you stop moving, they're able to cinch down and a solid, tight hold on you.

And that usually means you die.

I kept trying to buck Cho off of me.

If I could get my hips moving, I'd stand a good chance of displacing his body weight. His balance would be compromised. He might very well fall off.

But Cho had done this enough to read my moves. While I tried to buck him off, he kept his knees moving faster than I was.

He countered my counters.

His right elbow slammed into my throat just under my larynx.

I gagged.

My eyes welled up.

A little harder and he would have collapsed my trachea.

Not good.

Spittle flew out of his mouth as it drew even with mine. "You're finished, Lawson. I'll kill you for not doing what I told you to do."

The elbow shot to the throat had rendered me speechless.

I could hardly breathe. I wanted to gag.

I headbutted Cho instead. I caught his lazy eye socket and heard a bone snap.

Cho grunted and that was the moment I needed.

His body's reaction to the blow momentarily shifted his weight.

I rolled my hips and bucked him off.

He rolled away.

I scrambled to my feet.

"Lawson!"

Even now, her voice sounded so soft and feminine. I turned.

Teresa's hand moved.

"Here."

I saw something fly through the air. I reached for it. Felt it hit my flesh.

My hand wrapped around it.

In my peripheral vision I saw Cho coming for me. Fast. I pivoted.

Dropped to one knee.

And brought my gun up.

My vision tunneled, focusing on Cho.

His arm came down once.

Was he throwing something?

My finger squeezed.

And I felt the gun buck.

Once.

The report filled the room and I winced. Even though it was a small caliber, it still sounded loud.

The single shell spun out of the chamber and clanged off the stone floor in the dying thunder, but not before it hit Cho.

Cho's chest broke apart into a million pieces of singed red goo.

He flew back into the wall, crumpled to the ground, and lay there.

I approached him cautiously. He might be faking it. He might still be alive.

I didn't want him alive any longer.

One look told me he was done.

His voice came in small rasps. "You haven't won."

If only he knew how many times I'd heard that one before. "You're finished, Cho."

"This isn't over. You have no idea of how far up this goes."

I shook my head. "Shut your mouth and die already."

"I shall."

"Good."

His stubby index finger lifted from the floor and pointed. "And so...will she."

I frowned.

Turned.

Teresa.

Shit.

She lay against the opposite wall. Cho's blue hypodermic stuck out of her neck at an obscene angle. I could see half of the blue Saber fluid inside had already emptied into her.

Her eyes looked glassy. She reached out for me as I came to her.

"Lawson."

I held her hand. "Hang on. It'll be okay."

She grabbed tighter. "It won't. I can already feel it killing me."

"Fight it. Stay with me."

She smiled weakly. "Can't . . . it's too . . . cold."

I could feel it in her hands. Her pulse had gone thready. Weak. And the cold seemed to seep right out of her skin into mine.

Like death itself.

"Lawson?"

I had trouble seeing again. "Yeah?"

"What was this . . . all of this . . . what was it all about?"

I told her then. I figured I owed it to her.

I told her about us. Me. Who we were. Who I was. I told her all about the vampires. About how we've always existed alongside humanity. About how evolution split us into two forks. About how we hunted. I told her how our laws came to be established. How we transformed ourselves from a vagrant, parasitic band of outlaws into a cohesive society built upon laws and traditions.

And when I finished, I looked into her eyes. I could see the moisture in them. I could see the tracks her tears had made as they'd wandered down her cheeks while I told her of my history.

I could see the sadness.

I could feel the regret.

And for a long time I sat on that cold stone floor, holding her body, and rocking back and forth, not wanting to let go.

If I'd had the power to bring her back, I would have.

But I didn't.

And even doing my job the best way I knew how hadn't saved her life.

What the fuck was the point?

I looked over at Cho—long since gone off to burn in Hell—and frowned.

Someone had controlled him.

There was someone else.

Above him.

Boxcar, Kohl, Cho, D'Angelo, Raoul, Rebecca—too many traitors. Too much ambition. Too much bloodshed.

The body count had been too high on this one.

And there were too many loose ends.

Too many shadow players still playing the game.

I hugged Teresa's body tighter.

"I'll find them. All of them. I promise." It sounded like a cheap greeting card, but I meant every word of it.

I owed her that.

And so much more.

Nothing would keep me from honoring my pledge.

Thirty-nine

By the time I drove back to Boston, I felt like I'd been used as a litter box and then left to ferment for weeks. Much as I didn't want to see anyone, I had to do a debrief with my Control. Protocol waits for no one.

Lucky me.

Niles and I met at a park near my house. He sat on the bench wearing a long overcoat. His shoes looked shiny in the dull sunlight.

I had on my jacket and jeans. I think some of Cho's blood had stained them, but I didn't give a shit.

He looked me over as I sat down. "You look like hell."

"I appreciate your keen observation skills."

"Whoa. Grumpy too."

I looked at him. "You been through what I've just been through and I don't think pleasantries'd be on the tip of your tongue, either."

"Was it as bad as you said on the phone?"

"Worse."

"I haven't heard from anyone on your STA-F team."

"You won't either. They're dead."

"Jesus."

I nodded. "I'm the only one left. Two of them—Pinkie and Gopher—they died in an ambush planned by the third—Boxcar."

"Boxcar." He frowned. "You mean Samuelson?"

I looked at him. "Yeah."

"Don't forget, Lawson—I've seen your entire dossier. Everything. I saw the records from the Academy."

"Well, Samuelson—Boxcar—they both went bad. He was working on this thing as much as Cho was."

"He worked for Cho?"

I shook my head. "Not what I said. I said he was guilty of treason, yeah. But he wasn't a flunky for Cho. Samuelson wasn't into taking orders from anyone he felt was beneath him."

"Which leaves us where?"

I shrugged. "Did you know that Cho knew some form of magic?"

"What?"

"Did some sort of funky thing on me back in New York. Ripped my gun right out of my hand. Tossed it across the room."

"Really?"

"I would have chalked it up as some sort of telekinesis, but then he managed to somehow create the illusion of some of my worst cases coming back to get me for good."

"Like how?"

"Cosgrove. Arvella. Petrov. Shiva even. I don't know how he did it. But it was damned convincing."

"You ever hear anything about that kind of skill before?"

"Me? No. It's not my specialty to know about it. I just kill shitbag vampires. But then again, just because I haven't heard of a lot of this stuff doesn't mean it doesn't exist."

"Too true."

"He also had some sort of weird cloud of darkness he used as a burglar alarm back at the pad in the city."

"Another illusion?"

"Maybe. Maybe something different. I'll have to ask Wirek next time I see him."

"But in the end you killed Cho anyway, right?"

"Yeah. But only thanks to a friend."

"This friend—is she still alive?"

I started to ask how he knew it was a she but then stopped. Niles was a good Control. It was his job to know that stuff.

To know me.

I tried to smile. But it didn't feel very happy. "Cho killed her."

"I'm sorry."

"Me, too."

We sat there while the autumn winds blew around us, scaring up leaves and twigs and dragging them from one end of the park pavement to the other. An unseen force that could exert untold amounts of control over the environment.

The allusion to my present situation did not amuse me at all.

I sighed.

Niles looked at me. "At least it's over."

"It's not."

"Cho's dead. Boxcar is dead."

"And so are Kohl, D'Angelo, and Rebecca, and Raoul. Lots of bodies, yeah. And a lot of traitors uncovered. But it's not over."

"Is that what's eating you up inside?"

I didn't tell him I felt like shit because Teresa had died because she was involved in something she'd been dragged into. It was my fault she'd gotten mixed up in it. My fault alone. That was something it was going to take me a while to get over.

Truth was, most vampires didn't care that much about humans. I didn't see it that way. It was my job to preserve the Balance. But to me, that preservation went on to include lives whenever possible—be they human, vampire, or whatever. If I could spare them instead of take them, I counted that as a good thing.

I'd failed in a big way and it hurt like hell.

I took a deep breath and looked at Niles. "Someone's still out there. They might have had their plans cut short for a while, but they're still out there. Planning. Scheming."

Niles glanced away. A jogger ran past us wheezing in the afternoon air. "Let me guess: you want to go after them."

I smirked. "Since when does desire ever have anything to do with my job?"

"All right. We both know you *have* to go after them."

"That's the trouble with this destiny shit. It gets to be a real pain in the ass sometimes."

"Sometimes?"

"Most times."

"There's the Lawson I know."

A few kids went skipping by, chasing leaves. Their parents followed behind, chattering among themselves. Were they all truly aware of the world around them?

How aware was I?

"I'll get started soon."

Niles looked at me. "What's stopping you from going now?"

"Fatigue. Depression. A general sense that I make no difference in the world whatsoever."

"So, get a nap."

"That's one helluva bedside manner you got there."

He frowned. "What the hell do you want me to say, Lawson? You're a Fixer. You kill bad guys. You preserve our anonymity. Sometimes things get fucked up. A lot. That's no reason to turn into a victim on me." He sighed. "I'm sorry things went real sour on this one. Especially when it looked like anything but that."

I nodded. "It'll take more than a nap."

He grinned. "How about a vacation?"

"That might be a good thing."

"I'll get the leave approved."

"They won't like me leaving. There's no one covering New York right now. Lots of holes make the Council nervous."

"The hell with them. They'll approve the leave if I have to shove it in their mouths and work their jaws to swallow it."

I almost chuckled at the thought. "I can use a good break."

"Where will you go?"

Overhead, the sun worked toward the west, staining the blue sky a brilliant orange. It glowed in my eyes and made me squint.

"Japan."

"Japan?"

"It's been a while since I was there."

"You have friends over there?"

"A few. Not sure if I'd call them friends, per se."

"Rest and relaxation in the land of the rising sun."

Niles's voice drifted away. I was already thinking about the trip. I was already wondering how I could get in touch with Talya. Maybe we could rendezvous somewhere over there.

"You'll have to check in with the local Fixer in Tokyo."

That snapped me back to reality. "Can't I go off the books?"

Niles frowned. "If it was up to me, sure. But you know I have to put your trip into the logs. We need to know where you are, in case we have to recall you."

"Niles. If this thing goes as deep as I think it might, me being on the logs will also provide information to the potential bad guys. I don't want to spend my whole vacation having to look over my shoulder."

Niles sighed. "What do you want me to do?"

"I don't know. Use a fake name or something. Just make sure it's not me."

He nodded. "You owe me one for this, Lawson."

I looked at him and smiled again but there was still no joy in it. "If only you knew how many others I owe, too."

"A long list?"

"It's a lot longer than anyone should ever have."

I stood, felt the next wind come dancing across the pavement, and let it propel me out of the park.